The Vicarage Murder

ALSO BY FAITH MARTIN

DI HILLARY GREENE SERIES
Book 1: Murder on the Oxford Canal
Book 2: Murder at the University
Book 3: Murder of the Bride
Book 4: Murder in the Village
Book 5: Murder in the Family
Book 6: Murder at Home
Book 7: Murder in the Meadow
Book 8: Murder in the Mansion
Book 9: Murder in the Garden
Book 10: Murder by Fire
Book 11: Murder at Work
Book 12: Murder Never Retires
Book 13: Murder of a Lover
Book 14: Murder Never Misses
Book 15: Murder at Midnight
Book 16: Murder in Mind
Book 17: Hillary's Final Case
Book 18: Hillary's Back
Book 19: Murder Now and Then
Book 20: Murder in the Parish
Book 21: Murder on the Train

MONICA NOBLE MYSTERIES
Book 1: The Vicarage Murder
Book 2: The Flower Show Murder
Book 3: The Manor House Murder

TRAVELLING COOK MYSTERIES
Book 1: The Birthday Mystery
Book 2: The Winter Mystery
Book 3: The Riverboat Mystery
Book 4: The Castle Mystery
Book 5: The Oxford Mystery
Book 6: The Teatime Mystery
Book 7: The Country Inn Mystery

THE
VICARAGE
MURDER

FAITH
MARTIN

JOFFE
BOOKS

Revised edition 2024
Joffe Books, London
www.joffebooks.com

First published by Robert Hale in 2015
as *An Unholy Mess* by Joyce Cato

This paperback edition was first published
in Great Britain in 2024

Cover art by Nick Castle

ISBN: 978-1-83526-741-7

PROLOGUE

The Bridge and Wagon, as the police were later to discover to their cost, was just the sort of dozy country pub where a shotgun *could* go missing without being the cause of too much fuss.

Not that it was an establishment set in an area rife with crime and thick with malefactors — in fact, just the opposite. Nestled amongst picturesque thatched cottages overlooking a peaceful village square, the possibility of theft and murder being committed on their back doorstep was something that would never even cross the minds of the people who regularly drank there.

A tradition-loving landlady owned the freehouse, so it was not that most soul-destroying of all things — themed — and only a token gambling machine lurked in one particularly dark corner where it remained virtually unmolested. Nor was loud modern pop music ever allowed to darken its hidden speakers. And since the village itself was situated at the end of a no-through road, hardly any strangers came passing through the peaceful Cotswold village of Heyford Bassett to cause any trouble.

There was not even the diversion of a nervous company executive sneaking out for a quick drink with a pretty secretary to break the monotony.

1

On that particular Saturday lunchtime, as on most other days, there was only a handful of Heyford Bassett's oldest regulars to be found in the pub, but many more of the newcomers to the village.

June Cowdey, the attractive owner and barmaid, watched the amiably noisy crowd in the far corner with a tolerant glint in her dark green eyes. The eight or so men all looked exactly like what they were — gentlemen farmers — and were busy acting like men who'd just had a successful morning's pigeon shoot. Moreover, most of the members of the older generation had shown their usual touch of class by leaving their weapons propped up in the dusty and dark boot room, along with their walking sticks and muddy spaniels.

Clem Jarvis, the owner of one of the biggest farms around, and one of those gentlemen who'd thoughtfully left his pigeon-potter outside, was now happily well into his third pint of real ale, and reliving that morning's glories.

'Of course, poor old Bill there couldn't hit a bird if it flew down and landed two feet in front of him and waggled its tail feathers in his face,' he chortled loudly, catching June's eye and winking at her admiringly.

June, with her naturally red hair, pale skin, hourglass figure and mysterious reputation, was undoubtedly one of the most popular women in the village. Well, with the male contingent, anyway. Rumour had it that there was a Mr Cowdey lurking about somewhere, but June neither confirmed nor denied this sad state of affairs.

Now she smiled back automatically at Clem and carried on polishing glasses, her eyes settling briefly on a couple of newcomers in the little window seat.

The village's huge old Georgian vicarage had just recently been converted into a set of twelve luxury flats, and June, for one, was glad to see some new blood coming into the village — and her pub. Most of the locals, however, had bemoaned the loss of the vicarage to flats as just the latest assault upon their national heritage.

Back in the nineties, mock-Tudor houses had been erected on the other side of the river, and the resulting cul-de-sac had been coyly named Church Court. The village had grumbled about it for years of course, but inevitably two other paddocks had gone the same way. Valley Dene had been built a little further down Ford Street, and finally, only last year, River View had been constructed.

People living in homes that had once had pretty views over the river were particularly resentful about this blight on their bucolic idyll, and bad feelings about developers still tended to simmer just below the surface.

As the lunch hour progressed, however, the pub began to fill more quickly. Yet more strangers from the vicarage began to trickle in, and Sally, a cheerful part-timer, came to take over at the bar, apologizing for being late.

'Sorry, June, I got caught by that Muriel Larner. I swear she deliberately lies in ambush by that gate of hers.' She rolled her eyes expressively. 'I just couldn't get away from her. If nattering were an Olympic sport, she'd be up there with that cyclist fella.'

June, who knew the garrulous Muriel well, told her not to worry and retired to the kitchen, whilst the pigeon-shooting party became ever more boisterous, not to mention downright drunk.

But the newcomers to the village didn't seem to mind. After all, talk of pigeons, barley blight and the state of Clem's silage was just the kind of authentic rural atmosphere they'd come to the countryside to find. Or so they repeatedly told themselves.

* * *

By three o'clock the pub began to quieten down as, in dribs and drabs, it slowly emptied, with the pigeon-shooting party being the last to stagger collectively to the door.

It was then that Clem Jarvis noticed his shotgun was missing. But by then he was, as the locals so quaintly put it, pissed as a newt, and besides, he vaguely remembered — or thought he did — one of his cronies asking if he could borrow it for a rabbit shoot scheduled for the next weekend.

It was either that or some bugger had pinched it.

But Clem didn't really believe that his shotgun had been stolen since crime was practically unknown in the village. So it was that he merely shrugged and lurched his way home with the help (or hindrance, depending on how you looked at it) of his equally pissed-as-a-newt cowman.

The next morning he had a prize hangover, his wife was in tip-top nagging condition, and he was utterly sure now that it had been Bill who'd asked him if he could borrow the shotgun to get in some practice. The silly sod certainly needed it.

And Clem simply never gave it another thought after that. Until it was far too late, of course.

And that was how, a little while later, the police were to learn just how easy it was for a killer to steal a shotgun from the Bridge and Wagon.

CHAPTER 1

Monica Noble rubbed her itching nose with the back of her flour-smudged hand and her smoky blue eyes narrowed slightly in worry. Would two apple pies, one peach pie and two black cherry pies be enough? It was hard to judge when she wasn't sure just how many guests they could expect for the party. If everyone only brought the odd friend or family member it wouldn't be a problem. But what if everyone turned up with hoards of them?

Then she shrugged. Why worry about it? With Vera Ainsley about, nobody was likely to starve at the garden party scheduled for tomorrow, come what may!

Vera was quickly growing in fame as a minor celebrity cook, and there was even a rumour going around that she might get her own television show if she played her cards right. Well, on one of those small Freeview channels, anyway.

Monica, who wasn't particularly blessed with culinary professionalism, reached somewhat guiltily for a supermarket tin of cherry pie filling and began spooning the sticky red goo into a pie dish lined with, it had to be said, rather patched and indifferent home-made pastry.

'What's *that*?' a reedy voice suddenly piped up. 'It looks absolutely gruesome.' It was almost as if her conscience had been given a voice, and anyone more sensitive might have given a little yelp of alarm and started to wonder about karma or the way the cosmos actually worked. But Monica, recognizing that only a teenager could reproduce the scorn that had been prevalent in the voice, merely glanced over her shoulder at her fifteen-year-old daughter Carol-Ann and smiled.

'That's prime cherry pie gunk, as you'd know if you ever bothered to do any cooking,' she responded lightly.

Carol-Ann wrinkled her nose. 'Huh, Vera says those things are all full of E numbers and additives and who knows what else. And she should know — she's a *real* cook.'

To which, of course, Monica had no comeback whatsoever. 'Be a love and pour me a glass of lemonade, will you?' she said instead. 'It's sweltering in here.'

Carol-Ann pouted but obliged, pouring out a glass for herself as well. Monica took a grateful mouthful of the fizzy drink, bought yesterday from the nearest supermarket, and sighed. No doubt Vera would have made the real thing from scratch, complete with floating slices of lemon and lime, with plenty of added ice as well. And probably with a grating of chilli floating in it, or something. From what she'd seen of the myriad cookery programmes on television nowadays, practically everything came with some chilli in it.

But despite feeling sometimes uncomfortable or inadequate in her new and vague role as 'vicar's wife,' Monica Noble didn't feel particularly threatened by the super-cook living in flat 8 of the newly converted vicarage. She'd always managed to feed her first husband and daughter to their satisfaction, and her second husband wasn't complaining either.

Likewise, she felt no particular sense of rivalry towards the rather touchy Pauline Weeks, who occupied a top-floor flat, and for some reason took a perverse delight in talking down to her whenever the opportunity arose.

In fact, Monica Noble was far too comfortable with herself and her life to worry about such petty things as social status. Or her skill — or lack thereof — in the kitchen.

At thirty-five, widowed and remarried, with an ex-life in London and an ex-career in advertising behind her, she was reasonably confident that she was as seasoned, wise and competent as the next woman. Whoever *she* was.

And besides, now she had a whole new and challenging life as a country village vicar's wife to think about. Which was more than enough for anybody to be getting on with, Monica felt. All in all, she just had no time for unnecessary angst.

'Do you think I should cut my hair?' Carol-Ann suddenly asked, making her mother glance around sharply and with real alarm.

Carol-Ann had lovely long, naturally pale blonde hair, inherited from her late father. She opened her mouth to advise strongly against such a drastic action, then stopped herself just in time. Cunning and deviousness were art forms that she'd quickly learned to cultivate, ever since Carol-Ann had first hit puberty.

Instead, she forced herself to relax, and shrugged nonchalantly.

'If you want to,' she said blandly, turning out the last of the red sticky ooze into her pie dish and then tossing the can aside with deft flair towards the waiting kitchen bin.

It missed, of course, and bounced off onto the floor, leaving a slight cherry-red smear on the shiny kitchen floor in its wake. Monica sighed, but decided to leave it where it was until she had finished baking.

Carol-Ann, who hadn't even noticed her mother's misdemeanour, shot her a quick, suspicious look. Monica pretended not to notice the shrewd teenage scrutiny and pulled the pie dish towards her and rolling-pinned a piece of pastry onto the top of it. Lopsidedly, of course. Tugging it into place and hoping it wouldn't tear, she absently glanced up at the lounging teenage girl.

'I thought you liked my hair long?' Carol-Ann challenged, her big blue eyes narrowing ominously.

Monica shrugged. 'I do. I thought you did too. Didn't you tell me that all models have long hair?' she added casually, for her daughter had announced a year ago that she was going to become a supermodel. Either that or a computer games designer. The game design Monica could just about deal with. It only meant spending vast sums of money on the latest hardware and games and girding her loins to pay out for her degree at uni.

Coping with Carol-Ann's modelling ambitions was something else entirely. But Monica lived in hope that she'd grow out of it.

'Huh,' Carol-Ann said.

Monica began to cut out what she hoped looked like cherries from the leftover pastry to decorate the top of her pie. She rather suspected, though, that the end result looked more like the dessert had developed a severe case of measles.

'Some models have short hair,' Carol-Ann said, unwilling to let it go. She suspected that her mother was pulling a fast one, but hadn't learned enough yet about the subtleties of reverse psychology to be absolutely sure.

Monica hid a sigh. She supposed, philosophically, that if Carol-Ann came home one day with a crew cut like an American marine, she'd survive the shock. Whether or not Graham would, though, was another matter.

Monica's lips twitched as she thought about her mild-mannered husband and the shocks Carol-Ann sometimes imposed on her long-suffering stepfather.

Having criticized her mother's cooking and dropped her little bombshell, thus feeling that her work here was now done, her daughter wandered away, waif-like, through the door. Already standing at just over 5'9" tall, and with a naturally slender frame, she was very good at doing waif-like.

Monica began to clean up the kitchen, starting with the recalcitrant tin can, and hummed contentedly to herself as she did so. She liked this room, with its windows that opened out onto a wonderful view of the gardens, the fitted pale pine cabinets and cheerful sunny yellow tiles. In fact, she liked the rest of the flat too, and far preferred it to the days when she and

Graham had had the whole enormous building to themselves. Not that *that* had been an issue for long. She'd only been married to her new husband for less than six months before they'd learned from his bishop that the diocese was selling the huge barn of a building to developers.

The Nobles had been given the first choice of the converted flats, however, and naturally they'd picked flat 1. It was the only one with its own private access, being in the front and on the ground floor, and had views of both the large gardens and the river opposite.

Graham Noble, unlike some of the more conservative members of his flock who had been none too pleased to hear that their vicarage was being sold off, had in fact agreed with his bishop on this issue. Living in a huge, three-storey eighteenth-century building was no longer a viable proposition in this brave new millennium, either financially or ethically.

And the more dire predictions that had circulated about it all ending in aesthetic disaster had proved to be somewhat overegged.

The local firm that had been hired to do the renovations had not only installed wooden-panelled lifts that were sympathetic to the decor, but had also managed to separate the rooms into distinct residences without butchering the overall harmony of the interior of the building. Flats 2, 6 and 10, (one on each of the three floors) had been configured to be slightly larger and thus more expensive than the rest, but all the homes on offer were spacious and airy, with their fair share of retained original features. Fireplaces, cornices, ceiling roses and wainscoting had all been meticulously conserved. There were still a few unoccupied flats for them to finish, but it wouldn't be long before the renovation was complete.

Now, as she rinsed out the dishcloth at the sink, Monica glanced out of one such retained feature — the large elegant sash window — and watched as John Lerwick, who also had a flat on the ground floor, trundled past with a wheelbarrow full of weeds.

Although the large grounds were supposed to be a communal garden, and as such a joint responsibility, only a few of the residents so far had shown any inclination to tackle the undergrowth. But a few of the flats had yet to be sold, so who knew who might buy one of those. Monica wondered if it would be wrong to pray for a couple of green-fingered retirees with plenty of time on their hands to spend on their favourite hobby, and after some thought supposed that it was. When it came down to it, she thought that most of the residents would probably rather chip in and pay for professionals to keep the grounds looking nice.

Regardless, right now the gardens were slowly improving under John's slow but steady prowess, so perhaps it would be better if they just left him to get on with it as he saw best. After all, if somebody else came in with their own horticultural preferences, it might cause friction. And Monica didn't particularly want Graham to be drawn in over arguments about topiary or ornamental bedding. As a vicar, her husband was often appealed to as arbitrator in any squabble going.

And she was all for the quiet life.

'Oh, come off it, Marge, the flat's fine,' a harassed male voice suddenly blew into her kitchen, along with a rose-scented breeze. 'You're just nit-picking now and you know it.'

Monica had no trouble identifying the voice as belonging to Sean Franklyn, who, along with his wife Margaret, had moved into the last of the smaller flats on the ground floor, number 4. Monica had, of course, made all the usual friendly overtures to them, but hadn't really been surprised to have her offer of a drink one evening politely ignored.

Now she sighed as the married couple wandered into view carrying towels and suntan lotion. The taller of them, Sean, was a lean man, with vaguely if somewhat unimpressively handsome features, with dark brows, hair and eyes.

Margaret, who had short and very stylishly cut red hair (helped no doubt by the application of a first-class dye), shot her husband a speaking look. She was thirty-eight, almost anorexically thin, and was wearing a loose sundress over a matching bikini that had cost far more than her husband knew. On her wrist was a truly fabulous bracelet, a pagan-looking, intricately beaten copper dragon inset with turquoise, which had a tail that curved almost all the way up to her elbow.

Monica couldn't help but admire it, even from a distance, and wished that she had been blessed with a more creative nature. Margaret designed and made her own jewellery, and sold it regularly to local shops and at craft fairs for nice little sums. And she was very careful indeed that everyone should know just how well it sold, Monica thought with a small smile.

'Oh? You call it nit-picking not even to be consulted about where we're going to live?' Margaret sniped back, the look on her face, even from several yards away, unmistakably ferocious.

Monica hastily ducked her head and wiped her work surfaces vigorously. She contemplated closing the window, since she hardly wanted to be a witness to anyone else's marital spats, but then a small trickle of sweat running down her spine quickly changed her mind.

It was the first week in July, and absolutely sweltering. The news was full of the heatwave, and promised more record-breaking temperatures to come. And why *should* she be forced to roast, Monica wondered, somewhat resentfully. If the Franklyns *would* insist on arguing in public, they surely had no reason for complaint if they were accidentally overheard?

'Oh come off it, we got a bargain and you know it. This place is great,' Sean's whining voice echoed back as the couple found a spot in the sun and disappeared from view behind a bed of exuberant and rather rampant roses.

'I'd have preferred to stay in Bath, as you bloody well know,' Margaret snapped.

Monica tried to close her ears to the discord, but it was all but impossible. As soon as the oven was up to the required heat, she would put the pies in and go seek sanctuary in the den, where the latest mystery thriller by a writer that she particularly liked was waiting to tempt her.

'Our lease was almost up and you still hadn't found anywhere good enough for you,' Sean's voice was more of an angry growl by now. 'You were wasting so much time being so bloody picky. Would you rather we were out on the streets? Anyway, what's wrong with this place? It's a genuinely old building, a fact that should please all your antique-mad cronies. It's in a pretty village, it's central, and it's quiet. What the hell more could you ask for?' The volume of his voice rose higher still.

'Oh it's quiet all right,' Margaret snapped.

Monica sighed and muttered something not particularly Christian under her breath.

With lots of long, wavy dark brown hair, a trim figure, and possessed of a good fashion sense, she knew that she was not exactly most people's idea of a typical country vicar's wife. In fact, she flattered herself that she could look quite presentable when she put her mind to it, and had a modern outlook on life that didn't always sit well with the older ladies in her husband's parish.

Graham's fan club, as Monica had quickly nicknamed his middle-aged female admirers, had been shocked to their collective bosoms when their vicar had suddenly got married, and hadn't been shy in gossiping about it. Especially when he'd just reached his fiftieth birthday and his long bachelorhood had seemed to be safely confirmed.

Monica grinned somewhat smugly now as she contemplated her husband, and perhaps not surprisingly, for Graham Noble was one of those really good-looking men whom age only seemed to improve. At just over six feet tall, slim, with nearly black hair that was keeping its natural colour and dark brown, melting eyes, he looked a good ten years younger than he actually was. With attractive crow's feet at his eyes and an air of kind, bookish wisdom, it was not surprising that he could still make female hearts flutter.

As Carol-Ann had grudgingly put it, he resembled a sitter for one of those portraits of scandalous nineteenth-century poets — all dark and brooding and wickedly handsome.

But for all that, Graham Noble was an ideal vicar. He wore the long cardigans his parishioners knitted for him every Christmas, and managed to look good in them. He drove an old car, left to the church by an eccentric widow, and used it to make himself genuinely useful, shopping for the bedridden and taking others to doctor's appointments and generally making life easier for a lot of people. More than this, he actually *listened* to them. He was always there for anyone who needed him. He gave good services, and was a popular choice far and wide for marriages and christenings. He even gave interesting sermons. Well, sometimes. And if the fact that his church was inhabited more than most English churches were on an average Sunday morning was because of how good he looked in a cassock, nobody was complaining.

Not the fan club, not the bishop, nor Graham. Not even Graham's wife.

Marrying a much younger woman, and a widow with a teenage daughter to boot, he had shocked many of the locals with this display of what they saw as uncharacteristic rashness. And even though they'd been very happily married for some time now, tongues still hadn't ceased to wag. Which just went to show, Monica thought placidly, how little happened in Heyford Bassett!

Glad to leave the arguing Franklyns behind, she put the pies into the oven, and was just about to leave the kitchen when Margaret's strident voice started up again.

'And I still haven't found those earrings — not the ones I made, the ones I bought in Travinia's in the High Street, the diamond and sapphire ones.'

Monica had quickly cottoned on to the fact that Margaret, although she liked to model her own eye-catching wares, also frequented some of Cheltenham's swankiest jewellery shops to buy the 'real' thing. Monica had noticed a few diamond rings on her fingers from time to time. Not that she was envious, naturally. Well, not much, anyway. As a vicar's wife it didn't do to go coveting your neighbour's ox. Or his wife's bling, for that matter.

'I had them on when I was sunbathing here the last time. And that little teenage bimbo was hanging around — I saw her. It wouldn't surprise me if they fell off and that little pest found them and pocketed them, instead of returning them to me like any decent person would.'

This latest outburst made Monica's hackles rise, like a dog catching sight of a stranger lurking in the doorway.

'It's been nearly two weeks now, and they still haven't come to light,' Margaret moaned. 'I'm telling you, that Carol thingummy must have taken them.'

By the kitchen door, Monica began to simmer. She was going to damned well march right out there and give that woman a piece of her mind. How dare she suggest that her daughter had any interest in her precious earrings!

'I hope you haven't accused her,' Sean warned quickly. 'She's the vicar's daughter for Pete's sake.'

'Stepdaughter,' Margaret's voice corrected, making Monica's hackles rise even further.

'Are you sure you couldn't have just lost them?' her husband's mollifying voice sounded ineffably weary now. 'Perhaps you took them off and left them on your towel and forgot about them. Then, when you got up and collected the towel they could have fallen onto the grass without you noticing them. Shall I look?'

'Oh for—'

Monica grimaced, as the language became fouler and fouler. 'They're sapphires and diamonds, Sean!' Margaret finally yelled, at the end of her patience. 'If they were in the grass they'd sparkle and be seen. I'm telling you, someone stole them.'

But not *my* daughter, Monica thought silently. And if you so much as *dare* accuse her, you'll get your ears roasted! She stalked from the room, trying to calm down. Margaret was just a sour, spiteful woman with nothing better to do than create dramas around herself, Monica told herself firmly. Get a grip and get some perspective! If she couldn't quite manage

14

to turn the other cheek yet, as Graham seemed to be able to do so easily, the least she could do was refrain from rising to the bait.

She took a deep breath and headed for the bathroom. First she'd have a cold shower and simmer down, and then lie naked on the bed, allowing the water to dry naturally on her skin. That always made her feel cool and refreshed on a hot summer's day. And if Graham just happened to be around, well — even better.

And just what *would* Graham's fan club have to say about *that*!

CHAPTER 2

Trisha Lancer parked her neat little Metro under a big yew tree at the end of Church Lane and turned off the ignition. Through the trees, she could see the handsome Cotswold-stone vicarage she remembered so well and chewed nervously on her lower lip.

She suddenly felt ridiculous. Here they all were, in a brave new world full of science and modern psychology, and yet here she was, bringing her troubles to the *vicar* of all people. Just how last century was that?

Like the vast majority of Heyford Bassett children, Trisha had been raised, half-heartedly, as Church of England. And, also like everyone else, she'd found Graham Noble to be both approachable and human. But since getting married and moving to Stroud, her visits to his church had become fewer and far between.

But now here she was, back again, and needing help.

Taking a deep breath, she got out of the car, clutching her handbag close to her chest and already wishing that she hadn't come.

It had all seemed so clear-cut when she'd made the appointment to see him. She was in trouble, and Graham Noble might be able to help her. He was one of the very few people whom she could trust not to go blabbing her troubles about to all and sundry, as her so-called 'friends' were wont to do. But he was also a very clever man, with a surprisingly practical nature considering his calling, and those two attributes were just what she needed now. If he couldn't see the problem clearly, and didn't set about helping her, then no one would.

But now she'd almost talked herself out of it. It was ridiculous, wasn't it, really, turning to a vicar for help? Besides, she'd hardly spoken to him for ages. And yet, for all that, here she was, psyching herself up to tell him things that she wouldn't even dream of telling anyone else.

Above her, a blackbird began to sing sweetly. It was a beautiful, hot summer's day, and mallow bushes were bursting into pale pink and peach blooms all around her. But she was feeling utterly depressed, and incapable of appreciating the beauty on offer.

I'm desperate, she thought suddenly. And as that simple statement filtered into her subconscious, she found it created hardly a ripple. It was, perhaps, not so surprising — she'd been desperate for some time now.

Taking a deep breath, she squared her shoulders and walked through the big iron gates, a short, slightly plump, rather scantily clad woman with tear-bright, desperate eyes.

Her mother had told her about the vicarage being made into new flats, of course, and so she was careful to check that she had indeed come to flat number 1 before ringing the doorbell.

A pretty, dark-haired woman wearing a loose floral dress answered it almost at once.

Trisha, who'd seen Monica Noble around the village only a few times and never spoken to her, looked at her helplessly.

'Hello. It's Mrs Lancer, isn't it?' Monica smiled gently. Trisha nodded and nervously tucked a strand of hair behind one ear. Her hand shook as it did so. Recognizing all the signs of embarrassment and need, Monica's blue eyes softened in sympathy.

'Please, come on in, my husband's expecting you. He's in his study. Would you like something cold to drink? It's so hot, isn't it?'

Trisha shook her head to the offer of a drink, but followed her hostess into a cool and pleasant hall.

'It's right through here.' Monica led her to the first door on the right, and tapped firmly. She opened the door and looked inside. 'Graham, it's Mrs Lancer to see you.' She smiled and stood aside, and Trisha, with no other option now, stepped hesitantly into the room.

Graham came from behind the desk and held out his hand. 'Trisha! How lovely to see you again; come in and sit down.'

His pleasant, deep voice was instantly soothing and it was some moments before she realized that her hand was being engulfed in a warm, strong grip. When she looked up, the dark brown eyes looking down at her were full of concern.

She managed to drag in a breath. 'This is silly,' she said, then blushed deeply.

'Perhaps it is,' Graham said mildly, and smiled. 'Then again, perhaps it isn't.' He led her to a comfortable armchair, and as he turned, his eyes met those of his wife, who gave him a long, gentle look and backed out.

Over the past year, Monica had quickly discovered that Graham's job, unlike those of a lot of people, actually *meant* something. He wasn't in the business of just creating or moving money around, or producing throwaway items for a throwaway society. He didn't care a fig about such things as the media, PR or quality control and time-and-motion efficiency.

Instead, she'd watched her husband visit patients in hospitals who had nobody else to care about them, to bring them a bunch of grapes and a magazine and to just sit and chat and make them feel less alone for an hour or two. She'd been awakened in the dead of night by the telephone more than once because somebody was having a crisis that required a man of God. And, sometimes, like today, she'd shown people into Graham's study who had that same look of desperation about them as the young and obviously troubled Mrs Lancer had now. And, more often than not, Monica had seen them leave his study looking like very different people, as if some weight had been miraculously lifted from their shoulders.

As an ex-advertising executive, it made her feel distinctly humble — and grateful — to be married to such a man. It was during moments like these that Monica, who already loved her husband at a steady, calm and comforting level, loved him just that little bit more intensely.

Inside his study, Graham reached for a carafe of water tinkling with ice cubes, poured out a glass and handed it over to Trisha. He'd officiated at her wedding in the church just across the road, and had subsequently christened her son Carl just a couple of years or so ago. Right now, though, it was hard to equate the happy, carefree young girl he remembered with this woman. She looked downright haggard.

She accepted the glass of water and sipped it. It was good — and had a nice but faint tang of lime. And suddenly, coming here didn't seem so ridiculous anymore.

'I've come because I need help,' she said simply.

Graham nodded. 'I'll help if I can,' he agreed, just as simply.

'You won't tell Mum I've been, will you?' she asked anxiously. 'She'll fuss so.'

Graham quickly assured her that nobody would know of her visit unless she herself told them.

'It's my husband, Jim,' she said flatly. 'We've got a problem.' Graham crossed his legs slowly, resting his hands on his knees in a comfortable gesture.

'What sort of problem?' He'd heard many things from many people during his twenty-six years as a vicar, and honestly believed that it was not his place to judge. What's more, he knew that voicing pain and fear out loud was often the hardest thing of all, and added gently, 'Just take a deep breath, and take your time.'

'He's . . .' Trisha bit her lower lip, glanced uncertainly at the man in front of her, and sighed. 'This is going to sound so ridiculous. But it's really, really becoming a problem.'

Graham nodded. 'Go on,' he encouraged gently, and Trisha sighed.

'He's got this thing about bodybuilding,' she finally blurted out. 'He thinks he can win Mr Universe.'

Graham blinked, and hoped he didn't look as surprised — or as amused — as he felt. There was a treacherous tug at his lips and he ruthlessly suppressed his urge to smile. Instead he nodded.

'I see. That's a little unusual, I agree. How old is he exactly?'

'Oh, he's three years older than me. Twenty-nine.'

'Hmm. And is he likely to win Mr Universe?' Graham asked. Trisha began to laugh, and once started, it took her a long time to stop.

'In a pig's eye,' she said finally. 'Not that *that's* going to stop him. Every day he's down at that damned gym, pumping iron. He won't eat what I cook for him any more — it's not got the right balance of carbohydrates, he says. I wouldn't mind so much, but he's started talking about taking Carl with him to work out, and *that* I'm not standing for,' Trisha finished militantly.

'Carl?' Graham said, taken aback. 'You mean your *son*, Carl? But how old is he?'

'Only five, for pity's sake.'

And that was when Graham quickly lost all desire to laugh. 'Yes, that does sound worrying,' he agreed a shade grimly. Nobody living in modern times could fail to be aware of the issue of child abuse — and abuse came in many different guises. Not that he thought he was dealing with that here, but obviously Jim Lancer couldn't be thinking quite straight if he wanted his five-year-old to start pumping iron.

'I'm scared we're going to lose all our money too,' Trisha carried on, a definite wobble in her voice now. 'He's spent so much money on equipment, our house looks like a hardware shop for weightlifters. And he's gone right off . . . you know . . .' She suddenly blushed furiously.

Graham nodded. Yes, he knew.

'How long has this been going on?' he asked quietly.

'Nearly a year now,' Trisha sniffed. 'Ever since he joined that gym. At first, I thought it was a good idea, and when he started coming home with some muscles and all my friends said how buff he was looking, I felt sort of proud of the silly sod, you know?' Trish's voice started to rise. 'But now he's spending all our money on vitamins and equipment, and letting everything else go to rack and ruin. The lawn's not been mowed in months. People have started to look at him sideways, you know, as if they're not too sure that he's all there anymore. And I'm so scared that he'll get the sack, because he's not doing his job properly. He's sold a few flats recently, but he hasn't sold a proper house in ages, and that's not just because the market's flat, even though it is; it's like he just can't think of anything else but putting on more inches around his biceps.'

'It's become an obsession, in fact,' Graham put in quietly.

'Yes, and that's not good, is it?'

'No.' It was beginning to sound more and more as if the man had developed a definite kink in his psyche. The obvious answer was for him to see a therapist or mental health expert of some kind, but that, Graham was sure, was going to be very tricky to arrange. Given the ever-perilous state of the male ego.

Trisha, surprised to have her worst fears so calmly confirmed, suddenly seemed to wilt.

'Can you help me?' she asked forlornly.

Slowly, Graham leaned forwards and took her hand. 'First of all, Trisha, I'll have to do some research and some reading up on the subject. Find out a little more about it. I'm not really *au fait* with the bodybuilding culture or what causes men to develop an obsession with it.'

Trisha cast a quick look over his own lean and fit frame, opened her mouth, and then quickly closed it again. He was a vicar, after all. And a happily married one at that.

'Then I'll talk to a friend of mine who's a psychologist and a counsellor,' Graham went on. 'And I'll see what he recommends.'

Trisha nodded. When it came right down to it, she hadn't really expected the vicar to actually *do* anything for her. She'd only come because then at least she'd have felt as if she'd *tried* something, and could tell herself that at least she'd *done* something positive. But now she was actually beginning to feel optimistic.

'But I shall need to speak to your husband too,' Graham said firmly, and Trisha instantly began to gnaw nervously on her lower lip. Jim would have a fit if he thought she'd been talking about him behind his back to the vicar.

But before she could start to object, Graham swept on, 'After all, he might not think he has a problem. Perhaps he *doesn't* have a problem. It might not be as bad as you think.' Graham was always very aware during any consultation that he was only hearing one side of an argument. 'I'll do some reading and talk to my friend. Then we'll see what he advises. How's that to begin with?'

The last phrase seemed to work magic. Trisha's pinched and anxious face suddenly relaxed. It implied further action. That she was no longer on her own. Two things that gave rise to that most needful of all things — hope.

'All right,' she agreed tremulously, even managing a smile now.

Graham rose, ushering her to the door.

Monica, reading in the lounge, glanced up as she heard the study door open and got to her feet. She was just in time to see a very different woman from the one who'd entered turn and smile into the study.

'Thank you, Vicar,' Trisha said gratefully, then turned and walked confidently to the door.

Monica smiled and went back to her magazine.

* * *

In flat number 11, Pauline Weeks poured a long, cold drink for her attractive visitor and handed it over.

At forty-three, Pauline was a fairly recent divorcée, and living well off her alimony payments. Too humiliated to stay in Wimbledon, where her well-heeled husband and his newer, younger wife had set up home as well, she'd decided to move and 'be something' in the country set. A whole new way of life was so appealing, or so she told all her friends. Or so-called friends, since most of them had decided to stay in her ex-husband's camp after the split. So when she'd spotted a small but pretty flat being advertised in an upmarket country lifestyle magazine, the idea of living in a 200-year-old plus converted vicarage, situated in a pretty village in the heart of the Cotswolds, had seemed just the ticket.

But after only a couple of weeks of it, she had been beginning to wonder. The countryside was so . . . well, *quiet*. But then Paul Waring had moved into another flat, and things had definitely begun to look up.

Now she smiled at him provocatively, glad that she'd spent so much money on a good dentist, and showing her whiter-than-white teeth to their best advantage.

'I would suggest we take our Pimm's outside and soak up some rays, but I've got a feeling that the Franklyns are already out there, and I don't fancy having to make small talk with that charming pair. Why she ever left Bath I'll never know. To hear her talk, you'd think she was practically the mayor of the place.'

She smiled down at the blond Adonis lounging in her best armchair and observed him shrewdly. She hadn't yet been able to wheedle out of him his exact age, but she put it somewhere in the early to mid-thirties. Not young enough to be called a toy boy, at any rate, surely? That is, if she ever managed to pin him down. So far, he was proving adept at slipping out of all of her carefully laid nets.

But she was determined to persevere. At just over six feet tall, he would have towered over her ex-rat Jeremy, that was for sure, she thought now with savage satisfaction, picturing the two men side by side. Paul had a mass of thick, attractive sandy-coloured hair, whereas poor old Jeremy was definitely going thin on top. What's more, Paul Waring was a walking advert for his business, with finely honed pecs and a washboard stomach. Jeremy, the last time she'd seen the cheating bastard, had been developing a distinct paunch.

In her best fantasies, she'd roll up at one of her old Wimbledon set's parties with Paul in tow, and waft him under the nose of her stupefied ex and that bimbo of a new wife of his. One day . . . Reluctantly dragging her mind from such thoughts, she brought her mind back to the here and now.

'Didn't you say that your friend, you know,' she snapped her fingers restlessly, 'the estate agent . . . ?'

'Jim?' Paul Waring drawled idly, not paying much attention to her chatter but enjoying the drink. One thing you could say about Pauline, she never stinted on the good things in life.

'Yes. Jim, that's the one,' Pauline agreed. 'The last time I was at your place working out, he was telling me how you introduced Sean Franklyn to the flats here, and practically helped him to sell flat 4 to them. What's more, he said you were happy for him to earn the commission free and clear. How come?'

She tried to keep the suspicion out of her tone, but the truth was, she'd taken against Margaret Franklyn in a big way, and at first sight. If ever there was a praying mantis in human form it was that one, Pauline thought grimly.

Paul Waring, owner of a number of gyms in the county, took a long gulp of the cold drink and sighed happily, his Adam's apple bobbing attractively in his tanned throat, a fact that didn't escape Pauline's eagle eye.

She caught him looking at her, checking out her newer, even more slender figure, and preened a bit in her white summer dress. For once she'd learned what her new and dishy neighbour did for a living, naturally she'd wasted no time in applying for membership of his nearest gym. And the results of all those workouts with him were now paying off real dividends with an even more honed body to show off. Which was especially satisfying with the stick-thin Margaret now on the scene.

'Oh that was nothing,' Paul said airily, finally answering her question. 'Jim Lancer's a really good client of mine, so when he told me that he hadn't had many sales commissions recently, and that his boss was beginning to give him the evil eye, I remembered how Sean was looking for a place. I insure the gyms with Sean's insurance company, that's how I know them,' he tossed out casually. 'So I just helped them both out by steering them towards this place.' He waved his glass around vaguely, indicating Pauline's nicely appointed apartment, and, by implication, the wider environs. 'It's a nice enough development, after all, and the Franklyns are the sort of tenants we want if we want to keep up standards.'

Pauline snorted. 'You think? I think that Margaret is positively a poisonous reptile.'

Paul laughed at her gently. 'Maybe she is, but she's a well-heeled, upper-middle-class poisonous reptile, and her husband is in insurance. You couldn't get more solid, safe bets when it comes to keeping up the tone of the place.'

'You know them well then, do you?' she asked, wondering jealously just how close he might be to the very fashionably thin and ever-elegant Margaret.

'Actually, Margaret was a member of one of my gyms once. I didn't really know her though; she worked with one of the personal trainers. I know Sean a lot better.'

Pauline had taken care of herself, he had to admit, but he wasn't sure that he was in the market for a Mrs Robinson figure of his own just yet. Not even a slim and youthful-looking version, with a thick cap of dark brown hair, attractive, foxy face and immaculate make-up.

'Yeah, so Sean's all right,' he said, deliberately leading the conversation away from the jewellery designer.

What was it with women that they always felt the need to compete with each other? Still, it could be entertaining to wind them up and watch them spit fire. And with that in mind, he decided to do just a little bit of gentle stirring.

'He's got the reputation for being a bit of a lad, mind you. Rumour has it that he's been casting his net a little too close to home this time though. I doubt if Margaret is going to stand for it.'

'Oh?' Pauline's dark brown eyes instantly lit up with spiteful enjoyment, her mind racing. 'Who's he seeing then?'

But Paul merely shrugged. 'Gentlemen never tell.'

Pauline bit back her annoyance at that, and eyed him thoughtfully. Dressed in what was nearly a uniform for him — pale shorts, white ankle socks, trainers, and a short-sleeved T-shirt bearing the logo of a famous designer on one shoulder — she was very much aware of the strength implicit in his tanned legs and arms. So what if he was a handful of years younger than herself? Didn't she deserve a bit of a treat, after all the crap that life had been throwing at her lately?

All she had to do was think of a way to manoeuvre him more firmly into her life — not to mention her bed — and things could start to look rosy again.

Unless he had someone else in mind. She knew he wasn't married, and was pretty sure he wasn't gay. So was his eye on someone else?

'I daresay what's sauce for the gander can be sauce for the goose,' she said, her lips tightening very unattractively. 'I don't expect Margaret is exactly faithful either. Sure you didn't get the Franklyns to join us in our merry little camp here just so you could see more of *her*?'

Paul sighed heavily. Pauline might be very much the available and eager divorcée, but it was also obvious that she could be hard work.

'Don't be daft,' he said mildly. 'I didn't have any ulterior motive in helping Sean or Margaret get a flat here, I assure you. I was just helping out Jim, like I said. In fact, I helped him earn two commissions, because I also put good old Maurice into flat 6 too, as it happens.'

'You did?' she asked, clearly surprised. Now that she thought about it, Maurice Keating, the retired Oxford don, had been the third one to move into the vicarage after herself and Paul. 'Why?'

'You've got to have a professor or two to give the neighbourhood a touch of class,' Paul drawled.

Pauline laughed. 'You're wicked,' she said. 'Mocking poor old Maurice like that.'

Paul grinned. 'Don't tell me the old duffer hasn't already pigeonholed you and bored you witless going on about the major opus that he's writing.'

Pauline rolled her eyes dramatically. 'Hasn't he ever? The metaphysical poets, isn't it? Or something like that.'

Paul nodded. 'Sounds about right. I'm not sure, my eyes start to glaze over whenever he starts to speak about it. It's all those perfect vowels and ever so proper BBC announcer's voice that does it.'

'He's not a fan of Margaret's, though, is he?' Pauline said with a small smile, unable to let the subject of her nemesis go. 'Have you seen the way he glares at her whenever they pass each other in the hall?'

'She probably rebuffed the randy old sod, and he's bearing a grudge,' Paul said carelessly.

Pauline chuckled, then her smile abruptly fled as the blond man drained his drink in a gulp and rose lithely to his feet. 'Well, thanks for that, but I must be off. The staff at the new gym need a collective kick up their backsides. Subscriptions are falling off.'

'Oh, OK. Fancy coming over for dinner tonight? Something healthy,' she added hastily. 'I've got some organic vegetables in, thought I'd make a stir-fry. Virgin olive oil, naturally.'

Since she'd moved to the vicarage, she'd been swiftly converted to healthy eating and exercise.

Paul shot her a beaming but regretful smile. 'Sorry, I'll probably still be working. Besides, it's too damned hot to eat. I haven't had an appetite since this heatwave struck. Maybe some other time, eh?'

Casting around desperately for something to stop him leaving so soon, she grasped the first thought that came to her. 'So what are you going to be doing for this garden party thing the vicar's wife has saddled us with? Aren't we all supposed to be bringing a casserole or something, à la Women's Institute?'

'Oh, are we supposed to bring our own goodies?' he asked vaguely. He'd received the invitation through his door, of course, but hadn't paid much attention to it. A week or so ago, Monica Noble had decided that, with most of the flats now sold, it would be nice to get all the residents of the big old house together for an official getting-to-know-you do. 'I thought it was a housewarming party.'

'Whatever,' Pauline said, rolling her eyes. 'It'll hardly be the "do" of the season, will it? I thought I'd bring some salads and perhaps some of those artisan breads they sell at the farmer's market.'

Paul grinned, unsurprised. He couldn't imagine Pauline baking a Victoria sponge. 'When in doubt, bring booze, I say. I'll bring along some good bottles of wine, I think. Maybe splash out on some champers. What do you think?' Although he rarely drank much alcohol himself (the Pimm's just now being too good to pass up), he knew it went down well with others.

Pauline's eyes glittered. 'Super. I love champagne.'

'Right, that's settled then,' he said, and headed for the door. As he thankfully escaped the divorcée's clutches to go back to his own flat (the problems at the new gym having been slightly exaggerated), he passed Joan and Julie Dix, the mother and daughter who'd recently taken flat 9.

Joan Dix, noting the number of the flat he'd just come out of, smiled grimly to herself, then caught her nineteen-year-old daughter's curious eye and shook her head slightly. It was nothing to her what her neighbours got up to. She had problems enough of her own to think about.

Once inside their own flat, Julie went straight to her bedroom, no doubt to use her mobile phone. She was hardly ever off it these days, Joan thought uneasily. Wearily, she sat down at a table and rubbed a tired hand over her face.

She was going to have to do something about the way things were going. Her old mother had always said that it was best to just nip things in the bud before they had a chance to get worse. It might hurt in the short term, but in the long term it saved a heap of trouble.

Now all she had to do was work up the courage to act. The trouble was, she didn't know if Julie would ever forgive her. After taking a gap year to do some travelling before starting uni, Julie was at just that age when she thought she knew everything. When, in fact, she still knew so little of the world, her mother acknowledged solemnly. And just what foul things it could do to you.

A still-attractive woman, with blonde hair and tired eyes, Joan Dix contemplated her next move with grim determination.

* * *

As Trisha Lancer walked back to her car and began the drive home, somewhere in the big converted vicarage behind her somebody sat at a table making lists. To an observer the list wouldn't have made much sense, but to the author it was a complete blueprint for murder.

Each item was gone through minutely and ticked off. Reminders got underlined. A memo to hide clean clothes in the darkest alcove of the stairs was heavily underlined — as was the note to burn the old clothes after changing.

The maker of this list then slowly put down the pen, stretched, yawned lazily and leaned back in a chair. It was amazing how *easy* it was going to be to murder somebody and, even more importantly, to get away with it.

After all, all you really had to do was carefully plan each and every step beforehand, time it, hone it, and then finally have the nerve to go through with it. To leave nothing to chance, to calculate all the odds, and be prepared to take just the odd, well thought out risk.

And, of course, make clever use of a few everyday household items.

CHAPTER 3

The next day, Julie Dix pushed a lock of long, honey-coloured hair behind one ear and glanced out of her third-storey window into the gardens below. She was sitting in her favourite place — the wide window seat in the largest window in the lounge — on a padded cushion that her mother had covered herself with some lovely, old chintz-style curtain material that they'd found in a charity shop.

Ever since she'd been a little girl, she'd loved exploring such shops with her mother, on the hunt for 'treasures.' These could be the genuine thing, like a piece of undiscovered Moorcroft pottery, or a piece of atypical Clarice Cliff, which her mother would inevitably swoop on, or simply some cheap but pretty costume jewellery that appealed to a little girl, and had Julie happily forking out her pocket money. So when she'd come back from Thailand and had moved into her mother's new flat for the summer before starting university, it had seemed natural for them to pick up old habits.

For as long as Julie could remember, it had always been her and her mother against the world. But she was grown up now, and the sooner her mother accepted the fact, the better.

She gave a small sigh as the ancient church clock struck ten, but a quick glance at her watch showed her that it wasn't yet even a quarter to. The warm air wafting in proclaimed another blazing day was on its way, making her lift the sash window up even higher to let in more of a breeze. Lazily she lifted the hair off her neck and let the breeze play around her nape.

It seemed almost a shame to be leaving the country during such an unusually fine spell. Still, Sean was right. It was now or never.

Down below, Vera and John were putting out the folding tables, ready for this shindig that Monica Noble had arranged, and Julie smiled as she watched them. It was kind of nice to see the two, lonely, middle-aged people getting tentatively together. A bit embarrassing maybe, but sweet. At nineteen, Julie was still inwardly convinced that true love, *real* love, was really only the province of the young. But she liked Vera Ainsley, who never seemed to give her growing success and fame much credence, and although John Lerwick rarely said much, and Julie hadn't got the faintest idea what his life story was, she found herself liking him as well. There was something about a quiet, strong, mature man that made her feel safe. Now she felt her lips give a small twist as she thought about that. Did she still have daddy issues or what?

Yet on that fine, lovely morning, looking down at the mundane scene below and contemplating with excitement what was to come, Julie felt calm, certain and committed. Love, she supposed complacently, did that to you. The silly little teenager that she'd been before, doing the whole gap-year thing but really learning nothing from her travels, was now long gone.

Instead, she was becoming a woman, and her mother would just have to deal with that. If she, Julie, could analyse herself enough to see what was happening to her, why couldn't her mother do the same for herself? Perhaps she should just sit her mother down and explain things to her. Just because her only daughter was about to leave the nest, didn't mean her life was over. OK, so she was in her late forties now. She was still an attractive woman. If Vera could find love at her age, why couldn't Joan?

Julie's contemplation was interrupted by a sharp sound from below.

John Lerwick yelped as a folding table inexplicably snapped shut on his fingers and he cursed under his breath, grimacing at his own clumsiness, making Julie, from her lofty perch, giggle. Hearing it, he looked up and gave a cheery wave.

Everyone, Julie supposed, liked John — even that snobby Pauline Weeks, ever since she found out that he was the creator of a cartoon strip in a big daily tabloid, and was thus a minor celebrity in his own right.

Julie found his cartoons, always set in the animal world, to be invariably hilarious and well-drawn, and they were always the first thing she went to over her morning cornflakes.

Her mother, of course, only read the *Guardian*.

With a small sigh as she thought of her mother once more, Julie turned away from the window. All complacency aside about how all her mother really needed was to get herself a life, she was feeling rather worried about Joan. Her mother, as Julie well knew and sometimes to her cost, was not an easy person to deceive, and Julie was beginning to feel distinctly nervous now. Joan Dix's radar for trouble had always been finely honed, no doubt as a result of her disastrous marriage, and Julie knew she needed to be treated with caution.

So no matter how much Sean explained how easy it would all be once they'd made the initial effort, she knew that there were still so many things that could go drastically wrong. And her mother finding out what was happening and messing it all up was definitely one of them.

Usually a placid person, Joan had a side to her that could be surprisingly frightening.

Julie wished that it would soon all be over, but the garden party wasn't even due to start until two. Even as she heard more laughing voices coming from below, she felt herself shiver and, rising from her seat, walked restlessly about the apartment, ending up in her bedroom, where she lay stretched out on her bed, staring at the ceiling morosely. In here, she couldn't hear the preparations being made below.

The old vicarage had been built like a big square 'C' with two wings looking out across one another over a small expanse of central formal gardens. The party was being held in this part of the grounds, which meant that those with flats overlooking the back of the vicarage wouldn't have a view of it at all.

Julie tossed restlessly onto her side. She was sure that Margaret suspected something, and might become spiteful enough to pick an argument, or maybe even create a public scene — which would ruin all their plans.

'What's that big sigh for?' Joan asked from the open doorway. Julie jumped, then shrugged.

'Oh, nothing.' She smiled brightly and sat up, swinging her legs over the side of the bed and regarding her painted toenails thoughtfully. 'It's just this party. I wish we didn't have to go.' She didn't realize it, but an edge of real desperation had sounded in her voice, and Joan frowned, suddenly looking her age.

Joan's husband had died several years ago, but not before leading his long-suffering wife a merry and utterly demoralising little dance. Fidelity hadn't been a word that Roger Dix kept in his personal dictionary, which had, not surprisingly, given Joan's personality a certain twist.

She simply didn't trust men anymore, and had never even been tempted to date during the last five years of her widowhood. In her philosophy, men simply led you on, got you in trouble then left you to cope alone. And she wanted more than that for her Julie. Much more.

Julie had always wanted to go to university and study to become a vet — a worthy ambition that her mother had always heartily supported. In her opinion, a woman needed a good profession and to be self-sufficient right from the start. And to that end, she'd scrimped and saved and made sure to invest her late husband's insurance policy money wisely, to ensure that her daughter wouldn't be saddled with student debts that would hang around her neck like a millstone. Her daughter's future had thus always been set in stone, and was therefore one less thing for her to worry about.

Now, as Joan looked down at her, she noticed the dark smudges under her daughter's pretty green eyes, making her wonder what was keeping her from sleeping at night. Her lips tightened as the suspicions that had been festering in her for the last few weeks suddenly erupted. Unconvincingly, she told herself not to anticipate the worst.

'Oh, I don't know. You might surprise yourself and actually enjoy it. Monica's gone to a lot of trouble to make it a success. And she strikes me as the sort of woman who usually succeeds in doing what she sets out to do. I'm sure we'll all have a good time.'

Julie shrugged. 'Oh, it's just not my kind of thing, that's all,' she muttered evasively. 'I mean, it's so retro.'

Joan tried to relax. Teenage tantrums she could cope with — if that's all it was. 'Come on, love, it won't be as bad as you think. Monica only suggested it as a way for us all to get to know each other better. It'd be silly not to be friendly. You like Vera and John, don't you? And the others will probably turn out to be quite nice too, once we get to know them.'

'Sure. Look, forget I said anything,' Julie said, backtracking quickly. 'Besides, it's you who has to live here, not me,' she added thoughtlessly.

Joan nodded, turning away quickly, lest her daughter see her sudden tears. Julie, an only child, had been Joan's whole world for as long as she could remember. Unloved and neglected by her husband, the birth of their daughter had finally given Joan a reason for being. She'd finally found someone to love without fear. And love her she had. Sometimes so fiercely that even Joan's friends had worried about her. There was something almost unnatural about the devotion Joan had to her only offspring.

So when Julie had finally enrolled at university, Joan had felt bereft. Relocating here — to be nearer to Julie's chosen university — had seemed like the thing to do. She knew Julie was hoping that she would be able to make a new life for herself here, and indeed, life in the country was actually suiting Joan very well. She liked Monica Noble and her husband, and was already making friends in the village. She'd found herself a job in the pretty nearby market town, which had done wonders for her self-confidence, and had even joined the WI.

So when Julie had first come here, she had been relieved to see that her mother had looked more relaxed than she had in a long time — which went a long way towards assuaging her guilt for what she was about to do now.

But there was no help for it. Julie *had* to have Sean. Life simply wasn't worth much without him.

Now Joan sighed heavily. It still caught her on the raw to be reminded that Julie wouldn't be living with her full time anymore. Sometimes she felt on the verge of panic, and during the day she'd sit for hours, thinking up ways to scare the men away from her daughter. And one man in particular.

'Look, Mum, why don't I make a proper fruit punch for this party?' Julie said, guessing the reason for her mother's gloom and desperately seeking to distract her. 'I'll even sneak some rum into it.'

'Don't you dare!' Joan squeaked, thinking of Monica Noble. Not that she thought Monica would mind, but, well, she *was* still the vicar's wife. And such things still meant something to someone of Joan's upbringing, which had been rather conservative and traditional, being the only daughter of parents who'd waited late in life to start a family.

Julie firmly ushered her mother out and towards the kitchen. 'Why don't you start on it for me? You know, peel some oranges and stuff. I'll be there in a minute.'

Joan moved off to the kitchen. But once there, she paused abruptly in the middle of the room, thinking furiously. Her daughter's tactics didn't fool her, not for one minute. Besides, she'd been thinking about things, and had already decided what she'd have to do.

She would have to tackle Margaret Franklyn. Yes. That was by far the best thing to do. After all, the woman had as much to lose as Joan did. It only made sense for them to get their heads together and sort it out once and for all.

Julie watched her mother go and sighed. Then, unable to prevent herself, she crossed to her dresser and reached into her underwear drawer. There, she pulled out a piece of dark cream paper and read the loving words, then gently rested the letter against her lips, kissing it and feeling foolish but happy.

Who said that romance — real romance that is, not the poor imitation that passed for it today — was dead? She felt excited and scared and just a little bit sick. What they were going to do was so final. A proper, grand gesture. But for her lover, she'd take whatever risks he asked of her, she thought with a delicious pang of fatalism.

Reluctantly, she put the letter away and sighed. She'd told him she'd destroyed all his letters long ago, as per their checklist. But she hadn't been able to bring herself to consign this last letter to the flames.

If only he wasn't married. And to such a bitch! Things would have been so much easier. They wouldn't have had to do any of this. It just wasn't fair!

Sean was such a great planner and clever thinker, though, Julie comforted herself nervously. Surely nothing could go wrong? Even so, she felt sick with nerves.

* * *

One floor down, Dr Maurice Keating checked his appearance in the mirror, and fiddled restlessly with his thick silver mane — secretly his pride and joy — wondering if his present barber cut his hair as well as the old one had. He thought not on the whole, but he *was* cheaper. Not that such penny-pinching need concern him for much longer, he thought with a smile. Soon he'd be able to afford again all the fine things in life that he'd once taken for granted.

The thought made his smile widen even further with satisfaction, and he adjusted his cuffs before wandering back to the lounge to read his paper. From time to time he heard noises outside in the garden, but felt no inclination to go down and offer his services. He was not the sort to enjoy manual labour, not even the modest kind required on golf courses or croquet lawns.

Besides, he was doing his bit by bringing cheese and pickles to the party, and had already cut off the whitening crusts from the old cheese that he'd bought on sale at one of Cheltenham's lower-end supermarkets. The jar of pickles had been a Christmas present from an allotment-owning friend who grew all his own shallots. And since Maurice was far too fastidious to eat them, having always had a horror of getting bad breath, they'd been pickling away merrily in a dark corner of his larder ever since.

He frowned, and hoped that the sound of the party wouldn't spook his rather shy friend, who was due to visit later that afternoon. But he'd warned him about it, and had explained everything that he needed, ad infinitum. He wouldn't let him down, surely?

Maurice tried not to worry about it. Unlike Julie, Maurice had been looking forward to the party enormously. He was very much a social animal and liked the way people responded with satisfying reverence to his brains and erudition. So when he'd first received his invitation from the vicar's good lady, he'd accepted with alacrity.

And then the new arrivals had moved in, and completely out of the blue, his world had come crashing down around his ears.

Getting to his feet now, he walked over to the window. It was still only ten thirty, and already distressingly humid. Along with fear of developing halitosis, Maurice hated the thought of sweating, too. Body odour was yet another of his pet hates.

'Damn, it's going to be hot,' he murmured, watching that wonderful woman Vera Ainsley arranging vases of roses on the tables. If it wasn't for that moonstruck John Lerwick always hanging around her, he might have made moves in that direction himself. Her cookery books sold very well indeed, or so he'd heard. And a wealthy woman was always that bit more attractive than one who lived in Penury Street. But now, even setting off on that simple little adventure was out of the question.

Maurice prowled around the room restlessly. He felt uneasy, deep in his bones, now that the time had come for action. But the visitor due to arrive wouldn't take kindly to being put off at this late stage, and might even turn nasty. Besides, other events had also been put into motion. So even if he'd wanted to, there was no backing out now.

* * *

On the ground floor in flat 4, Margaret Franklyn lay back in the tub, a small contented smile on her face. She'd just purchased a gorgeous new Jaeger dress, white lace over cream silk, and she was determined to wear it to this ridiculous little garden party. She'd had her hair done that morning, and it was now carefully protected in a shower cap. She had hours left yet to do her make-up, and was utterly determined to be the most lovely thing around this afternoon, just to show them all.

To show that silly little teenager what a real woman could look like, for instance. Oh yes, she knew exactly what Julie Dix was up to, and boy did she have a great big spoke to put in *her* wheel. She also couldn't wait to see her husband's face when her lawyer served the divorce papers on him. Margaret laughed happily to herself, soaped her skinny legs, and thought about jewellery.

Jewellery was her one great love. It had been the fact that she couldn't afford to buy the really spectacular pieces that had started her designing and making her own. Selling the pieces after she got bored with them had been an afterthought, but had led to her forming her own small business, which was proving to be a nice little earner.

It was ironic that now she could afford to buy almost all the baubles her heart desired. Especially thanks to her two most valued — and strictly private — clients. The thought of how much those two had spent on her projects was truly lovely to contemplate. Then she frowned, remembering a nasty event just over a year ago, when the two of them had almost met, due to one of them arriving way too early. Watching it all from the window, she recalled how sick it had made her feel, for it wouldn't do for them to be aware of each other. But luckily she'd got away with it. One of them had just been pulling away in his car as the other one had driven in, and taken advantage of the free parking space.

She sighed amid the bubbles, wondering how much longer that lucrative deal would continue, and returned her attention to her outfit. With a white dress she could wear almost any-thing of course, and just yesterday she'd finished some stunning pieces in aquamarine and moonstone. She'd look sensational.

If only those diamond earrings hadn't been stolen! Still, she'd fixed that Carol-Ann's thieving little wagon all right. The police sergeant she'd talked to on the phone that morning had been given a right rocket. There'd be some action soon on that front, she was sure of it.

She was so looking forward to seeing Monica Noble's superior nose put out of joint when her precious little chick was hauled off to the cells. Something about the vicar's wife had always rubbed her up the wrong way; there was something so knowing in those big baby blues of hers that made Margaret feel petty and small.

With a snort, Margaret forced herself to think of some-thing far more amusing. Like the pathetic Pauline Weeks for instance. Not that it would be hard to put *her* in the shade. Perhaps, just for the hell of it, she'd create a little mischief there. Pauline was so obviously panting for Paul Waring — a situation just brimming with laughter-making possibilities.

Oh, she was going to have fun this afternoon! And when she thought about her secret meeting and all the goodies that *that* entailed, she laughed even louder.

* * *

Most of the old-time villagers, plus a good portion of those from the new estates, were also contemplating fun just then. A small, old-fashioned fair, complete with dodgem cars, round-abouts and a Ferris wheel, had come to Cheltenham, oozing nostalgia (and goldfish in plastic bags) like a leaky tap, and thus proving irresistible to many. Monica had noted its adver-tised arrival just three days after issuing all the invitations to her own party, and had felt like spitting. She'd contemplated changing the date of the party, but by then Vera had enthusi-astically taken up the challenge, and there was no going back.

And, to be fair, most of the vicarage residents probably hadn't intended to go to the fair anyway. It was certainly below Maurice, who wouldn't be seen dead at such a place, and both Pauline Weeks and Paul Waring probably consid-ered themselves far too sophisticated and modern-minded to be lured there.

But for most of the residents of Heyford Bassett, a sum-mer visit to the fair was high old entertainment, and already the place was becoming unusually deserted. Streams of cars had been seen steadily disappearing up the hill — the only route out of the village — which led to the main B-road about half a mile away, leaving behind an almost eerily silent, and near-empty village. Only, in a small country village, there was always someone watching and listening.

* * *

In his study, Graham Noble blinked rapidly.

40

'Venus?' he repeated, staring at the gum-chewing, enthusiastic young mother in front of him. He glanced helplessly across at her pimply, equally young partner. 'Venus?' he repeated again.

They were unmarried, and, in his judgement, were likely to remain so, even though they'd come to him to discuss the christening arrangements for their week-old baby daughter.

'You want to call her Venus?' Graham said again, as if repeating the fact often enough would make it sink in.

'Venus Marjoram,' said the mother, popping a gum bubble enthusiastically and nodding. 'Right. We haven't registered her yet, because we couldn't agree on a name, but now we have, right, Stevie?' By her side, the proud father shifted uncomfortably in his chair.

'I see.' Graham swallowed hard. He glanced at the lad, remembering him vaguely from long ago days when he'd sung in the choir. Or rather, caterwauled in the choir.

Steven Marsh blushed and looked distinctly uneasy.

'And do you, er, like this name, Steven?' he probed mildly. Steven quickly looked down at his trainers and Linsey gave him a nippy but sharp-elbowed dig in the ribs.

'Yeah, I love it. It's different, right?' he added hopefully.

'Oh it's certainly that,' Graham agreed dryly. 'Yes, well, I'll have to call around and visit, er, little Venus,' he bit the bullet bravely, 'sometime soon.'

'Well, don't make it tomorrow,' Linsey drawled. 'We took her to the doc for her check-up this morning, and she's been grizzling ever since. We're gonna have to miss the fair today 'cause of her. Can't get no one to babysit, see?'

It was nearly eleven o'clock before the proud parents left for the short walk home, arguing about the merits of 'All Things Bright and Beautiful' versus 'Onward, Christian Soldiers' for the service.

* * *

Julie nimbly negotiated the stile, jumped off the wooden plank onto the other side of the field, and began walking the short distance along the footpath that led behind the church. She squealed as a pair of arms shot out from behind an elder bush and dragged her to the ground.

Above her, Sean Franklyn's face grinned down at her.

'You!' Julie sighed with relief, her heart pounding. 'You scared me!' But, of course, she was utterly thrilled.

'I know. Not long to go now.' Sean's lean, handsome face slowly became serious. 'You know what you have to do?'

'Of course,' Julie said, her own grin fading. 'We've gone over it enough times.'

Sean nodded. 'It's just that we've got to get the timing just right.'

'I know. I'll remember.' She sounded a touch angry now.

'OK,' he said, a conciliatory smile coming to his dark, swarthy features. 'I know you won't let me down.' His hands splayed across her slender waist, the fingertips just nudging her under her small breasts.

'Did you go to the safety box this morning?' Julie asked, running a hand up his sleeve.

'Yes. I've got all the money. Spain will be great. You'll see.'

Julie nodded. 'Sean,' she said tentatively. 'It will be OK, won't it?'

Sean smiled and bent his head to kiss her. When he lifted his head again, he was satisfied with the starry look in her eyes. Hell, she made him feel twenty again, and as if anything in life was possible.

'Of course it will,' he whispered, his voice gruff and a bit impatient. 'You'll see.'

* * *

Noon came and went, and the temperature soared. Showers were run, and last-minute food items were prepared. And as the time for the garden party to start drew near, somebody intent on murder did a quick tour of the vicarage and grounds.

Checked that the back doors were unlocked and free of any obstacles. Checked that the recess under the stairway on the second floor was definitely out of clear view of anybody standing in the garden-party area. Checked that all the equipment was working properly. Had a large Scotch, and waited.

It would be soon now.

CHAPTER 4

Monica reached for the thinnest of her summer dresses and slipped it over her head, then realized that you could just see the outline of her bare legs through the cool, multi-coloured, flower-patterned silk, and muttered something vaguely mutinous.

'Oh, *très* daring,' Carol-Ann drawled mockingly from her prone position on her mother's bed, munching industriously on an apple. 'What *would* the fan club say? Daring to show that you actually have . . . gasp, shock, horror . . . legs.'

Monica grinned back at her. 'Don't be so cheeky. Anyway, the fan club won't be here for once. This is strictly a residents-only bash, and besides, most of them have gone off to the fair anyway. So if I'm to blow caution to the wind and ruin my reputation, now is the time to do it.'

Carol-Ann cast a jaundiced eye over her mother's demure dress and snorted. *She* wouldn't be caught dead in it! Her own outfit for the afternoon consisted of a pair of very short designer shorts and a top that tied into a knot at her navel, exposing most of her midriff. Only she hadn't told her mother that yet.

'Oh, by the way,' Carol-Ann said, reaching into one of her pockets. 'I bought these this morning, from the shop.

44

Think they'll look good on me?' And she held out a paste set of diamond and sapphire drop earrings that looked suspiciously similar to the ones that Monica could remember Margaret Franklyn wearing a few weeks ago. So Carol-Ann had clearly got to hear about Margaret's suspicions.

Monica fought between the impulse to laugh and the need to take her mischievous daughter to task.

'I take it that Mrs Franklyn has been asking you some pointed questions about her missing pair of earrings?' she asked archly instead.

Carol-Ann snorted. 'As if I'd want her . . .' and she mimed sticking her finger down her throat and retching, '. . . earrings.'

Monica sighed and reached for a bottle of Miss Dior, and Carol-Ann promptly shot off the bed and headed for her own room, lest any of the naff scent should get on to her. 'Say what you like, it's for the young at heart,' Monica sing-songed after her retreating back, grinning at her daughter's pithy response.

Then she sighed and glanced at herself in the mirror again. Her newly washed wavy hair gleamed nut-brown in the bright daylight, and sensible, cool sandals encased her small, neat feet. She looked ladylike, but not too obviously like a vicar's wife, which was just how she liked it.

She glanced at her watch, saw that it was nearly two, and rushed for the front door, tapping on her husband's study door in reminder as she went. Then, remembering that she'd promised John to give the roses in the front garden a final watering before the party got properly underway, she quickly nipped back down the length of the flat. Exiting through the door that led from the Nobles' flat into an interconnecting communal corridor, she walked swiftly towards the exit.

This corridor ran the entire length of the converted building. Passing flats 3 and 4 on either side of her as she went, she wondered if anybody could have started the party early, and hoped not. John would kill her! She reached the back door almost at a run and fairly erupted out into the blazing heat of the afternoon. The crunch of the gravel in the car park that

45

had been made out back sounded loud under her feet as she tramped across it.

The back garden was even more of a jungle than the front, with thick rhododendron bushes, silver birches and weed-strewn herbaceous borders running riot everywhere. But John's rain butt was kept out here in the shade of two big oaks, as was his tool shed, a rather dilapidated greenhouse and a cold frame that was currently growing cucumbers. She made her way to the shed and quickly filled a watering can. As she walked back to the rear door, she dodged a car, which had, very unwisely, been parked in the full blazing glare of the sun. Skirting the smart dark blue Jaguar XJS, recognizing it as Paul Waring's car, she winced as she glanced inside at the cream leather upholstery. Anyone trying to sit on that now would get a scorched behind, and no mistake!

Luckily for Monica, everyone had decided to be fashionably late and the party area was still free of guests, with only the volunteer workers present. John, a padded fifty-two-year-old with blond hair fast becoming silver, twinkled at her as she began to guiltily water the standard roses.

'I know, I know,' she called to him as she flitted from rose bush to rose bush like a demented hummingbird. She then tucked the empty watering can out of sight under the tables. 'Shall I go and get my fruit pies now?' she asked cheerfully, turning to Vera, who nodded at her fondly.

Almost a female equivalent of John, she was also blonde turning silver, plump-figured, and easygoing. And right now, the celebrity cook's own contributions lay scattered along the length of the tables, looking, as always, in a class of their own. Crisp green salads of every description, tempting seafood platters, delicious-looking little quiches and tarts, trifles and towering gateaux all combined to set Monica's tastebuds watering.

When she came back, towing a complaining and pie-laden Carol-Ann in her wake, Pauline Weeks and Joan and Julie Dix had also emerged with their own offerings. And if Pauline's chicken and ham pie looked suspiciously like the huge pies you could get in the local Sainsbury's, nobody was going to say as much.

Within half an hour, everyone else had arrived. Maurice Keating looked set to go punting on the Cherwell, with a rakish boater hat atop his head, very smart white cotton trousers and a matching white shirt with a navy blue trim. Paul Waring, typically, was dressed in shorts that revealed the strong columns of his hairy and muscular legs, and a plain white T-shirt that stretched impressively across his broad and even more muscular chest. Margaret Franklyn was dressed as if she were about to go to Ascot. The lace and cream dress she was wearing was set off with a hat so outrageously wide-brimmed that it offered shade from the sun to anybody standing within a few yards of her, and the jewellery she had on quite literally took one's breath away.

Monica eyed the dramatic aquamarine necklace, which was comprised of interlocking irises, and wondered if she dared ask her to make one for herself. Then she realized that Margaret would probably only sniff superciliously and say that *every* piece she made was a unique one-off, and that only the desperate and tasteless wanted replicas made.

'Wine, dear lady? I should get in while you can if I were you, as I can only see one bottle.'

Monica jumped then turned and smiled at Maurice, who had somehow appeared beside her.

'No, thank you, Maurice, it's far too hot for that,' she declined, fanning a hand in front of her face for emphasis.

Maurice, who could always drink wine, especially if someone else had paid for it, refilled his own glass, and offered to bring her a glass of Julie's fruit punch.

'I've heard tell that it's very good. And chock-a-block with ice.' At that they both turned to look automatically at Julie, who was just selecting a jumbo prawn from the seafood platter.

'Thank goodness they're being eaten quickly.' Vera, having walked quietly up to them, nodded at the platter. 'Seafood in this heat needs to be consumed right away.'

Maurice sneaked a quick glance at his watch.

Monica noticed but didn't mind, since she rather liked Maurice. She could see right through him, of course, as could everyone else, but there was something endearing about the front he put up. An essentially lonely man, missing the collegiate life, and perhaps living just a little above his means, he reminded her a bit of a character out of a book, one where the hero was trapped living in an age that didn't suit him.

Vera caught her eye and smiled, as if reading her thoughts, then said brightly to him, 'I wouldn't mind a glass of punch, since you're giving it your own personal recommendation.'

'Oh now, I wouldn't say that—' Maurice began, turning the talk to fine wine, which, apparently, was his real forte.

Monica, content to let Maurice flirt with the cook, tuned out their conversation, and instead glanced around at the rest of the throng. Off in one corner, beside a table on which a big blackcurrant cheesecake predominated, Pauline was button-holing Paul, so no surprises there. Joan had wandered over to her daughter's side. Julie, it had to be said, looked studiously bored, but was maybe just a little bit nervous. Her eyes kept darting about, as if afraid to land on any one spot, Monica noticed.

Further down the table stood the fabulous Margaret, and her rather less-than-fabulous husband. Sean, like the rest of them, was beginning to look a bit wilted in the intense heat. A more mismatched couple Monica couldn't imagine — and not a happy one either, if their perpetual arguments were anything to go by.

Moving on, her eyes softened. Graham was handing Carol-Ann a glass of fruit punch, and pretending not to notice her daring attire. He himself was wearing a short-sleeved blue shirt, his ever-present dog collar, and a pair of lightweight grey trousers.

Monica noticed Margaret detach herself from her husband's side and wander over to Paul. Even from where she was standing, Monica could see the way that Pauline bridled at her sashaying approach, and rested a hand possessively on Paul's forearm.

'Oh-oh,' said Carol-Ann, who'd sidled up to her mother and followed Monica's line of sight. She now gave a brief chortle of glee. 'Poor old Pauline's gonna get her knickers in a twist now, just you wait and see.'

'Carol-Ann,' Monica chided automatically. 'You know Graham doesn't like you to talk like that.'

'Sure.' Carol-Ann shrugged. That was why she did it.

To Carol-Ann, life had been good in their small Clapham flat. So when her mother had met a country parson at a PR party in Cheltenham and then one day calmly announced that she was getting married and that they were moving to the countryside, Carol-Ann hadn't exactly been overwhelmed with joy.

Having a vicar for a stepdad stripped her of her street cred overnight, in such a cruel way that it bordered on child abuse! And as for having to change schools at such an impressionable age, well, her mother would have only herself to blame if her schoolwork crashed and she had to leave school at sixteen to become a waitress. Which meant that she'd never be able to find a decent boyfriend, and would die a dried-up old maid. Monica would never be a grandmother.

None of these dire predictions, it had to be said, had seemed to make any great impression on Monica, and now here she was, lumbered with Graham for a stepfather. Carol-Ann sucked moodily on a spoon. In her other hand was a bowl filled to the brim with one of Vera's coconut and chocolate meringue trifles. Then she suddenly smiled.

'See, I told you. Just look at Pauline. She looks set to explode,' Carol-Ann crowed. 'Margaret's all over Paul like a rash.'

Pauline's sharply raised voice and Margaret's sultry answering laugh wafted across the party like an uninvited guest. Paul deftly broke up the potential catfight by simply shrugging off Margaret's red-painted hand from his other arm and saying something quietly in her ear. Margaret, giving a little shrug and a wide, predatory smile, returned to her husband, who'd been trying to avoid looking at Julie Dix.

Pauline said something pithy to Paul and stomped off, disappearing inside the house. Maurice, who'd failed to hold Vera's attention for more than five polite minutes, wandered back to the table in search of more wine. As he did so, he glanced yet again at his watch. The solitary wine bottle was empty. Seeing him put the empty bottle back on the table, Paul came up to slap him on the back.

'Sorry, Maurice, old boy, my fault,' he said, making the older man jump. 'I said I'd bring the booze, and damned if I didn't forget. Monica, does the village shop stay open on a Saturday afternoon, do you know?' he called across the table, and Monica nodded back.

'Righto, everybody, booze coming up. Who wants ale or beer?'

John jauntily agreed that that would be a good idea — and maybe some stout. Grinning good-naturedly at the progressively tall orders that were being playfully tossed his way by the others, Paul jogged back into the house and disappeared.

Sean glanced across the lawn and caught Julie's eye. Carefully, inching one hand up to the other, he surreptitiously tapped the glass in his watch.

Vera, just about to raise a glass of fruit punch to her lips, caught the little by-play and looked nervously around. But she needn't have worried. Margaret, having put Pauline into a satisfying bad mood, was now more than happy to turn her attentions to Julie, but had turned around just a shade too late to see the silent message being passed between her husband and the other woman in his life.

* * *

Pauline stomped into her flat and slammed her shoulder bag onto the settee. 'That *bitch*!' she hissed, walking to the kitchen and reaching for a bottle of vodka. Paul was hers, damn it. And she wasn't about to let a Venus flytrap like Margaret get in her way.

She took a slug of vodka straight from the bottle, and coughed.

* * *

Julie, wearing a skimpy halter top and shorts, flushed nervously as Margaret bore down on her. By her daughter's side, Joan visibly stiffened, and a look of hate crossed her face as Margaret began to speak. Her voice was so low that nobody overheard her opening comment, but whatever it was took the colour right out of Julie's face.

Joan made a sudden lurching movement to one side, and for one brief second, it looked to the startled and nervous John Lerwick, who had been keeping a careful eye on them, as if she were getting ready to thump the elegant Margaret right on the nose. He saw Joan's hand clench into a fist and then slowly uncurl again. He glanced instantly across the lawn towards Vera, wondering if she had noticed.

Maurice returned to Monica, wondering if he should think up an excuse to return to the house and voice it, or if he should just casually leave. Which would seem the more natural?

'A very nice turnout,' he said heartily, waving a hand over the assembly, and trying to ignore the increasingly tense atmosphere that was stealing over the little party. 'I must say, it's really rather hot. It's quite enervating, isn't it? I think I might go in and change.'

Monica smiled, thinking that only someone like Maurice would ever use the word 'enervating.' Not that he didn't look washed out, poor thing, she thought with sudden guilt. Maurice, when all was said and done, was a man of advancing years.

'Why don't you do just that, then come down and find some shade? I'll bring you something cold to drink,' she advised gently.

51

Maurice nodded, pleased with his nonchalant exit, and moved away.

* * *

Pauline Weeks tried the handle of the door, not really thinking it could possibly be unlocked, but it was! For a moment she felt terrified, and told herself not to be so lame. You had to take risks sometimes. Pushing open the door, she walked inside and looked around. It took her only a minute to do what she needed to, and then she was once more back at the door.

She pushed it open and listened carefully, but heard nothing.

* * *

Once inside the cool of the house, Maurice walked quickly to the stairs and mounted them, pausing once to look around, thinking that he'd heard something. A door closing, perhaps? But after a moment, he decided he was probably letting nerves get the better of him.

With his heart hammering in his chest he resumed climbing, and once outside his own door was rather disappointed to find the corridor empty. Yet again he glanced at his watch. He hoped his new friend wasn't going to keep him waiting. You'd have thought, though, in his line of clandestine business, it would pay to be punctual.

He fished his keys out of his pocket and unlocked the door, taking a few steps inside, then stopped abruptly. From the sofa a smallish, squat man with ginger hair was slowly standing up.

Maurice gaped at him foolishly, then quickly shut the door behind him.

'How the hell did you get in here?' the ex-Oxford don demanded. 'The door was locked.'

The ginger-haired man smiled almost cheerfully. 'Do us a favour,' he mumbled. 'You got the money?'

Maurice, sweating now, walked to the bureau and extracted an envelope, heavy with notes. It represented the last of his savings. But he had no other choice. He hesitated a moment, then handed it over. His companion calmly counted it out. When he was finished, he nodded. 'Right. Let's get to business then.' There was hard look about his face now that made Maurice shiver.

He was so far removed now from the civilised dreaming spires of Oxford that it wasn't even funny.

* * *

Carol-Ann sighed heavily. So far, Margaret hadn't even noticed the earrings she was wearing, and she was beginning to get bored. Not seeing her adversary anywhere, she was left without any other option but to sharpen her claws on her stepfather instead. It was beginning to annoy her that the more she got to know him, the better she liked him, and she was determined to do something about it.

'Hiya, Pop,' Carol-Ann beamed at him. 'I've had a great idea for a sermon. I've found a passage in the Book of Deuteronomy that actively forbids surprise tests in school. Next time you get any teachers in on a Sunday, could you tell them about it?'

* * *

Time passed the way all time passes at a party, filled with meaningless chitchat, the consumption of more food than necessary, and the telling of jokes that a lot of people had heard before.

Sean watched Julie talking to her mother with narrowed, worried eyes. It was nearly three o'clock, and the afternoon sun was killing.

Paul Waring returned at last, triumphantly carrying heavy crates of beer as if they were feather pillows, whilst at the same time miraculously clamping four bottles of wine under his armpits. A conquering hero couldn't have been given a more enthusiastic welcome.

Vera rescued the bottles of wine and promptly took them to the ice buckets. Noting that the ice had long since melted into tepid water, she beckoned John over and asked him if he had any ice left in his fridge. Obligingly, John trotted off to get some, just as Sean and Carol-Ann began to crowd around the beer crate.

Monica smiled her thanks as she accepted a cold can of pale ale from Paul that she didn't particularly want, and snatched a similar can from the hands of her offspring as she attempted to saunter casually off with it.

'Oh, Mother!' Carol-Ann sighed. 'I *am* fifteen.'

'Drink punch,' Monica said flatly. Carol-Ann huffed and puffed and slouched off with a truly impressive display of bad grace. Monica smiled after her daughter's hunched back, took a sip of the ale, and glanced back at the bodybuilder. 'It's not like you to advocate something as calorific as beer, is it, Paul?' she chided teasingly.

'Ah well, a little in moderation won't hurt,' he said half-heartedly, popping the ring pull on a can of lager. 'Besides, I'm celebrating. I just sold one of my gyms for a huge profit. I'm thinking of diversifying into leisure shops, selling sporting gear and clothes. What do you think — a good idea? Are we still riding a high on the crest of the Olympics, or are we all going to revert to being couch potatoes any time now?'

'I'm not the one you should be asking. I never was much good at sports,' she admitted ruefully. And it was just as she was lifting the long can of light ale to her lips for a second sip that it happened.

From the house, and making everyone jump out of their skins, came the loud, shattering sound of a small explosion.

Paul dropped his can of lager onto the lawn, and then stooped quickly to pick it up, froth foaming over his sun-tanned hands and wrists as he did so. 'What the hell was that?'

Everyone froze. Monica, who'd heard the sound before, but never this close, had recognized the sound at once as that of a shotgun being discharged. Usually such a noise meant that somebody was shooting rabbits or pheasants in Chandler's Spinney.

But not this time. This time the shot had come unmistakably from inside the house itself. It was so bizarre that for a moment, Monica's brain couldn't seem to process the information it was getting. What on earth? In that moment of utter bewilderment, the scene around her seemed to freeze.

Almost unaware that it was happening, everything became superimposed onto her mind's eye.

Paul Waring stood in front of her, his hand covered in spilt beer, gaping towards the house. Over by the punchbowl, her husband turned his startled face towards the vicarage, a look of growing fear coming into his eyes. Joan Dix and Vera Ainsley stood close together, Joan grasping Vera's arm so hard the cook's skin was turning white. And Sean Franklyn stood on his own, slowly lifting a glass of wine to his lips and gulping it down in one go.

And, for some reason she couldn't explain, a list of the people not present suddenly leapt into Monica's mind.

Margaret Franklyn. John Lerwick. Julie Dix. Maurice Keating. Pauline Weeks. And Carol-Ann.

Carol-Ann! Her baby! With a wordless cry of fear, Monica sprinted for the front door of her flat, leaving several people gaping after her like a small shoal of startled fish.

CHAPTER 5

Graham, seeing Monica dash for their front door, moved swiftly after her, his heart in his mouth. Gesturing to the others to stay where they were, he was still moving fast enough to be just a few seconds behind her as Monica ran into the hall, her eyes enormous.

'Carol-Ann! Carol-Ann!' she yelled frantically.

The Nobles' flat was very simple in design, with a central corridor. The kitchen, dining room and living room were all situated on the left, looking out across the grounds towards the rest of the village. Graham's study, Carol-Ann's bedroom and the bathroom all opened off from the right, and looked across the central garden, towards the other wing of the big house. The master bedroom intersected the two halves of the flat, stretching across the bottom end of the corridor.

Monica headed straight for her daughter's bedroom and almost collapsed in relief when she saw Carol-Ann standing there, a blouse clutched to her bra-clad chest, staring, wide-eyed, out the window. Monica could see that her big blue eyes were wide with shock and she was looking a shade pale.

'Did you *hear* that?' Carol-Ann finally gasped. 'It sounded like it came from right here. That was a *gunshot*, wasn't it? Or am I going bonkers?' she asked, all in one breath.

Monica, who was clinging onto the door handle for strength (since her knees seemed to have to turned to jelly), realized she was gasping like an old steam train, and took a deep calming breath.

'What? It sounded like it came from this room, do you mean?' she asked, still a bit fuddled.

Carol-Ann sighed elaborately. 'Duhhhh! Not from right here, Mother,' she rolled her eyes theatrically. 'Or else I'd have seen who fired it, wouldn't I? I meant from here, in this house, somewhere. Heck it was loud!'

Just then Graham appeared behind them, and with a small squeak, Carol-Ann lifted the blouse a little further across her chest.

'Dad!' she yelled.

Graham, confounded by two shocks at once — being called 'Dad' for the first time ever, and catching a glimpse of his stepdaughter's bra-clad frame — turned bright pink and hastily backed out into the hall. Monica grinned and went out, slowly closing the door behind her.

'Thank G—' she hastily stopped herself from taking the Lord's name in vain, and said instead, 'She's all right! When I heard the gunshot, and she wasn't there, I thought . . .'

She shook her head and leaned back against the cool wall, managing a weak laugh and closing her eyes. Instantly Graham was beside her, holding her hand.

'It's OK. She's all right. You saw for yourself, she's in her usual sparkling form,' he said, gently teasing.

The warm, comforting contact and the sound of his soothing voice calmed her, and her thundering heartbeat began to quieten down to a more normal rhythm. Then her eyes snapped open, and at the same moment met Graham's.

'But she was right. That *was* a gunshot, wasn't it?' Monica asked faintly.

Graham nodded grimly. 'Yes. I'm no expert on firearms but I think it was a shotgun.'

He moved to the front door and looked out at the garden party, and saw that everyone had instinctively gathered together into a little huddle in the middle of the lawn, as if they could find comfort in numbers. Seeing a shepherdless flock in need instantly galvanised Graham into action, and he walked purposefully outside, Monica not far behind him.

'Sorry,' Graham said obliquely as he reached them. 'We just had to check on Carol-Ann.' They all looked at him blankly, and Graham spread his hands in silent appeal.

'Look, I don't want to alarm anyone unduly, but I think that was some sort of a gunshot we heard just now. It was probably just some lads on the way back from potting some rabbits up in the wood, and they thought it would liven up the day for them to fire a shot in the grounds or something. Maybe somebody thought it would give him some kudos if he fired into the air over our heads to wake us all up a bit. You know how juvenile lads can be. But, to be on the safe side, I think it might be a good idea if everyone went back to their flats and just checked that everything's—'

'Julie!' Joan Dix suddenly shouted, white-faced, and hurried away.

'Oh. Right,' Paul said vaguely, glancing at the beer can still held in his hand. And then he too headed back to the house. The others followed suit, and soon the garden was empty.

Monica looked at Graham helplessly. 'Do you really think it *was* just a practical joke by one of the village lads?' she asked. But even as she asked it, she felt a deep sense of foreboding begin to stir inside her. 'I thought most of them would be at the fair.'

Graham looked back at her solemnly, and she remembered the tension she'd felt in the air earlier on, caused mostly, it had to be said, by Margaret. She remembered, too, the way Joan had clung to Vera, as if she had also sensed that something awful had happened. Then there was the very stillness around them. Even the birds had been momentarily silenced. No doubt about it, she felt distinctly spooked.

'I say, did you hear that racket?' It was almost inevitable that it should be the returning Maurice, with his carefully cultivated upper-class accent, who should break the silence and bring an almost farcical sense of comic relief to the moment.

Monica turned to him and smiled as best she could. 'Yes. Were you in your flat?'

'That's right,' Maurice said, and smiled, showing just a fraction too many well-maintained and even teeth, indicative of someone who wore dentures. 'Cooling off, and all that. My blood pressure's not what it should be, or so the quacks keep telling me,' he said with a shade-too-hearty laugh.

He's nervous, Monica noted, then gave a mental shrug. Well, weren't they all?

'Was anything wrong in your part of the house?' she asked rather obscurely, and wasn't surprised to see Maurice blink.

'Wrong?' he echoed blankly. 'Don't think so. Why? What sort of thing do you mean? Broken windows or someone's television aerial crashing down? Can't say as I saw anything amiss.'

Monica glanced at Graham helplessly, and then shook her head. 'Oh, it's probably nothing.'

John, moving as quietly and unobtrusively as usual, was almost upon them before anyone noticed him.

'Was that a shot I just heard?' he asked. Monica jumped visibly, such was the fraught state of her own nerves, and John shot her an apologetic look. 'Sorry.'

'We think so,' Graham answered his question in such a matter-of-fact tone of voice that John merely nodded. It was one of Graham's more priceless traits that he always seemed able to bring calmness and a sense of normalcy to any situation. 'The others are just checking their places to make sure that there's been no upset,' he added, with masterly understatement.

'Well, my place is all right,' John said, equally as matter-of-factly, and held up a big plastic bowl of ice. 'I've just come from there.'

Pauline came back next, looking around the small group, her face tense.

'What was that awful noise? And where's Paul?' she asked sharply.

59

'He'll be back soon,' Monica said automatically, and he was. He came loping across the lawn at that moment, looking like he could run for miles without getting out of breath. As he no doubt could.

'Well, there's nothing wrong with my place,' he said, then was forced to give Pauline a blow-by-blow account of what he meant.

During the next few minutes everyone slowly filtered back, Joan and Julie bringing up the rear. At the sight of the young woman alive and well, Monica felt herself relax, and it wasn't until that moment that she realized just how tense she'd been.

That was when she realized that Sean Franklyn still hadn't returned.

'Well, it looks as if it was just a storm in a tea—' Vera began to say, when Sean, at last, came back, out of the door in the left wing of the house. Even before he reached them, they sensed that he was bringing trouble.

'I can't find Margaret,' Sean said flatly, as soon as he was within talking distance. 'I've searched every room in the flat, the car park and gardens round back, even your garden shed, John. She's just not here. Does anyone know where she's gone? Did anyone see her?'

Monica licked lips that had gone suddenly dry. 'Did she say anything when she left the party, Sean?' she asked quietly. 'That she had an errand to run, or had to leave for a while, maybe, and would be back soon?'

'No. Well, not that I know of,' Sean replied sullenly, then flushed as everyone looked at him in some surprise. 'I mean, she wasn't talking to me. She was talking to . . . Julie,' his voice trailed off, and he looked as if he could kick himself.

Naturally everyone turned to look at Julie, who in turn went white.

'She didn't say anything to me,' Julie yelped defensively. 'She just sort of floated off.'

Nobody said anything to that. They'd all experienced the way that Margaret could just 'float off,' leaving you feeling about as uninteresting and unimportant as a gadfly.

'I think it might be a good idea to check the empty flats,' Graham said into the sudden and rather ominous silence. 'The decorators leave them unlocked. It's a very hot day — perhaps she's fainted.'

'But what would she be doing in one of those?' Sean asked scornfully, then glanced uneasily around the group as nobody spoke.

'All the same,' Graham said softly. 'Let's just make sure she isn't in the house. I think we'd all feel better if we searched for her. Agreed?' He turned to Paul, who blinked then nodded.

'Yeah, OK. I'll take number 12. It's the only one empty on my floor,' Paul muttered.

'I'll come with you,' Pauline said, adding defiantly, 'it's right next door to me, after all.'

'There's an empty flat next to me, too,' Vera added quietly. 'Number 7. Oh, and number 5 is also empty.' She looked questioningly at John, who nodded briefly. Without a word, the two of them turned back towards the house.

'And Monica and I will check the empty flat opposite us,' Graham added. 'Maurice, why don't you stay here with Joan and Julie? Make sure they're OK. Maybe get them something to drink and set up a few deckchairs in the shade for them?' he added, giving the older man a dignified, less physically arduous task more suited to his usefulness.

Maurice brightened up at once.

'Delighted. Ladies,' he said gallantly, leading them off to the table where the fruit punch languished.

Then Graham glanced across at Sean, who was staring down at his feet. He looked more puzzled than anything else.

'Sean, why don't you have a glass of wine?' he advised quietly. 'You look like you could do with a drink.'

Sean glanced up. 'What? Oh, yes. I think I will.'

They all watched him pour a glass and take it to a shady part of the lawn, where he sat down heavily. It didn't look as if he tasted it when he drank.

It wasn't until the Nobles had entered the main hall that led, amongst others, to the empty flat number 2, that Monica said out loud to her husband what everyone else had been privately thinking. 'You don't think anything's *really* happened to Margaret, do you?'

Graham smiled reassuringly and reached out for her hand. His long, gentle fingers felt warm around her own, and she squeezed them gratefully.

'No. I just think it's sensible to check out all the possibilities, that's all,' he said mildly. 'Knowing Margaret, she probably decided the drinks on offer weren't good enough, and has just gone off to buy herself some fancy liqueur or something in town, and just hasn't bothered to tell her husband. Or anybody else for that matter.'

Monica smiled. 'That certainly sounds like Margaret,' she agreed wryly. They were now at the door to flat 2, and the smell of fresh paint and plaster was stronger here.

'Here it is,' Graham said rather unnecessarily, and reaching for the brass door handle, pushed it wide open.

Flat 2 echoed the layout of their own flat, in that it had a central corridor and doors leading off it, but this flat didn't have the long room at the end. The uncarpeted corridor was speckled with paint and gritty with dirt.

'Do you know how far the decorators have got?' Graham asked, for some reason whispering now.

Monica too felt the need to lower her voice. 'No,' she whispered back. 'You take the doors on the right, I'll take the doors on the left.'

Graham nodded, and promptly disappeared into one of the rooms, leaving Monica hesitating in the gloomy corridor.

There was something eerie about a house that was bare of furniture and carpets, she thought nervously, something cool and unlived in. It raised the hairs on her forearms.

When they'd first moved here, Carol-Ann had insisted that the nearly 300-year-old house was bound to be haunted. And now, for the first time since coming to live in the old place, Monica felt herself actively shiver.

Firmly she took herself in hand, telling herself not to be such a ninny, and determinedly glanced around. The first room she entered had been done out in pale peach and mint green, with newly sanded wooden floorboards, and was really quite pretty. Evidently it was either meant to be a bedroom or a living room. It was utterly empty, and as such, it took about three seconds to see that there was nobody there, and suddenly, Monica felt absurd.

There was nothing wrong here. It had just been kids having a lark after all. She was acting like some silly heroine in a Gothic novel.

She bit her lip, returned to the corridor and tried the next room down. This room was different, in that it was in the process of being decorated, and tarpaulins were hung against every wall but one. She looked up and sure enough, the ceiling was in the process of being painted a matt white. The floor, too, was littered with discarded dustsheets, roller trays, brushes standing in jam jars full of smelly turpentine, and in the middle of the room a rickety-looking wooden stepladder had been left upright and ready for use. Monica glanced around, wincing at the bright red splashes of paint on the tarpaulins opposite her. Surely they weren't going to paint any room that colour?

A slow, sick feeling began to churn in her stomach, but it wasn't until she saw one very vivid patch of red begin to trickle slowly down the stiff, dirty tarpaulin that she realized why she was feeling so sick.

The paint was still wet. And it shouldn't be. Monica blinked, her mind scrambling for an explanation. Surely any paint stains would have long since dried overnight? The decorators didn't work on a Saturday, and tended to treat Fridays as a near half-day as well. She seemed to remember that they were all packed up and gone by half past three yesterday. And in this heat, any paint would dry within a matter of hours.

Fighting off the weak-kneed urge to call for her husband, Monica forced herself to walk slowly towards the far wall, and gave a small yelp as she nearly fell over something on the floor. Windmilling her arms fruitlessly, she half-bent and put one hand out in front of her to stop herself falling right onto her nose. As she did so, her hand touched something heavy and soft and yielding under the tarpaulin on the floor.

It was only when she looked down that she saw she'd disturbed the dustsheet enough to reveal a leg. A shapely, human, female leg.

Monica swallowed hard. Feeling acutely nauseous, she quickly clamped her other hand to her mouth. She swallowed hard again, several times, telling herself firmly that she was not going to be sick.

She was *not*.

But she couldn't seem to drag her eyes away from the sight of the bare limb, which was extremely thin, tapering to a narrow ankle, the foot of which was attached to a very good quality, white leather high-heeled shoe.

And Monica knew that only one woman had worn heels that high to the party. Unable to help herself, Monica felt repulsed as she lowered her hand to the leg. Her fingers hesitated for a moment, and then gently touched the pale calf.

The leg was warm! Very, *very* warm. She must still be alive! Perhaps she'd merely fainted with the heat like Graham had theorised earlier! With a cry of relief, Monica yanked the tarpaulin completely off the supine figure of Margaret Franklyn, and then fell back with a single, sharp scream.

For one thing was certain. Margaret was not alive. Margaret was very, very dead indeed.

* * *

In the opposite room, Graham heard his wife's cry and came rushing out into the corridor. Seeing her kneeling form through an open door he hurried in and then stopped dead.

For one moment, as his brain processed what he was seeing, the grisly red-and-white vision on the floor began to swirl, clouding his vision. Then he blinked and determinedly shook his head. Instantly, he reached down for Monica, hauling her to her feet with surprising strength.

'Come on. Come away, darling,' he said gruffly, and, again with surprising strength, turned her around and led her back out into the corridor.

It was then that Monica's legs finally buckled beneath her, and without a word Graham stooped, lifted her into his arms, and walked out with her into the gloriously bright afternoon sunshine. With a shudder, Monica turned her face into his neck and closed her eyes.

'Oh, Graham,' she sobbed. 'Did you see her? Did you see what somebody *did* to her?'

Graham nodded. 'Yes,' he said grimly. 'I saw.' And he wished with all his heart that Monica *hadn't* seen it.

Maurice Keating's jaw dropped at the sight of the vicar carrying his wife across the lawn towards them.

'I say,' he began, but fell silent as Graham glanced sharply across at him.

Ignoring the retired Oxford don, he walked right past him and carried Monica to the shady part of the lawn. There he gently lowered her to the ground. As he was doing this, Vera and John returned from their own searches.

'There's nothing amiss in the flat near us—' John began cheerfully, and then, seeing Monica's stricken face and the vicar's equally grim one, he shut up abruptly.

Vera wasted no time in going straight to Monica's side. 'John, fetch me a glass of wine,' she ordered simply. Listlessly, Monica shook her head, but when John brought the glass and Vera pressed it against her lips, she drank obediently. Wordlessly, Graham indicated to John with a jerk of his head, and the older man followed him a few paces away from the ladies, where they couldn't be overheard.

'Go and call the police,' Graham said quietly. 'And an ambulance. Tell them there's been a fatality.'

John's tanned face paled a little, but after one swift, searching glance of the vicar's face, he nodded and strode away, glancing across at Sean as he did so. Graham followed his gaze and felt his heart sink.

Slowly, he walked towards the husband of the woman he'd just found so cruelly slaughtered, and hunkered down on his knees in front of him. Seeing this, and sensing the reason behind the heaviness in the air, Julie made a sudden movement in their direction, and was quickly checked by her mother. Joan, in fact, almost yanked her daughter off her feet in her determination to keep Julie away from the two men.

Maurice began to sweat. He gulped down the last of his glass of wine, and looked longingly at the ice bucket. Dare he pour himself another? No, perhaps not. Best to keep a clear head.

'Sean,' Graham began quietly, and reached out to touch the man's shoulder.

Sean looked up at him, his handsome, rather dissipated face a curious mixture of hope, resentment and understanding.

'She's dead then?' Sean said flatly.

Graham nodded. 'Yes,' he confirmed simply. 'I'm afraid she is.'

Sean Franklyn, it had to be said, didn't look particularly surprised.

CHAPTER 6

Detective Chief Inspector Jason Dury narrowed his pale blue eyes against the glare of the full summer sun as the unmarked police car overtook an articulated lorry. Once safely by, his sergeant, Jim Greer, who was driving, quickly eased back to sixty. He was relatively new to the Cotswolds, and didn't yet know his way around the picturesque countryside as well as he would have liked, and the narrow lanes and twisting village roads sometimes took him by surprise. He wondered if his boss knew this, for a few moments later he said helpfully, 'The turning's coming up on the right.'

Jason pointed out the typical country sign, a faded white wooden signpost practically hidden in the hedges by rampant and fragrant dog roses, and with the words 'Heyford Bassett — Village Only' barely visible in faded black lettering.

Jim indicated, and a few hundred yards down the narrow lane, they crested the hill with a panoramic view of a meandering river cutting its way through a small but picturesque valley, and started to head down into the village itself.

'Pretty little place, sir,' Jim murmured appreciatively, wondering ruefully at the size of house prices in such a rural idyll, and Jason nodded.

The river cut the village in half, with the older buildings, the manor house, church, and vicarage on the nearest side, and the newer estates plus access to a large farm, on the other side. The narrow, old Cotswold stone bridge crossing the water and connecting the two parts was probably centuries old, Jason surmised, and would once have been almost the sole province of sheep and the farmer herding them to market.

'Did the chap who called in give any details?' Jason asked quietly.

'No, sir, he didn't seem to know anything much at all,' Jim explained. 'Just said that there'd been a gunshot in the house and that something bad had happened, and could we come out right away.'

'Might be nothing then,' he grumbled. 'Some idiot might have been cleaning his air rifle and accidentally shot the cat.'

Jim grinned. 'Let's hope so, sir. Not that I've got anything against cats,' he added hastily, lest his new boss should think him heartless.

Of all the officers at Cheltenham, though, Jim liked Chief Inspector Jason Dury the best. Like Jim, he came from a working-class background, and had attained his rank through sheer hard work, patience and (unlike Jim) a judicious understanding of office politics. And just like Jim, Jason was also ambitious. In other ways, though, they were very different. At thirty-eight, Jason Dury was still unmarried, despite the fact that he was the heartthrob of the detective division, whereas the younger Jim was comfortably settled with a wife and family.

They turned off into a narrow lane just before they got to the bridge and a little further on, discovered Church Lane branching off on their left.

'Park in the shade if you can, otherwise the car will bake,' Jason ordered, as they reached the end of a rustic little beech-lined cul-de-sac and found themselves facing an attractive Norman church, with its typical, plain, no-nonsense tower. He sighed heavily as he got out of the car. 'Right, well, let's see what we have.'

Opposite the church, the roof of a substantial building could be seen, and the sergeant pushed open one of the big iron gates set into a passageway between dark towering yews which obviously led on to the vicarage. As they got past the dark trees, a man stepped out in front of them from the shade of the more colourful bushes that bordered a gravel path. Jason stiffened instinctively for a moment, like all policemen, not liking to being taken by surprise, then noticed the white dog collar and marginally relaxed.

Graham approached, hand outstretched. 'You must be the police,' he said gravely. 'I'm Graham Noble, the vicar here.'

As Jason introduced himself, all thoughts that this might turn out to be a minor incident quickly fled. The vicar looked visibly upset, but he was controlling it well. A tall, handsome man, Jason judged that he was probably older than he actually looked, and Jason sensed a quiet intelligence and kindness at work behind his troubled eyes.

Graham cast an assessing look over the two men, who were physically very different from each other, wondering which would have the higher rank. The older man was about 5'11", with corn-coloured blond hair and startlingly blue eyes. Character was stamped on his face in the crow's feet at his eyes, which had a steely look to them. He looked like a man who'd seen a lot. His companion was younger, shorter and darker, and gave the impression of an eager dog straining on a leash.

Jason helped him out of his dilemma by introducing himself and his sergeant, and the three men solemnly shook hands.

'Were you the one who telephoned us, Reverend?' Jason asked mildly once the preliminaries were over.

Graham shook his head. 'No, that was John Lerwick. Perhaps I'd better give you a quick explanation.' He turned and began leading them up towards the big, impressive house.

'The vicarage was sold to developers nearly eight months ago, and is in the process of being made into a set of twelve flats. My wife and I live in flat 1. There are, at the moment, four flats still empty and waiting to be sold. We were having a little garden party for all the residents, a kind of house-warming if you like, in the front garden. About . . .' Graham checked his watch, 'half an hour ago now, we all heard a shot. It sounded very close, as if coming from the house. When we checked we found one of our party in one of the empty flats, flat 2. A Mrs Margaret Franklyn. And, er . . . she was dead,' Graham finished.

It all sounded so blunt and hideously final, put into words like that, and he felt a wave of helplessness wash over him. He felt he should be doing something, helping somebody, but he was not sure how.

Jim, unaware of the vicar's angst, shot his superior a quick, excited look but said nothing. In spite of what tel-evision programmes would have the general public believe, murders or even suspicious deaths were quite rare, and he'd only ever worked two such cases before.

'I see,' Jason said flatly. 'Jim, send for forensics.'

Jim nodded and reached for his mobile. Jason followed the vicar to the front garden, where the food-littered tables and half-full glasses of wine gave mute evidence to a party that had been rudely interrupted. A series of white faces turned their way, and Jason had an overwhelming impression of a sea of anxious eyes.

The vicar, somewhat awkwardly, showed him around, and introduced everyone.

'And finally, this is Joan Dix and her daughter, Julie. Julie's only here for the summer holidays. She starts uni in September.'

'Thank you, Reverend. Perhaps you can show me flat 2?'

Graham paled but nodded. 'Certainly, Chief Inspector. This way.'

Monica and the others watched the two policemen disap-pear into the far wing of the house, and a small ripple seemed to go through them all. Relief that the moment was over,

Monica wondered — or renewed tension? She couldn't be sure. Although she was beginning to emerge from the fog of her own shock, she wasn't, by any means, up to interpreting complex body language right now.

'Do you think we should stay out here?' Joan asked tentatively. 'Or should we go to our flats?'

'I think we should stay here for the moment,' Vera said. 'At least, until someone tells us that we can go.'

They were all grouped in the shady part of the garden, but Monica could see that both Maurice and Joan were beginning to suffer from the heat.

'Let's have some more fruit punch,' she said, which had the effect of brightening the others far more than it should have done. It was as if such a normal, everyday little suggestion had driven away the spectre of that more outrageous thing that had come to visit them.

Inside the house, Graham pushed open the main door to flat 2, and indicated with a pointing finger the room they wanted. Jim noted that the vicar had every intention of remaining outside, and as they walked into the room he'd pointed out, he could understand why.

The victim was a mess.

Grimly, Jason walked very carefully towards the body, aware of the cardinal sin of disturbing a crime scene before forensics had been and gone, but also noting that the crime scene had been considerably disturbed already. He went only far enough to see for himself that the victim was dead, which didn't have to be very far at all.

Margaret Franklyn had been hit by a shotgun, at close range and right in the middle of her torso.

'She looks as if she might have been beautiful once, sir,' Jim said weakly, and Jason nodded thoughtfully. Was that relevant?

The victim had been wearing a white dress, he noted absently. Blood speckled her face, which was half-turned away from him. He moved back and glanced around the walls at the blood spatter pattern they depicted.

71

'When the photo boys get here, make sure they take plenty of pictures of these bloodstains on the tarpaulins,' he said quietly.

'Sir,' Jim said flatly.

'Meanwhile, stay here and make sure nobody else comes in.' Back at the entrance, Graham watched as Jason Dury came out. The faces of both men were grim and solemn.

'Is that how you found her, Reverend?' Jason asked.

Graham shook his head. 'I wasn't the one to actually discover her, Chief Inspector. That was my wife.'

'I'll have to talk to her, I'm afraid.'

Graham nodded and together they returned to the garden. Jason regarded the wary-eyed group of people looking back at him and cursed his luck. He knew that witnesses, when grouped together, naturally tended to talk things over. It was only human nature, after all. Unfortunately, and without meaning to, they also began to distort facts and remembrances to fit in with what the others were saying. Still, the harm was already done. Best now to just get the initial statements first, then separate them and do a fuller interview later.

He reached for his notebook and pencil. Unlike a lot of other senior policemen, his shorthand was excellent.

'I'd like to begin by asking each of you where you were when you heard the gunshot.'

He didn't imagine the sudden stiffening of shoulders, or the sense of sudden panic, but he didn't read anything of major significance into it either. People tended to be scared when asked questions by the police, whether they were actually guilty of anything or not. He turned to Graham, instinctively sensing that he was the best one to break the ice.

'Reverend?'

Graham nodded, then frowned. 'Yes. Well, I was here, at the table. I was, I think, near the punch bowl.'

'Thank you. Mrs Noble?' he glanced around, trying to locate the vicar's wife. He'd had a vague impression of a bowed dark head during their fleeting introduction.

Monica looked up at the mention of her name, and Jason, suddenly confronted by a pretty, elfin-shaped face and big smoky blue eyes, blinked rapidly.

'Mrs Noble?' he said again, more firmly.

'I was standing nearly where you are now, talking to Paul. He'd given me a can of ale.'

'That's right,' the big, well-muscled man in shorts and T-shirt confirmed, and Jason cast him a quick look. The man looked vaguely familiar to him for some reason. He made a mental note to try and place just when and where he'd seen Paul Waring before when he had the time to give it some more thought.

'Mrs Dix?' he swept on.

'I was here too. With Vera. Just over there, I think,' she indicated a spot vaguely.

As Jason looked questioningly around, a plump woman self-consciously half-raised her hand.

'That's true. We were talking about shortbread,' her voice trailed off apologetically.

Jason smiled and nodded. 'And you, sir?' He caught the eye of Maurice, who flushed and looked deeply uncomfortable.

'Oh. I was in my room, dontcha know. Getting changed and er . . . using the facilities.'

Jason nodded. In his notebook he wrote, 'On the loo.'

'And Miss Dix. Miss Julie Dix?' he added, as the silence dragged on. He saw Joan give her daughter a nudge, and his eyes sharpened on the pretty girl, who seemed to come out of a deep trance long enough to look at him vaguely.

'Sorry?'

'Where were you, Miss Dix, when you heard the shot?'

'Oh. In my bedroom.'

'She was putting on a long-sleeved blouse,' Joan said, her voice almost ferocious. 'She was getting sunburned,' she added, her voice almost daring him to call her a liar.

Jason had heard that tone of voice before. Usually it came from a parent determined to prove that her boy or girl had nothing to do with whatever was being claimed.

73

Monica, who'd been listening to everything carefully, found herself becoming almost fascinated by the remote, good-looking, fair-haired man. He's so obviously apart from us all, Monica thought with a flash of understanding. Rightly or wrongly, it's suddenly become us against him.

Jason looked over the thin-lipped assembly, and settled on Pauline Weeks. 'And you, Mrs Weeks? Where were you when you heard the gunshot?'

Pauline shrugged in a masterly gesture of unconcern. 'I was getting some fruit salad from the fridge. The food down here was getting too warm, and I thought some ice-cold fruit would go down a treat. I nearly dropped the bowl when I heard the shot go off, I can tell you,' she laughed nervously.

'I see. And that leaves Mr Lerwick and Mr Franklyn.' At the mention of his name, Sean seemed to twitch. John spoke hastily, feeling, for some obscure reason, suddenly compelled to come to the other man's rescue. 'I was getting some ice for the ice bucket. Paul had just gone to the shop for some beer and wine. Vera asked me to get it.'

'So you were in your flat too?'

'Well, no. I'd got the ice and had just come out the door when I noticed some Whisky Mac roses that needed dead-heading. Just over there, in the Nobles' border. I was just pinching some heads off when I heard the shot and then hurried on over here.'

Jason glanced across the central garden to the other wing of the house. There were a lot of plants, plus the tables in between, but he should have been in plain enough sight.

'Did anyone notice Mr Lerwick over there when the gun went off?' he asked quietly.

There was a sudden shuffling of feet and embarrassed half-met glances, but no one volunteered to give the cartoonist an alibi. It was Graham who cleared his throat.

'I should imagine, Chief Inspector, that everyone did the same as I did when they heard the shot. Namely, looked in the direction of the other wing, where it seemed to have come from. So I doubt that anyone would have noticed John, even though he was standing there in plain sight.'

Jason saw John Lerwick glance at the vicar. Instead of looking grateful for the vote of confidence, he looked merely thoughtful.

Which was interesting, but was it relevant?

'I see. And Mr Franklyn?' Jason asked softly.

Although his voice was as neutral as before, everyone suddenly seemed to sense danger. Into Monica's mind, as with most of the others, flashed the thought that the police, in cases like this, immediately suspected the spouse.

'Mr Franklyn was here,' Monica said sharply, then flushed as the policeman's blue eyes instantly fastened onto her face. She felt herself blushing even more deeply and wished she didn't feel so wrong-footed. 'I saw him by the table, drinking wine,' she added, just a touch defiantly. Damn it, did he have to look at her like that? She did see him. He was there.

'I see,' Jason said, casting a quick look at the husband. The vicar's wife had been very quick to defend him. But Sean didn't look a particularly wholesome sight just at that moment, and for some reason, that made the policeman feel quite pleased. 'Is that true, Mr Franklyn?'

Sean nodded vaguely. 'That's right. I was here,' he said dully. 'Drinking the fruit punch, actually. Not the wine.'

'Did anybody else notice Mr Franklyn's whereabouts at the time of the shot?' Jason persisted.

'Yes, I did,' Vera said crisply. 'He was here, like Monica said, drinking wine . . . or something in a wine glass anyway.'

Graham cleared his throat. Jason's eyes went straight to him. 'Mr Franklyn was definitely present at the time of the shot, Chief Inspector,' he added his own two pennies' worth, holding his gaze steadily.

So, the husband has an alibi, Jason mused. Curiouser and curiouser.

Of course, the culprit might not be amongst these people at all. It could have been a complete outsider.

'I'd like to see the rear exits of the house,' Jason said. 'Perhaps you could show me, Reverend? And would everybody else please return to their flats. Somebody will be along to take a full statement shortly.'

Graham glanced at the house. 'Do you want to go into the east wing or the west?'

Jason indicated the entrance that led to flat 2. Inside, Jason quickly realized that a rather dark and narrow corridor ran the entire length of the building. So anyone could have gone through the house and out through the rear exit without being seen. This hypothesis was confirmed as they reached the back of the house, where a lift was located at a right angle to a pair of big double doors which in turn led out onto a gravelled car park and a dense jungle of garden.

The door was unlocked. Jason glanced at the gravel, which as he'd expected, showed no sign of bloodstains. It was also, of course, impossible to tell the individual movements of footsteps or tyre tracks in the gravel, which had been regularly used. He nodded.

'Can I use your telephone, Reverend? It'll save me going back to the car.' He had, of course, a mobile on him, but he wanted to see inside the vicar's flat.

Once in his study, Graham tactfully left him alone, and Jason reported in and asked for more manpower. As he looked around the pleasantly masculine and tidy room, he noted — unsurprisingly — several old Bibles lining the shelves, along with tomes on theology, philosophy, archaeology and a huge *Roget's Thesaurus*.

Jason knew that understanding the setup at the vicarage was imperative if he was to solve this crime.

Sean Franklyn had looked shocked enough, and he had an alibi, but there was something about him that had that look of a man caught out in some way.

Then there was the vicar. Outwardly calm, Jason instinctively wanted to trust him. And since he also had an alibi, he could see himself relying more and more on Graham Noble to give him the inside picture.

Monica Noble now. He'd have to talk to her himself about the discovery of the body. He was looking forward to speaking to her again, and that made him frown.

Then there was Paul Waring. If the police hadn't run across him before, Jason would be surprised.

The mother and daughter were definitely nervous, and there was something there, without a doubt.

Maurice Keating had the look of an academic about him. Once, Jason had had the pleasure of arresting a man who'd thought himself very clever indeed. The clever ones always thought they could get away with murder. If this wasn't a crime of passion, or a spur-of-the-moment act, then he'd have to take a really close look at Maurice Keating. Especially since he was one of those with no alibi.

Pauline Weeks was another one absent at the time of the shooting. Jason didn't feel anything about her one way or the other, except that she'd been acting just a shade too nonchalant for his taste. But that could just be a cover for nerves.

There seemed to be nothing outstanding about John Lerwick or Vera Ainsley, although John hadn't actually been seen at those roses.

He sighed and walked to the door, and as he pulled it open a long-haired waif tumbled into the room and all but fell over his feet. She just managed to save herself gracefully, then turned a young, defiant face his way.

'Sorry. I didn't know anyone was in here,' Carol-Ann lied magnificently.

Jason's lips twitched. 'No?'

'No. You're not one of Graham's bleeding hearts, are you? If so, you'd better scram. Someone's dead, and this isn't the time to start making confessions. The cops might get the wrong idea.'

And with arms akimbo she smiled at him challengingly. He was quite a hunk, Carol-Ann thought dreamily.

'I'm Chief Inspector Dury. And you are?'

'Carol-Ann Clancy.'

'Carol-Ann?' It was Monica Noble, drawn by the sound of her daughter's voice, who called her name from out in the hallway.

'In here, Mum,' Carol-Ann yelled back.

Monica put her head around the door, and her eyes flashed quickly at Jason. What was he doing, questioning Carol-Ann without her being present? Wasn't there a law against that?

Jason looked confused. Mum?

'I'm sorry, I thought you said your name was Clancy?' he turned back to Carol-Ann.

'Carol-Ann is the daughter of my first marriage, Chief Inspector,' Monica explained, entering and then closing the door behind her. 'I was widowed. Graham Noble is my second husband.'

'Oh, I see,' Jason nodded. Then his eyes narrowed. Nobody had mentioned Carol-Ann Clancy before. 'And where were you when the shot went off, Miss Clancy?' Jason asked casually.

Carol-Ann swallowed hard. 'In my bedroom. Getting changed.'

Without being aware of it, she was sidling up to her mother, who took her hand and squeezed it reassuringly. Monica noticed the quick, speculative look that flashed into the policeman's penetrating eyes, and felt her heart lurch in sudden fear. Surely he didn't regard Carol-Ann as a suspect? She was a *child*!

'That's right,' Monica said firmly. 'As soon as I heard the shot go off, I raced in here to see if she was all right.'

Jason sighed. More revelations.

'You didn't happen to see John Lerwick deadheading any flowers did you, Miss Clancy?' he asked dryly. 'He claimed to be in your flower border at the time.'

But Carol-Ann surprised him.

'Yeah, I did. He went past my window just a second before I heard the shot. Made me jump, I can tell you, but old John's all right. He's not a perv. He didn't even look into my bedroom window on the off-chance of getting an eyeful.'

Jason smiled. 'I see. Might I see your room?'

Monica paled, mostly at the thought of the state of it, but gallantly led the good-looking policeman into Carol-Ann's den.

But he merely glanced around the typical teenage chaos, then strode purposefully across to the window. The girl had a perfect view across the garden, he noted, as well as the other wing facing this one. He turned sharply.

'Did you see anyone come in or out of the front door over there?' he asked quickly.

Carol-Ann instantly shook her head. 'No. Nobody.'

Although she'd answered instantaneously, he got the feeling that it was the truth. Jason nodded. So the killer must have come and gone from the back. He needed to know who had flats overlooking that side of the house.

'You don't happen to have a plan of the house, do you?' he asked without much hope, and as expected, Monica shook her head.

'Sorry, no. But I could draw you a rough sketch if you like,' she offered, 'so long as you don't want anything too technical.'

Monica led Jason back to her husband's study. Once there, she sat behind Graham's desk, drew out a sheet of clean paper and a pen, and glanced up inquiringly. Jason had one hand resting on the desk. Leaning forward like that made his hair fall over his high forehead. She could smell the clean, sharp scent of his aftershave. She felt her heart trip just a little and hastily leaned back and away from him.

'What, exactly, do you need to know?' she mumbled.

'Just the positioning of the flats and who lives in them. Where the doors are, any windows that are in public-access areas and the location of the lift and the stairs.'

Monica, relieved to have some simple task to do, set to work, and a few minutes later handed him a rough sketch. Jason looked it over and saw that, of those not present outside when the shot was heard, only Pauline Weeks had a flat overlooking the back. John Lerwick did too, but he'd been in the central garden at the time of the shooting, confirmed by Carol-Ann.

'Right. Thanks,' he said. And clutching the piece of paper, he left.

Monica watched him go, and only then, slowly relaxed. When she looked up again, Graham was standing in the open doorway, watching her curiously.

'Was that the chief inspector I just heard go?' he asked mildly.

Monica nodded wordlessly.

'Why don't you come and lie down,' Graham said gently. 'You've had a really nasty shock. First you were white as a sheet, now you're quite flushed. Do you want me to call the doctor out?'

Monica reached for his hand and went quickly into his arms. 'No. I'm fine,' she said, resting her cheek against his chest and taking a deep, gasping breath. 'Oh, Graham,' she said softly.

* * *

Upstairs, on the top floor, Pauline Weeks was proving to be unhelpful.

Unfortunately, according to her version of events, she didn't look out of her kitchen window whilst collecting the fruit salad, and so couldn't say whether or not anyone had emerged from the back door.

'I notice your fridge is set right next to the window,' Jason prompted, staring at the appliance in question through the open kitchen door. 'I would have thought that it would have become a more or less automatic gesture to glance out-side whenever using it.'

Pauline shrugged. 'What can I say? I didn't.'

But her eyes refused to meet those of the policeman, and he felt a vague stirring of interest in his stomach. Just what was she holding back?

'The fruit salad must be downstairs now. Perhaps you'd like to retrieve it before the sun ruins it,' he offered casually.

Pauline started, then laughed nervously. 'Well, I didn't actually take it down.'

'No?' He raised an eyebrow.

'No. When I heard the sound of the shot, I clean forgot all about it,' Pauline explained carefully.

Jason nodded. 'I see.'

It all sounded, on the face of it, plausible enough. So why did he get the feeling that she was lying through her teeth?

CHAPTER 7

The arrival of the forensics experts was observed with intense interest by all those in the flats with a view to the front of the property. Monica, pretending to read, quickly abandoned her book as Carol-Ann bounded into the living room, breathless and pink-cheeked.

'Mum, you've just *got* to come into the kitchen and have a look at what's going on out there,' she squeaked excitedly from the doorway.

Monica sighed, not really in any mood to watch any of the gory and depressing details that must surely come with a murder investigation. But in the end, she thought that it was probably best to keep an eye on things, or at least keep herself up to date on what was happening. She suspected that Carol-Ann, by dint of being on her own at the time of the shooting, was actually on Dury's list of suspects, absurd as that seemed to her. And that thought really scared her. Teenagers had killed before, after all, and been tried and convicted of a variety of crimes, as the newspapers and news programmes on television were only too happy to demonstrate. And who was to say that a miscarriage of justice couldn't happen to them? Thrusting aside such unpleasant thoughts, she followed her daughter to the kitchen.

'What is it?' she asked, joining Carol-Ann by the sink, where the teenager was craning her neck to watch the alien-looking people in their pristine white boiler suits swarming all over the place.

Monica, spotting them, suddenly shuddered.

'Oh, come away, for pity's sake. Don't be such a ghoul! If that man Dury sees you watching, he's bound to wonder why you're so curious.'

'Oh don't be daft, Mum,' Carol-Ann wailed, but then observed, 'Oh look — he's got to be the one who takes all the pictures and things.'

But since the officer in question was festooned with cameras, it was hardly a massive feat of deduction.

'Carol-Ann, if you don't come into the living room with me right this minute, you're not going out for a week,' Monica warned stiffly.

Carol-Ann sniffed, but grudgingly followed her mother to the door.

* * *

In the small hall of the 'murder wing' — as he was beginning to think of it — Jason Dury watched the forensics people get to work.

'When the uniforms show up, each is to take an occupied flat and get a complete statement from the residents, starting from when they woke up this morning, but concentrating on what they did at the party,' he instructed his sergeant.

'Sir.'

'And then go on to more general stuff. Did you like Mrs Franklyn? Was her marriage a happy one? Did you see her leave the party, and if so, which door did she go into? Did you see her talking to anyone in particular at the party, and if so, how did she seem? You know the usual routine, Jim.'

Jim did. 'Where will you be, sir?'

Jason turned to him and sighed. 'I'll be with Mrs Noble. I want to learn everything she did when she found the body.'

Jim was just about to leave, but in the doorway he suddenly stepped aside to make way for a lean, neat man in a lightweight grey suit. He looked to be in his forties, with a dark moustache and a slightly thinning head of hair.

'Doc.' Jason greeted the pathologist with a laconic smile.

'Jason. What have you got for me?'

'Something messy.' He nodded his head towards the crime scene and the medical expert obligingly disappeared into flat 2. Jason hardly ever referred to pathologists by their name, usually finding it easier to just call them all 'Doc.'

This particular pathologist returned after a matter of ten minutes or so, peeling off a pair of rubber gloves as he joined the senior investigative officer in charge.

'Well, you don't need much telling, do you,' the medico said to Jason. 'She's been dead for no more than an hour. Cause of death was one wound from a shotgun to the torso. I can't say till I get her on the table, but I imagine it peppered every major organ she's got.'

'Killed at the scene?'

'With those spatter marks on the walls, I should say so,' the doctor agreed. 'As you say, a bit of a mess. Whoever killed her didn't intend to miss, and certainly didn't. She'd have died instantly, if that's any comfort.'

'Close range then?' Jason got to the point immediately.

'Yes.'

'Was the gun actually touching her, do you think?'

'Oh, I wouldn't say it was quite as close as *that*. But I would imagine that the killer couldn't have been standing more than a few feet or so away. But again, don't quote me until after the post-mortem.'

Jason grunted. 'So the killer would have got blood on him? Or her?'

'Hell yes,' the pathologist said. 'Lots of it, I would have said.'

Jason nodded. So, a quick change of clothes and a wash would have been an absolute priority. Especially if the killer returned to the party. But if the killer had been an outsider, maybe not so much. You could, after all, sprint to a car and drive off whilst badly bloodstained. In a car, on a road, nobody was likely to have time to notice if you were covered in red. With the speed of cars nowadays, you were lucky to get even a glimpse of people's faces as you passed them by. But if the car was going any great distance, the killer wouldn't have been able to risk it for long. Waiting at a T-junction or sitting at a traffic light would increase the risk greatly. After all, sitting still, any motorist coming alongside you could glance across, and then being blood-spattered would be very obvious indeed.

So if the killer had left in a car without washing or changing clothes, they would have been keen to get off the road fast and clean up. A local? Or could the killer have come in a car or van with tinted windows? That would solve the problem, and he made a mental note to get some poor uniforms watching traffic cameras and noting any vehicles with tinted windows in the vicinity at the time of the murder. Follow-ups on all of them would soon reveal any links to the Franklyns.

But in his gut, Jason Dury thought that the killer hadn't gone far. Not a betting man, he would, nevertheless, have had a little flutter on Margaret Franklyn's killer living right here.

'You'll have a full report tomorrow, if you're lucky,' the pathologist said, interrupting his thoughts. 'I can't see anything else more urgent cropping up and putting the post-mortem back, so I'll get started on your victim right away.' And with that, the two professional men parted.

Jason stood where he was for a moment, pondering. John Lerwick, according to Carol-Ann Clancy, *was* in the garden at the time of the shot. So that let him off. Unless, of course, she'd merely said that in order to give him an alibi. Or give herself one. Still, he was inclined, for the moment, to rule them both out. So that left Pauline Weeks, Julie Dix and Maurice Keating without alibis. All three of them would have had time to change their clothes and wash before rejoining the party, and in the case of Julie and Maurice, they'd both admitted that they'd changed their clothes. He'd check with other residents that Pauline hadn't changed her outfit too, but he didn't think she'd have lied about it. She struck Jason as the sort who'd expect any change in her appearance to be noticed by others and therefore wouldn't have bothered trying to conceal it.

In the case of Maurice and Julie, at least, each of them would have had access to their bathrooms. Where bloodstained water might, even now, be languishing in their U-bends or drains.

He ideally needed search warrants, but wasn't sure that he had enough to go on to satisfy a judge that warrants were justified. Still, you never knew your luck. He went back to the car and got on the radio to HQ, asking an experienced WPC to file the appropriate paperwork and see if she could sweet-talk a judge, then headed back to flat 1.

* * *

A few minutes after he'd gone, a group of uniformed officers reported in to Jim Greer. He quickly briefed and assigned them, picking at random John Lerwick to interview for himself. It was going to be a long afternoon. In his experience, questioning multiple witnesses was always a test of patience. No two people ever seemed to agree on even the simplest set of events. He foresaw nothing but a mass of confusing and conflicting statements ahead of them, but it had to be done.

* * *

In her top-floor flat, Pauline Weeks opened the door to a pair of surprisingly young-looking officers, one male, one female. She smiled and invited them in, poured them all lemonade, and proceeded to be very careful about what she said.

'So, you joined the party at about a quarter past two?' asked the male officer about ten minutes later, after her movements prior to the party had been carefully detailed.

'That's right.'

'And you spoke to Mrs Franklyn during the course of the afternoon?'

'Of course. It was a party,' Pauline answered calmly.

She felt cool now, and perfectly unfazed. It surprised her a little just how easy this whole experience was turning out to be. She'd have thought, under the circumstances, that she'd have been a bundle of nerves. But that wasn't so. In fact, it was just a little bit exhilarating, being questioned by the police.

'And what did you and Mrs Franklyn discuss?'

'Oh, this and that.'

'Can you be more specific?' he pressed, careful to keep his voice neutral and non-threatening. 'Surely you can remember *something* Mrs Franklyn said? It could be important.'

The female officer, who was very astute, recognized a sudden tension in the older woman. She cleared her throat softly, indicating to her partner that she wanted to take over the questioning.

'Did you like Mrs Franklyn?' she asked guilelessly.

Pauline glanced across at the young woman who'd just spoken, and hesitated. Then she smiled. 'Not really. Margaret could be a little difficult.' She was rather pleased with that. It made her sound all the more frank and honest.

'Oh? How so?'

Pauline shrugged. 'She was unpleasant to be around. She had the idea that she was superior to everyone else and so I avoided her whenever possible. So you see, we really weren't all that chatty.'

'Did you see her leave the party?' the male officer asked abruptly.

Pauline forced herself to lean back in her chair, to frown a little, as if earnestly thinking back. Then she said firmly, 'No.'

'Did you leave the party yourself at any time?'

She nodded. 'Yes, to get the fruit salad. I was keeping it cold in the fridge. That's when I heard the shot.'

The female officer glanced at her colleague. 'And you came straight here, to this flat, then went straight back to the party again on hearing it?'

Pauline smiled brightly. 'That's right,' she lied without a qualm.

'You didn't see anyone, or anything suspicious, either before or after hearing the shot?' It was the male constable who asked the question.

Again Pauline hesitated for just a fraction of a second, wondering if she should say anything. Then she gave a mental shake of her head.

'No,' she said, still firm. 'Nothing at all.'

After showing them out, she leaned for a moment against the door, aware that her heart was beating so hard it was making her feel slightly sick. She walked to a cabinet and poured herself a vodka and tonic, and sipped it slowly. Something tugged at the back of her mind. What was it? Something someone had said to her perhaps? No, not that. Something to do with clothing, maybe? Pauline narrowed her eyes in thought. She'd always had a good memory. She was confident it would come back to her.

* * *

In his flat on the floor below, Maurice Keating paced about restlessly. He knew the police would be here at any minute and he just couldn't decide how he should react. Should he be the cool and aloof academic, or a shocked, civilised man, rightly concerned and appalled by such violence? He walked to the sideboard and poured himself a glass of cheap whisky with trembling hands.

He glanced towards the closed and locked drawer of his desk. If the police ever searched his room he'd be for it. He finished the glass and continued pacing. There were no two ways about it. He was scared now.

A knock came on the door and he whirled around, his breath stalling in his chest. Then he straightened his shoulders, walked to the door, and opening it with something of a flourish, said cordially, 'Ah, the constabulary. Please, do come in. Drink, anyone?'

* * *

As the afternoon wore on, the less hardy members of Heyford Bassett began to return home from the fair, only to discover that something far more exciting had been going on in their absence, and right on their own doorstep.

Little old ladies and dignified gentlemen suddenly got the urge to walk their dogs down Church Lane, or to visit some long-forgotten relative's grave with a bunch of hastily picked flowers. And nor were they disappointed, for the uniformed presence at the vicarage gates confirmed the wild stories going around.

Some said a tramp had been found dead in one of the sheds whilst others would insist that it had been a naked woman found strangled in the bushes. Some even said the vicar was dead, and it was this last wild rumour that galvanised Graham's returning fan club into action. En masse, and dressed in their Sunday best with bosoms quivering with fright and curiosity, they began to descend on the vicarage.

The pimply constable on the gate, assigned to keep out sightseers, didn't stand a chance.

* * *

The pair interviewing Vera Ainsley liked her enormously, but quickly discovered, to their dismay, that she had the nasty habit of being discreet. She steadfastly refused to malign the dead, or speculate about Margaret's private affairs, and all they could get out of her was a crystal-clear account of the afternoon. But when asked if she'd observed Margaret leaving the party, Vera came up trumps. For she *had* noticed her go at about twenty-five minutes to three.

And she had gone not into the wing of the house where her body was later discovered, but into the opposite wing, where her own flat was located.

It was by far and away the most interesting tidbit of the afternoon, as Jason would say later, when he began reading through the reports.

* * *

In his flat, Paul Waring sighed and shook his head.

'I still can't believe it, you know? I mean, Maggie was a bit of a, well, you know . . . But for someone to *kill* her?'

He shook his head again. He was sitting cross-legged on the floor, a big, fit, impressive man, except perhaps in the brains department. That, at least, was the opinion of Constable Simms as he scribbled industriously in his notebook. Constable Simms, it had to be said, was a rather weedy-looking young man, with rather unprepossessing features.

'You sound as if you knew her well?' he probed craftily. Paul shrugged, fiddling nervously with the small, slightly raised panther logo on the shoulder of his T-shirt.

'Well, not that well, perhaps,' he corrected, 'but we talked some. She wasn't making a lot of friends here, and I suppose she was feeling bored. I felt a bit sorry for her, to tell the truth.'

'Would you say that she got on better with men than with women?' Simms summed it up accurately.

Paul nodded. 'Exactly. And she had a habit of going out of her way to make mischief. Like with Pauline this afternoon — that's Pauline Weeks, I mean.'

'Oh?'

Paul instantly began to look uncomfortable again.

'Not that it meant anything. You have to know them both to— Well, you see, it's like this. Pauline and I, well, we're getting sort of interested in each other, you know what I mean? Nothing definite yet, but there's definitely a "maybe" there, you know? But Margaret would insist on flirting with me, right under Pauline's nose. Oh, she didn't mean any-thing by it,' he added hastily, seeing the speculative look in the young policeman's eyes. 'I like her husband well enough, and I knew she wasn't serious. Not that I'd have been interested even if she was! No, she was just doing it purely because she knew it would get Pauline riled.'

'I see. And when was this?'

'Oh, I don't know — early on. Before I left to get the booze, anyway.'

'You left the party?' Simms asked, sounding surprised.

Paul started nervously. 'Only for a while. I'd meant to bring some booze, you see, as my contribution to the party. Only I forgot, so I just nipped down to the village shop,' he waved a hand vaguely towards the village square.

'And when was this?'

Paul blinked. 'I wasn't really noticing the time much. About a quarter to three, maybe? Or was it earlier. Maybe later. I'm not sure, you'd better ask the others. Someone's bound to know.'

The policeman hid a smile. Yes, just like he'd thought. He might have muscles where all the women liked them, but he had quite a few between his ears as well.

'Did you notice anyone hanging around the vicarage when you left?' he tried patiently.

Briefly Paul's face flickered, and Simms could have sworn he could hear the wheels grinding in his head. Slowly.

'No. No one,' he said at last, his eyes sliding away from those of the policeman.

Simms sighed, clearly not believing him. 'Sir, if you saw anything, anything at all, no matter how irrelevant it might have seemed at the time, we need to know about it.'

'Yes, I understand. But there weren't any strangers lurk-ing about or unknown cars or what have you. I promise, I'd tell you if there were,' Paul Waring said earnestly.

Simms, realizing he would get nothing more from this wit-ness now, nodded. 'OK, let's move on. Did you see Mrs Franklyn leave the party?'

'No.'

'Do you know anyone who had a grudge against her?'

'No.'

And on and on it went.

* * *

Vera Ainsley stepped out the back door, and walked to the small, fenced-off area where the refuse bins were kept. She dumped a load of rubbish into the big green wheelie bin marked with her flat number, and watched the colourful and, it had to be said, slightly odoriferous debris slide into the depths. She sighed heavily.

'You sound about as depressed as I feel.' A voice, coming from behind her, made her jump and look quickly around. Her face, which had been lined with worry, smoothed out into a half-hearted smile.

'Pauline, you made me jump!'

'Sorry.'

For a while the two women looked at one another awkwardly, then Vera smiled vaguely.

'Have the police talked to you yet?' she asked hesitantly.

Pauline nodded. 'Yes. Not that I could tell them much,' she added quickly.

Vera nodded. 'No. Me neither.'

Pauline frowned. 'You know, now that I've had more time to think about it, there *is* something that's been niggling away at me.'

Vera shut the lid of the wheelie bin with a snap. 'You shouldn't hold anything back from the police you know, Pauline,' she advised sharply, not liking the way the other woman instantly flushed an ugly red.

'I haven't!' Pauline denied hotly, the colour just as suddenly washing away from her face again and leaving it slightly grey. 'If I knew what it was, I'd tell them, but I just can't remember what it is that seems so off. It's probably nothing anyway.' Then she added reluctantly, 'I'm sure it's got something to do with clothes, though.'

Vera went very still, very suddenly. Her eyes, usually round and open, became abruptly shuttered. She cocked her head slightly to one side, observing the younger woman so intently that Pauline began to shuffle her feet.

'Maurice changed his clothes during the course of the afternoon,' Vera said slowly. 'So did Carol-Ann, I think. Maurice, I imagine, changed because he'd been perspiring, and you know how pernickety he can be about that sort of thing. And I think Carol-Ann had probably been told by her mother that what she was wearing wasn't appropriate. Could it be that?'

Pauline frowned, thinking it over. Finally, she shook her head. 'No, I don't think so,' she said hesitantly, then sighed and shrugged. 'Oh, it'll come to me eventually, whatever it is. All I have to do is stop trying to force it, and it'll just pop into my head. Probably in the middle of the night, when I'm trying to get to sleep,' she added, laughing falsely. 'That's how it usually happens with me. Anyway, I'd better follow your example,' she said, and as Vera looked at her suspiciously, held out a bag of rubbish and shook it.

Vera smiled, stepped to one side to let her pass, then walked back to the house and half-stepped through the open back door. She stopped halfway through, however, and turned to watch Pauline. Her eyes once again had a shuttered, blank look.

* * *

Monica opened the door at the sound of knocking, not at all surprised to find Chief Inspector Jason Dury on the other side of it.

'Chief Inspector,' she murmured. 'Please, come in. Would you like a drink? Something cold?'

'No, thank you,' Jason said, glancing up as Graham stuck his head out of his study door.

'Do you need me, Chief Inspector?' Graham asked mildly.

'No, sir. I've come to ask your wife a few more questions about finding Mrs Franklyn's body.'

He saw the vicar's eyes turn to those of his wife, asking silently if she needed him. It was an intimate, touching gesture that was only possible between two people who knew each other very well indeed. That sort of silent communication only came with people who were on the same wavelength, and Jason hastily looked away, feeling absurdly like a peeping Tom.

'This way then, Chief Inspector,' Monica said, and Graham, getting the message that she was OK, withdrew back into the study and the writing of his Sunday morning sermon that awaited him.

Jason followed Monica into a pretty little living room, decorated in shades of green, cream and pale orange, and sat down in a huge comfortable armchair. He got out his notebook.

Monica took the armchair opposite him, and Jason glanced across at her just as she was in the process of crossing her long, slim legs. He quickly looked back down at his notebook.

'Now, Mrs Noble. How well did you know Margaret?'

'Not at all well, really. She and Sean only moved in about a month ago. I don't think Margaret was very happy about it.'

'Oh? Why do you say that?'

Briefly, Monica told him about the spat she'd overhead, careful not to mention that she'd also heard Margaret practically accuse Carol-Ann of pinching her diamond earrings.

'So it was Mr Franklyn who chose their apartment?'

'Yes. I think Margaret would have preferred to stay in Bath.'

Jason nodded. This was interesting. Just because Sean Franklyn couldn't have pulled the trigger on his wife himself, didn't mean that he couldn't have set it up for somebody else to do so. Although it was extremely rare for people to hire a hitman, it wasn't unheard of.

But why buy a place that his wife didn't like? It sounded very odd to him.

'Mind you, Margaret picked fault with everything,' Monica carried on. 'She was the sort of woman who seemed dissatisfied with almost everything and everyone.'

'A discontented woman, then?'

'Yes,' Monica nodded. Then, feeling guilty about talking badly of a woman who had just been so brutally killed, added hastily, 'But as I say, I'd only known her for a short time. She might only have been going through a bad patch.'

Jason smiled. 'Mrs Noble, please. I'd rather you were honest and straightforward with me. Whatever you say can't hurt Mrs Franklyn now, but it might just lead me to whoever killed her.'

Monica felt a cold shiver run down her spine. Her killer — could that really be someone who was in this house, right at this very moment? For a second, she wanted to cry. This vicarage had always been a place of peace and sanity. Of, well, decency, as corny as that might sound. But now someone had brought evil into it.

'Mrs Noble?'

Monica blinked and the urge to burst into tears slowly faded. 'Sorry,' she said. 'It's just that it's all so horrible.'

Jason abruptly felt guilty. Finding a body, he knew, could badly affect some people for years afterwards. Some never really got over it.

'Do you want someone to come and sit with you, Mrs Noble?' he asked anxiously. Her husband, he thought, would be a rock for her right about now.

But Monica was already shaking her head and taking a deep, calming breath.

'No, thank you. I'll be all right. Just ask your questions and I'll answer them all as honestly as I can.'

Jason admired her pluck. 'Right. Well then, how did Mrs Franklyn get on with her neighbours here at the vicarage? Did she make friends with anyone in particular?'

Monica had to smile. 'No,' she said succinctly, and Jason caught on instantly.

'Did she make anyone particularly angry?'

'Well, there was Pauline Weeks,' Monica said reluctantly. 'Oh, it was nothing serious! It's just that Pauline is rather fond of Paul, and Margaret liked to tease.'

Jason wrote something down, and Monica wished she'd kept her big mouth shut. This was awful. Truly awful. She could feel her words being distorted even as she spoke, and she felt absurdly traitorous. Then she wondered what Pauline might be saying about her, right now. What, in fact, all the others might be saying, and she felt a little better. At least they were all in the same boat!

'So Mrs Franklyn was flirting with Paul?'

Monica flushed. 'That was just her way. She was also giving Julie Dix a hard time but that . . .' she trailed off miserably. Now she was dropping poor Julie in it! Jason looked at her and waited. 'It was just the way she was,' Monica finished lamely.

'I see. What was she giving her a hard time about?'

'I don't know, I couldn't hear what she was saying exactly, but I could tell she wasn't happy from her tone.'

'And how did Julie react?' Jason probed. 'Or her mother, for that matter?'

But this time Monica wasn't going to be drawn. 'I don't know, I wasn't really watching them. But Joan *is* rather protective of Julie.' Surely there was no harm in saying that? Besides, they'd quickly discover as much for themselves. 'I think she's an only child, and Joan is a widow, so Julie's all she's got,' she added pointedly.

Jason nodded. But it was not Joan Dix he was interested in. She had an alibi. Her daughter, however, didn't.

'Right. I want you to go over today with me. From the time you woke up till the time you heard the shot. Tell me what happened, as clearly as you can.'

Monica did her best. She had a good memory, and recalled every incident in detail, but to her own ears she sounded as if she was rambling. To Jason, however, she was a clear-headed witness, who also seemed to be totally unbiased and inherently honest.

Unless she was one hell of an actress and he was being a mug — a possibility he was determined to keep firmly in mind.

'And then you heard the shot?' Jason said, about half an hour later, as her dialogue came to a stumbling halt.

Monica tensed. Because now, she knew, he was going to ask her to relive that awful moment again when she first saw Margaret's body. But, all things considered, she handled it well. She was careful to keep calm, to speak slowly, to try and describe every detail.

'And then I tripped, and put my hand out onto the floor to stop myself falling, but instead of touching the hard flat ground, I touched something rounded and softer,' she finished, swallowing back a sudden urge to be sick. 'I pulled the tarpaulin away and — well, there she was.' She took another harsh swallow, and then said suddenly, as if making a discovery, 'Whoever killed her didn't really do a good job of hiding her, did they?'

That observation wasn't an exact echo of what Jason had been thinking, however. Rather, Jason had been thinking, why did the killer cover her up at all? He must have known people would hear the shot and come to investigate. Realistically, how much time would covering up Margaret's body have given him?

'Something doesn't fit,' he said, unaware that he'd spoken out loud until Monica looked at him questioningly. He shook his head impatiently. 'Never mind. And then you called for your husband?'

'I think so. Yes. He carried me outside. I was feeling unwell.'

'I understand,' Jason said quickly, the image of Monica being carried possessively and protectively by her husband suddenly flashing into and out of his mind. 'Well, I think that's all.' As he spoke, the front doorbell rang.

Jason frowned, and as Monica rose to answer it, he quickly followed. In the corridor they both saw Graham open the door, and then a veritable flood of twittering, anxious, middle-aged and elderly ladies fluttered in, all talking at once.

'Oh, Reverend, you're all right!'

'We heard you were dead!'

'Have you seen a doctor? The shock, you know . . .'

Monica watched Graham quickly and expertly handle the sea of anxious ladies as he quickly ushered them all into his study.

'That disappearing act was for your benefit,' Monica explained to Jason, grinning for the first time since finding Margaret. 'If they'd spotted you, you'd have been given a more gruelling third degree than any that you give down at the police station.'

Jason smiled back ruefully. 'I can well believe it!' Then he looked down at her. 'Your husband has a devoted parish, it seems,' he said, with just the hint of a question in his voice.

Monica grinned again. 'His fan club, Carol-Ann and I call them. And of course they're devoted. Graham has a way of making everyone love him.' She said it so simply and naturally, and without any covert overtones, that Jason, once again, felt a little stab of something perilously close to jealousy lance through his chest. He snapped his notebook shut with a little more force than was strictly necessary.

'Right. Well, that's all for the moment. I *will* ask that you remain in your flat for the rest of the night. I'll be asking the same of all the other residents,' he added, as she turned to him quickly, her mouth open and ready to protest. 'It's just a precaution.'

Besides, he wanted the grounds thoroughly inspected, and just on the off-chance that he got his search warrants today, he didn't want anybody else leaving the building.

CHAPTER 8

Evening came slowly, and the blackbirds continued to sing in the silver birches. With golden light bathing the flowers, and bumblebees gathering in their last cache of nectar and pollen, the evening was so beautiful that Monica, looking out from her living room window, sighed gratefully. Then, in the bushes, something stirred, and she could just make out the dark blue outline of a police uniform. Her mood instantly darkened.

She wasn't to know it, but Jason's WPC had failed to get a search warrant for the individual flats. Mainly because the judge had decided that they had no real evidence that any of the vicarage residents had been involved in the killing. But he wasn't taking the setback lying down. Not only did the police continue to watch the house, but tomorrow, he'd have forensics go over the public-access areas in the building, for which he *had* been granted a warrant.

For Monica, the beauty of the golden evening was now ruined, and Graham, seated on the sofa, looked up as she drew the curtains together with an angry tug.

'Something wrong?' he asked mildly.

'Depends on how you look at it,' Monica said wryly, picking up the television remote control as she sat beside him.

'We're being watched.' She told him about the continuing police presence.

'Well, think of them as being there for our protection,' Graham said, reasonably. 'There might be someone disturbed hanging around, and they're here to come to our rescue if we should need them.'

Monica sighed softly, concerned that it might be one of the residents that they needed protecting from. She leaned across to kiss him, and felt him stir with that mixture of surprise and near-guilty delight that had punctuated their entire courtship. She ran a hand lightly along his arm, and he trembled, just a little, at her touch. It always gave her such a delicious feeling of power and protectiveness when he did that!

'Monica,' Graham said huskily.

Just then the door flew open. 'Come on, Mum, turn on the telly! I want to see *Love Island*.'

Carol-Ann, oblivious to the atmosphere, leapt so hard onto the last available sofa seat that the other two actually bounced.

'Early night, I think,' Graham murmured dryly.

'Hmm, good idea,' Monica muttered, eyes gleaming, as she held out her hand and let him pull her to her feet.

* * *

John Lerwick shut and locked the shed door, pausing for a moment to look up at the first evening stars appearing in the sky. Since he was almost completely hidden by the shadows, the woman opening the back door and stepping out didn't see him, but in the twilight, John had no trouble at all in recognizing her. He was about to call out a greeting when she hurried over to a car and slid inside.

John felt himself tense. Since when had Julie owned a car? And hadn't they all been told they weren't allowed to leave the vicarage? The policeman on duty must be round the other side of the building. For a long moment John hesitated, an uneasy sensation creeping over him.

He'd just decided to go inside and make himself a mug of cocoa, when the door opened again and Sean appeared. He walked straight to the same car, got in and drove away. Although the moon had yet to rise, John could plainly see Julie turn her head to look at him as they pulled out of the parking lot.

John, thoughtfully, went indoors.

* * *

As soon as the village was left behind and they were on the main road heading towards Cheltenham, Sean pulled into a lay-by and switched off the engine. He was pale, and his hands trembled as they rested on the steering wheel. Julie, who had yet to say a word, finally turned and looked at him. A nameless dread as heavy as iron seemed to have taken up residence in her abdomen. His profile had a hard edge to it that she'd never noticed before.

'Where are we going?' she whispered.

'I'm going to a pub to get drunk,' Sean said flatly. 'I think you should go and see some friends or something. I'll drop you off.'

'Sean!' her voice rose in protest.

'No,' Sean said sharply, raising a hand to ward off any argument. 'It's best we're not seen together now. Surely you can understand that?'

Julie felt bitter tears stinging her eyes, and looked away. When he'd called her to ask her to meet him in the car park, she'd felt her heart leap with joy. All day long she'd been aching to see him and tell him how much she loved him, and that she'd do anything for him now.

'Sean,' she began again, tentatively, but once more he held up a hand to silence her.

'It all went wrong, didn't it?' he said flatly.

And Julie could only nod miserably. And now that wonderful, marvellous, careful plan of theirs lay in ruins.

* * *

The church clock had just struck two in the morning when Constable Brian Bradley thought he heard the crunch of gravel coming from the direction of the car park. He'd been bored witless all night, but now his adrenaline shot up. Crouching, he moved parallel to the rear of the house, pulling aside a lilac branch to peer across the car park.

A few cars were visible in the full moonlight, but nothing else. No sinister dark figures or shadows where they shouldn't be. And yet, he could have *sworn* he'd heard a crunch, like an injudicious footstep on the gravel. PC Bradley surveyed the vast area of garden. Go left or right? Not that it mattered much now — there was just too much garden for someone to hide in if they put their mind to it. Nevertheless, he set off on a scout of the gardens, and, as he'd expected, discovered nothing.

But someone *had* left the building. And, nearly an hour later, someone *would* sneak back in. Unfortunately, by that time, PC Bradley would be on the east side of the house, having a crafty fag.

* * *

The next morning being a Sunday, Graham was already up when Monica walked sleepy-eyed into the kitchen. He knew that he was the luckiest man alive to have found her — and at his age, too, when a long, quiet and essentially lonely slide into old age had seemed to beckon.

'Monica, I love you,' he said softly.

Monica glanced up from filling the kettle, read him like a sentence from a book, and smiled.

'I love you, too. But don't let Carol-Ann hear us! It'll put her right off her cornflakes.'

Graham grinned. Sometimes he worried that he'd been wrong to take this lovely woman from London and her well-paid job to bring her here, where she was simply labelled 'the vicar's wife' and was watched avidly to see whether she would sink or swim. Then, at other times, she seemed so confident of her place here, and really understood that his work was a vocation as well as a career, an essential part of himself that was indistinguishable from his personality. And at times like these, he felt humble and incredibly lucky.

Now he turned back to his toast and said dolefully, 'I expect, all things considered, we're going to have a full church today. Human nature being what it is.'

Monica grimaced, knowing he was right. The whole village would probably turn up to take their cue from their vicar, and see what new tidbit could be learned. She was about to say something encouraging, when, glancing up, she spotted Jason Dury striding across the lawn. He had a pair of uniformed policemen with him, and one of them was talking to him earnestly. Whatever he was saying, Jason didn't seem to like it, for even from this distance, she could see that he was frowning ferociously.

He was dressed in a dark blue suit and red tie, and the morning sunlight turned his hair to silver. As he glanced across the grounds towards the Nobles' flat, she quickly reared back from the window, not wanting him to see her watching him.

Her heart was beating just a shade faster than she'd have liked. Feeling absurdly guilty, she took her coffee to the table, sat down across from her husband, and lightly laid her hand on his. He looked up, smiled, squeezed her hand, and returned to his Sunday morning paper.

Monica sighed. And began to worry.

* * *

It was nearly eleven o'clock when Trisha Lancer pulled up at the entrance to Church Lane and slammed on the brakes. Everyone was just coming out of church, and she could hear the evocative and cheerful church bells pealing out across the countryside.

But the sight of the two police cars parked at the entrance to the vicarage gate made her panic. She'd not had the morning radio on or seen the local papers yet, making her one of the few people who hadn't yet heard about the murder in Heyford Bassett. Now she chewed on her lower lip in despair. She'd desperately wanted to speak to Graham today, especially after what she'd discovered last night, but the blue-and-white police cars filled her with the urge to run.

Graham noticed a car in the lane begin to reverse, and although he couldn't be sure, he thought he recognized the driver as Trisha Lancer. He took an instinctive step in her direction, then realized it was hardly the time or the place, with the whole village watching everything that moved, and checked himself.

'I'm sure the police will make an arrest soon, Gareth, so there's no need to keep Keith out of school,' he heard himself say reassuringly. Then he turned to smile and shake hands with a timid man who worked as the head gardener up at the manor. Now a big conference centre, the manor was the main source of employment for the locals.

He could only hope that Trisha's business wasn't urgent. Eventually, the congregation began to splinter and troop back to their various homes in the village. In her car, Trisha pulled onto the main road, her face tense. She kept glancing towards her handbag, and the frightening little secret she had hidden away in there.

She felt as if her whole world was on the brink of collapsing, and right now, the vicar of Heyford Bassett was the only person in the world that she trusted enough to tell. So she'd come back and see him tomorrow.

Perhaps.

* * *

Back at the house, the police had already set up an incident room in the big empty lounge of flat 2, forensics having given it the all-clear. Makeshift chairs and tables had been moved in, along with a desk, printer and a few boxes of files. Jason was sitting at a scarred wooden desk, laptop closed, reading the printed autopsy report.

It told him nothing that he hadn't expected. Margaret had been a reasonably healthy woman of thirty-eight. She had not been pregnant. She had probably not been rendered unconscious before her death. She had not been drunk. She hadn't taken any illegal drugs — or, at least, none that still remained in her bloodstream — and the only thing of note that the pathologist had to tell him was that she was, in his opinion, underweight. No signs, however, of bulimia or anorexia nervosa.

Cause of death, obviously, had been the shotgun wound. The technicians had identified the pellets, analysed the lead content, and given him all the information he could possibly want about the cartridge that killed her. Unfortunately, the shot used was one of the most popular brands around, and could have been bought in any sporting goods or gun shop in the country.

He tossed the report aside and rubbed the bridge of his nose wearily. At that moment, Jim Greer walked in.

'Still no sign of the gun, sir. We've got a couple of uniforms going through all those in the area with a licence for a shotgun, but we're in the middle of the huntin', shootin', fishin' brigade here, so we're looking at hundreds of licensees. It'll take time to talk to them all.'

'Too much to hope that anyone living here owns a shotgun, I suppose?' Jason asked, and his sergeant grinned back at him wordlessly. 'Yeah, thought so,' Jason sighed.

It had been one of their first priorities to try and find the murder weapon, and all yesterday afternoon and well into the evening, a team of policemen had been combing the grounds for it. Jason had reasoned that if someone living in the house *was* responsible for the murder, they wouldn't have had much time to get rid of the shotgun. It was far more likely to be only superficially hidden, as the killer wouldn't have dared to keep it in their flat.

And yet, the gun hadn't been found.

'Well, there's three possibilities, Jim,' he said tiredly. 'One: either someone from outside came in, shot her, left by the back door taking the gun with him, and by now could have disposed of it as far away as Scotland. Two: someone here shot her, then sneaked out last night and hid it a good distance away. And Bradley thinks he may have heard someone prowling about last night.'

Jim clucked his tongue. 'Bad luck not to catch him at it then.'

'We're short-staffed,' Jason said, a touch of bitterness mixed in with the fatalism. 'If I could have had as many men as I'd wanted, a mouse wouldn't have been able to get out of here unseen last night. And if the judge hadn't been so concerned with upholding people's rights, we could have searched the flats and found the weapon yesterday. Unless . . .'

'Sir?' Jim asked, his voice rising questioningly.

Jason sighed and leaned back in his chair. 'Unless, Jim, it's number three. Which is that somebody in this house has been very clever indeed. And we aren't even on the right track yet.'

'And that's the one you're going for, is it, sir?'

Jason shrugged. 'Let's just say I've got a feeling that this one is going to be a hard nut to crack.'

'There's nothing obviously wrong in Franklyn's flat, anyway,' Jim said.

It was standard police procedure to seal the premises of a murder victim, and Jim himself had gone through the entire place and found nothing. Sean had slept last night in an empty flat on the next floor, but would be allowed to return to his own flat later.

Flat 2, of course, remained sealed.

Jason reached for a pen. 'Franklyn has an alibi, remember? And if he did arrange for a hit to be made on his wife, he'd hardly be likely to leave anything incriminating lying around, would he?' He sighed heavily. 'What I just can't figure out is why she came here in the first place, Jim.' He looked towards the room where she'd been found. 'She'd been at the vicarage

106

long enough to know that flat 2 was empty, so why come in here at all? Unless she was forced to at gunpoint, she must have come voluntarily. To meet someone maybe?'

'A pre-arranged meet?' Jim said, nodding. 'It makes sense.'

'But who?' Jason said with frustration. 'Not someone already at the party, surely? It would be rather obvious if two people left the party together.' Suddenly he sat up straight. 'Paul Waring left the party briefly. Did you check with the shop that he'd actually been in? I know he came back with the booze but that could've come from somewhere else.'

'Yes, sir, one of my first priorities,' Jim said, a shade reproachfully. Did the boss really think he would let something as important as that slip? 'I managed to catch them just as they were closing. The owner remembers him coming in because he bought four of their priciest bottles of wine and a good stash of beer. She's not likely to forget a sale like that. Besides, she's the sort that notices everything,' he said wryly. 'You gotta love the nosy ones. She remembered more or less when he came in, too, and the time fits with when the other witnesses say they saw him leave and return to the party.'

Jason slumped back in his chair. 'There's going to be no easy answers on this one, Jim, I can feel it in my bones. So, what have we got? Margaret leaves the party, and according to Vera, goes into the opposite wing of the house from this one. Why?'

'Perhaps she wanted to get something from her flat first, sir?'

'Then she nips out into the corridor and down here to flat 2,' he mused, pulling the map of the house that Monica Noble had drawn for him a little closer. 'See, she bypasses this main foyer,' he pointed on the map, 'where the front lift is. The main door is probably only used by those on the second or third floors anyway.'

'Makes sense,' Jim agreed. 'John Lerwick, in flat 3, and the Franklyns would be far more likely to use the side door. It's like I said, sir, she must have wanted to go back to her own place first.'

'But for what? Nothing was found on her.'

'Perhaps the killer took whatever it was,' Jim said, his voice growing a touch excited now. 'Perhaps they met just so that she could hand it over.'

'So why then kill her?' Jason pointed out.

Jim sighed. 'Could be anything, sir. Perhaps they quarrelled and things got out of hand.'

'But raised voices would have been overheard by people at the party, surely?' he pointed out reasonably. 'They didn't have any music playing or anything like that. Besides, it couldn't have been a spur-of-the-moment thing. Whoever she met had a shotgun with him or her. You don't just lug one of those around for amusement.'

'Unless it belonged to Mrs Franklyn?' Jim pointed out, but he himself was dubious.

Jason acknowledged the point.

'Ask her husband if they own a shotgun by all means. But we already know that they don't have a licence for one, so it would have been illegal if they had. So he's not likely to cop to it, on that principle alone.'

'Sir.'

'Have the background reports on the Franklyns come in yet?'

'I think so. We managed to get on to their bank before they closed. And there's a report somewhere from the insurance office where Franklyn works.' Jim began sorting through files. He grunted. 'Here it is. The bank statements . . .' He quickly leafed through them, and nodded. 'They're a bit tight for money, especially after getting the mortgage on this place, sir, but they're not too badly off. No outstanding debts, at any rate.' He handed the report to Jason, who ignored it. He wasn't the sort of superior officer who thought a subordinate couldn't read a bank statement without help.

'And the insurance office?'

'A bit more interesting, sir,' Jim said, speed-reading the constable's report. 'According to the secretary who works there, a big promotion opportunity is coming up in the firm.

Whoever gets it rises well up in the managerial status and moves into the top job for the whole of Gloucestershire and the Home Counties. According to her, the boss was taking a good look at our Mr Franklyn as a possible contender.'

'So, things were looking up for them?'

'Yes, sir. But Mike Shaw — that's the chap who did the interview — makes a note here that he thinks the secretary was keeping something back. It might be worth talking to the boss himself. See what he made of Franklyn.'

'Right. Get on it, Jim.'

'It'll have to wait until tomorrow, sir. No boss I ever knew worked on a Sunday,' he grinned.

'Apart from our vicar, you mean,' Jason said, catching sight of Graham Noble, still dressed in his white cassock, entering his flat.

Jason looked up as one of the uniformed men looked in. 'Yes, Smith?'

'I attended the service, like you asked, sir. Everybody's talking about the murder, of course, but nothing untoward. No one acting suspicious.'

Jason nodded. 'I didn't really think there would be. Still, you never know.' Some of the more unbalanced killers really *did* hang around at the scene of their crimes, lapping up the action. 'I hope the service wasn't too much of an ordeal for you, Smith.'

The young PC grinned. 'It was better than I thought it would be,' the constable said. 'The vicar gave a right good sermon.' And with that, he departed to resume his sentry duty on the gates.

Jim glanced back at Jason, who was thinking not about the murder of Margaret so much, but the fact that Graham Noble gave a good sermon. Somehow he wasn't all that surprised. There were hidden depths in the vicar of Heyford Bassett that might yet prove useful.

Unless, of course, it was Graham Noble himself who had been so dead clever yesterday. In which case, Jason would take extreme pleasure in arresting him.

CHAPTER 9

Jason walked to the incident room window and pushed it open, wondering irritably when the heatwave was going to end.

'Jim, any chance of requisitioning a few fans?' he asked without hope. His sergeant looked up from the pile of reports he was reading and grinned. 'Thought not.'

It was nearly five o'clock, and all afternoon Vera, John, Monica and Graham Noble had, after being given permission to do so by the forensics team, been busy clearing away the remnants of the party. 'It's time to call it a day, Jim. Haven't you got a home to go to?'

Jim shrugged without enthusiasm. His in-laws had been invited over for Sunday lunch, and for once, he hadn't jibbed at having to work at the weekend. Not that he minded his mother-in-law so much, but his father-in-law was a total golfing fanatic who could talk about nothing else. And Jim had always been a rugby stalwart.

'I'll finish going over the forensic reports. You swan off for the night.'

Jason made his way back to his desk as his sergeant left, unaware that across the way, Monica had begun to open all the windows in her flat in search of a cooling breeze.

Jason sighed, undoing yet another shirt button, and began to read. He started with the fingerprint evidence at the crime scene. There were plenty of unknowns, probably belonging to the decorators, and tomorrow morning they'd all have to be fingerprinted and questioned. There were no prints belonging to the victim. Odd that, he thought. But then again, if Margaret had been meeting someone in there, she'd hardly have gone around finding naked surfaces on which to place her hands. Naturally, none of the other vicarage residents would have left their prints in flat 2, apart from the Nobles. But then, they were known to have been inside, so this meant very little. Of course, as any police officer could tell you, the person or persons finding a body were always put on the suspect list.

Not that Jason could seriously believe that a woman like Monica Noble would fire a shotgun at someone. Then he frowned, warning himself to be careful about jumping to conclusions. But then, she *was* one of those with an alibi.

Angry at himself for the way his mind kept see-sawing about when it came to the vicar's attractive wife, he tossed aside the woeful report and turned next to the detailed reports on the tarpaulins themselves.

And there was not much there for a copper to get his teeth into, either. Or rather, there was far *too* much there to be of any real use. The tarpaulins were literally smothered with forensic evidence. Paint. Turps. Plaster. Lichens. Dust. And food remnants, no doubt from dozens of packed lunches. A whole army might have trampled over it. He looked up as Jim reappeared, grumbling in the doorway.

'Forgot my damned car keys,' the younger man muttered in explanation, looking vaguely around.

'You ought to get one of those gizmos that you can put onto a key ring that beeps when you whistle,' Jason muttered. 'Hello, this is interesting,' he added, suddenly sitting up straighter.

'Sir?' Jim stopped his search and looked up, interested.

'The expert's comments about the bloodstains,' Jason said, distractedly speed-reading his way through to the end.

Although he spoke at a normal volume, on the still summer air his voice carried far enough to be distinctly audible to Monica Noble over in her flat, who was getting ready for a bath. She sighed, and began to walk towards the window to shut it.

In the incident room, Jason continued to speak. 'According to the expert, the spatter marks are consistent with Margaret being shot in the room at a distance of about six feet, but what do you make of these "mirror images" of certain bloodstains that they found?'

Monica clasped the window latch, her mind on a lovely cool bath.

'Like it says here, sir,' Jim said, 'they probably happened when the tarpaulin was folded over her. Where the two sides met, the bloodstains were transferred from one side of the tarpaulin to the other.'

'Yes, but—'

'Sir!' An excited young constable rushed in, his voice ringing loud with self-importance. 'We've just got this in.' The constable handed Jason a piece of paper. 'Apparently, the victim called the local station the morning before her death, sir. To report a crime.'

'I can read,' Jason said dryly. But why was he only hearing about this now?

Jim, tense and alert, watched Jason's face as he scanned the report.

'According to Mrs Franklyn, a very valuable pair of diamond and sapphire earrings had been stolen. She accused Carol-Ann Clancy,' Jason summed it up succinctly.

Jim whistled. 'Could it really be that simple?'

Jason shook his head thoughtfully. An accusation of petty theft wasn't much of a motive, he thought — unless they came across something to indicate that Carol-Ann was mentally unbalanced as well.

In her bathroom, Monica froze, appalled. She strained her ears, listening in vain for more conversation between the policemen, then when there was none, reluctantly closed the window. They must have gone into another room. Damn! She sat down abruptly on the edge of the bath, and in a daze turned on the taps.

She began to feel just a little bit sick. Carol-Ann was one of those who hadn't been present at the party when the shot was fired and that alone put her on the suspect list. Did the police really think that she could have done it? All over a pair of stupid earrings? She told herself she was panicking over nothing, and poured some bath salts into the tub. Then she stripped and climbed in. Although *she* knew her daughter wouldn't hurt a fly, how could she make Jason believe it? She couldn't just sit back and let Carol-Ann come under serious suspicion. She just couldn't!

But what could she do about it, short of finding the real killer herself?

* * *

Back in the incident room, Jim left, and Jason turned back once more to the reports. Something nagged at him, something that wasn't quite right. He reached for the pictures of the murder scene and spent several long minutes looking at them. But whatever had briefly teased at the back of his brain had gone. He was simply too tired to think properly anymore. With a sigh, he told everybody but a token PC to leave for the night, and headed to his own car.

* * *

On the top floor, in flat 9, Joan Dix sat on the edge of her daughter's bed, staring at the wall opposite. She was pale and trembling, and suffering just a little from shock.

Julie had long since taken the train to Cheltenham for some 'music and life,' as she'd put it to her mother. She'd had enough of death and police, and being cooped up in the house.

Thus abandoned, the hours had dragged by and Joan had started to do what she always did in times of crisis. She'd cleaned. Vacuumed every square inch of carpet and polished every wooden surface. No room had been spared her obsessive attentions — not even her daughter's bedroom. Which was how she'd come across the letter hidden in her daughter's lingerie drawer.

She'd just emptied the contents of all the drawers to re-line them with paper, as she'd done with her own vanity table drawers not ten minutes before. At first, she'd picked up the letter without a thought. Then she'd noticed the pink ribbon that was still looped around it, which looked as if it had once bound a whole stack of letters, and became instantly suspicious. In this age of emails and texts, who bothered to actually put pen to paper? Unless it was in the cause of romance, that is.

A quick glance at the masculine handwriting had got her heart thumping. Without a qualm she'd removed the pieces of expensive notepaper, and what she'd just read on them terrified her. And made her the only person in the vicarage on that sun-baked evening to actually feel cold.

She read the letter again, but its contents didn't change. And the enormity of her daughter's guilt and folly still remained, right there in her hands. Evidence of . . . And there, Joan's mind screeched to a halt and the numbness of shock suddenly shattered with that single thought.

Evidence.

The police had been searching the corridors, stairs and foyers of the house all afternoon. What they expected to find, or *did* find, she wasn't sure. But if they found these! The pieces of paper in her hands shook. For a moment, tears of panic flooded Joan's eyes.

Oh, Julie, Julie, what have you done?

She rose quickly and crossed over into the living room, which had a working fireplace. Without hesitating, she lit a match and held it to the envelope and pieces of paper, then knelt by the grate to watch them burn. When it was over, and only black ashes remained on the pristine grate, she took the poker to them and ruthlessly crushed even the ashes into dust.

She didn't want anyone, *anyone* to know what was in that letter. And it made her wonder what had been in the others, the missing letters. At least Julie had had the sense to get rid of those. Hadn't she?

Feverishly, Joan searched her daughter's room from top to bottom, but found nothing further that was incriminating. That done, Joan sat back numbly on the sofa and waited for her daughter to return.

They needed to talk. Julie was young and wild, and she might have some silly youthful idea of doing what was right, being open and honest with the police. And Joan would have to quash any such stupid desires right now. Her daughter, for all her intelligence, wasn't as wise to the ways of the world as Joan.

And Joan would fight tooth and nail to protect her daughter from the consequences of her actions.

* * *

Next door, in flat 11, Pauline Weeks mixed herself a stiff Scotch on the rocks and took it with her into the living room. There she sat down on a black leather settee and kicked off her shoes. She was smiling. She went to take a sip of the raw liquor, and paused.

'To you, Margaret,' she said softly, giving the empty room a mock salute. 'Cheers.'

All in all, she supposed that she could congratulate herself on getting away with things. No one had seen what she'd done when she came back into the house during the party, otherwise the police would be breathing down her neck by now. So *that* was one worry off her mind. Of course, the way things had turned out, it had all been for nothing anyway. Trust Margaret to ruin things, even when she was dead.

* * *

In the shrubbery at the back of the house, John's supple back served him well as he crouched up and down the flowerbeds, adding to the growing pile of weeds he was accumulating in his wheelbarrow. There was nothing like a mindless task to help you relax, he mused. To take away the tension and keep you calm and clear-headed. Besides, now that the worst was over, it was time to get on with life. If only he hadn't been witness to that clandestine meeting last night! He bent and pulled up a thistle. So what if Sean and Julie were involved? It was none of his business. For all he knew, Sean had simply been giving Julie a lift somewhere.

He sighed, knowing that he must speak to Vera about it. She'd know what to do. He tracked her down to her kitchen and once seated at the table, allowed her to cut him a piece of seed cake.

As she poured coffee into thick ceramic mugs, she turned to glance at him, her eyes soft.

'So, what's bothering you?' she asked quietly, an amused and indulgent look on her face.

'I've got something to tell you,' he mumbled.

Vera nodded. 'I thought you might,' she said comfortably. 'As it happens, I've got something to tell you, too. About Pauline.'

John sighed. 'Mine's about Julie.' He pushed a piece of the excellent old-fashioned cake about on his plate with a finger that wasn't quite clean. Then he looked up at her. 'Are we in the soup, old gal?' he asked gruffly.

Vera sighed. 'We might be. What do you know?'

* * *

In one of the three large, prestigious flats, Maurice was beginning to celebrate. He was free at last! He could hardly believe it. Now he could call his life his own again. His money was his once more to spend just how he liked — on himself. Of course, he'd gone to all that expense, but even so, he could hardly grumble.

He sat at his desk and began to type into his computer vigorously. His tome on the father of the metaphysical poets had once again recaptured his imagination. He almost managed to forget that Margaret had ever existed.

In the back of his mind, though, he was still afraid. If the police ever found out who killed her, and why, he'd be in deep trouble once more. But why should they? As far as he knew, they didn't even have a clue.

* * *

Sean Franklyn wasn't at the vicarage. Although he'd been given permission to go on living in the flat, when Dury had given him the go-ahead to leave the village, he'd jumped at the opportunity. Now he was sitting in a noisy and smoke-filled pub in a back street in Cirencester, getting steadily drunk.

He wasn't sure whether he was glad or sorry that his wife was dead. He was, however, very sorry indeed that he'd ever met Julie Dix. From a young bit of exciting stuff, she'd turned into a potential albatross around his neck.

* * *

Paul Waring was at home, doing press-ups in a spare bedroom that had long since been converted into a personal gym. His brawny arms, broad shoulders and deep chest were bathed in sweat. His sandy hair lay damply on his forehead.

'Sixty-one, sixty-two, sixty-three . . .' he muttered, keeping count religiously.

He worked without stopping until he reached the magical century, then leapt lithely to his feet and walked to the shower, whistling as he soaped himself under the cooling spray.

He didn't have a care in the world. Well, he was a *bit* worried, because if the police started digging around in his past they might come up with some embarrassing facts. But he could cope with that, if he had to.

* * *

Alone now in her high-tech, professional's kitchen, Vera sipped some of the experimental cold soup that she hoped to perfect in time for next year's cookbook and sighed. It just didn't work. Even if she added a bit more coriander, she didn't think that would rescue it. So it was back to the old drawing board. Oh well.

She poured the mixture down the sink. Luckily, she had other ideas to try. Ideas were her thing — that, and planning.

She and John had thrashed things out once and for all, and had come to the conclusion that silence and vigilance were the best answer. She only hoped they weren't going to regret it.

* * *

Darkness came, and brought with it a modicum of coolness to relieve the restless sleep of the vicarage residents. And, as if in answer to one of Graham Noble's prayers, Monday morning dawned with an early splash of rain and a marked drop in temperature, but by the time nine o'clock arrived, bringing a van load of decorators with it, the sun was once more relentlessly shining.

The constable on the gate told the foreman to go up to the house and see Chief Inspector Dury in flat 2. The rest were to stay in the van. They were all to be fingerprinted, and a man would be down with a kit in a few minutes. This produced some uneasy murmurs. Everyone knew about the murder, of course. But what they *didn't* know, because the papers hadn't got the information themselves yet, was that the murder had been committed in the very flat they were currently decorating.

Consequently the foreman, a beefy and perpetually cheerful man called Len Biggs, walked up to the house to tap on the closed door of flat 2, which was quickly answered by Jim Greer.

'Come in. You must be Mr Biggs? We've been waiting to talk to you.'

Len, not at all sure that he liked the sound of that, followed the policeman into a room crammed with office equipment, and gaped about at the hive of activity. He quickly snapped his jaw shut, however, when a blond-haired man who had authority written all over him rose from behind a chair and pointed to a seat.

He sat down gingerly in the chair indicated, as if expecting it to collapse under his weight.

'We 'eard about the murder,' he stated flatly.

Jason nodded. 'Well then, Mr Biggs, just a few questions. You and your men were working here last Friday? What time did you leave?'

Len hesitated. Technically they hadn't been due to leave till five, just like any other day, and the boss would have a fit if he found out they'd skived off nearly an hour and a half early. But after he'd taken a long look at the glittering blue eyes of the policeman opposite, he heaved a sigh and said reluctantly, 'Three thirty, or thereabouts.'

'Did you notice anybody hanging around who shouldn't be there?'

'Nah. Don't think so. I'll ask the lads if they saw anybody, but when you're plastering and painting, you don't do much looking outta the windows.'

'You were working in the biggest room on the left side of the flat, weren't you? The one that's been painted on the ceiling?'

Len nodded. 'That silly bugger Ron Jessup had already done the walls though. I told him to do the rooms on the right first. But would he listen?'

Jim, taking notes, grinned. 'So that's why the tarpaulins had been tacked up, to protect the walls from spatter?' he asked.

'Yup.'

'Did you ever see Mr or Mrs Franklyn around whilst you were working?' Jason asked next.

'Dunno,' Len said. 'What do they look like?' Patiently, Jason described the Franklyns.

'Seen him about a few times,' Len said judiciously, after some thought. 'Pleasant enough chap to speak to. But not her, I reckon.'

'Did you see him hanging around the flat on Friday?' Jason persisted, but as expected Len shook his head.

'Nah. Didn't see anybody much Friday.'

Jason sighed and nodded to him that he could go.

Len hauled himself to his feet, then looked around. 'When can we come back in then?' he asked. 'To finish the place off, like?'

'Not for a while. You got any other flats here to work on?'

'Yup, number 12. Right up on the top floor. It's the last one still to do.'

'I don't see why you can't start work on that one in a few days' time. You'll just have to tell your boss to reassign you until then.'

'Righto,' Len said agreeably, and left.

As he walked slowly across the garden, he paused every now and then to look back at the house. It was a funny old world, he thought to himself morosely. You weren't safe anywhere anymore. But you'd think that a little country place like Heyford Bassett, and in a vicarage too, you'd be safe enough.

'Hello, Len.' A cheerful voice broke into his thoughts, and he looked up to see the vicar's wife walking towards him, a bunch of newly cut flowers in her hand. Going to tend to the neglected graves in the churchyard no doubt, he thought, and smiled broadly. He liked Mrs Noble. She was the only one in the place to offer them fresh cups of tea and cold drinks.

'Sorry for your trouble, Mrs Noble,' he said simply.

Monica sighed. 'Yes. I hope the chief inspector didn't keep you long?'

'Nah, not long. He seemed interested in the room we were decorating.'

If his voice had risen a little at the end to make it more of a question, Monica couldn't really blame him. She was curious herself about how the investigation was proceeding. After all, she had Carol-Ann's welfare to think about. Surely it couldn't hurt to ask the odd question or two, and use some brainpower on the problem herself?

'Yes, well, that's where she was killed,' she confirmed briskly. 'I found her. It was horrible. All the blood splashed about on those tarpaulins on the walls. And the body covered by one of them.'

She shuddered, and Len quickly put out a meaty hand and laid it on her shoulder. 'You just forget about all that, missus,' he advised gently. 'You don't want to go givin' yerself nightmares. 'Ere, hang on, what did you mean, the tarpaulins on the walls?' he asked. 'We took all them tarpaulins down at lunchtime, when Kevin finished his painting.'

Monica looked at him curiously.

'No, Len, that's not right. The tarpaulins were still up on the walls. Well, all except for one wall, and that one was only uncovered because whoever killed Margaret pulled it down to cover her up with it.'

Len scratched his head and scowled down at his boots. 'Queer. I coulda sworn they'd been taken down . . .'

'Perhaps one of the others put them back up again,' Monica hazarded. 'Why don't you ask around?'

'I'll do that,' Len said. 'It was probably that Ron. He doesn't know his arse from his elbow. Oh, sorry for the language, like,' he said with an embarrassed mumble, and Monica laughed and said that it didn't matter, and thus reassured, the foreman lumbered off to rejoin his colleagues in the van.

Monica watched him go, but her amused smile slowly turned to a frown. She'd have to try and remember to tell Jason what Len had said about the tarpaulins the next time she saw him.

It might be important.

* * *

Jason looked up as Jim tossed a small plastic bag containing two sparkling items on the desk in front of his superior. The sergeant stood there, arms akimbo and looking disgusted.

'The team that searched the Franklyns' place found these behind the dressing table in the bedroom. They'd fallen down between the carpet and the skirting board. The carpet's a bit loose in there, apparently.'

Jason reached forward and peered at the diamond and sapphire earrings encased in the evidence bag.

'So much for Carol-Ann Clancy being a potential Lady Raffles,' he drawled — and promptly forgot all about them.

CHAPTER 10

Clem Jarvis hung up the telephone, and turned, grave-faced, to his anxiously hovering wife.

'Well, Clem?' she asked quickly, although after listening in to his side of the telephone conversation she already had a pretty fair idea of what he was going to say.

'Bill says he ain't got it,' Clem said flatly. 'And that's the last of 'em.'

They were in the hall of their old farmhouse, and Clem sighed heavily, sinking down in the chair beside the small occasional table.

'It's no use, Bess. It's gone. I'd best take a walk on down to the vicarage and see somebody about it, I reckon. Not that I'm looking forward to it. I feel a right idiot. And I don't know if they might not charge me with something, even. Carelessness like, or failing to do something or other.'

Bess bit her lip nervously. Nothing in her hard-working, honest, and rather sheltered life had prepared her for this.

'Clem, it's not your fault. And I really can't believe it's been stolen,' she wailed. 'You've had it years,' she added, as if this made any difference.

The farmer shook his head. 'Well, old girl, I 'ad it when I went into the pub with the others after the pigeon shoot that time, and it were gone when we left. And if none of the others borrowed it, then it's been stolen.' He delivered this piece of logical reasoning in a calm, fatalistic voice, but inside his stomach was churning. Would he have to go to court?

He walked outside, looking the epitome of misery, and cast a glance down into the valley, his eyes easily picking out the church tower and the big vicarage next to it.

'The coppers ain't gonna be any too happy with me, I reckon,' he murmured, in massive understatement.

Then, sighing heavily, he set off towards the village where he'd lived all his life, deciding to walk instead of taking the old Land Rover. It would give him more time to get it clear in his head just what he was going to say. But one thing was for certain — if it did turn out that his gun had been used to kill that woman, well, he'd never pick up a shotgun again.

Let the pigeons eat his crops.

* * *

Carol-Ann stormed into the living room.

'Right, that's it!' she hissed, slinging herself with teenage fury onto the nearest armchair. 'This afternoon I'm going into Cheltenham and I'm going to get a job in a shop.'

Monica blinked. Her daughter, volunteering to work! She must be coming down with something that made you delirious. Fighting the urge to go over and lay the back of her hand on her daughter's forehead to check for a temperature, she smiled instead.

'Why's that, honeybunch?' she asked mildly, looking up from the email she was writing to her old boss.

Sue Phelps, a forty-something, unmarried, dedicated career woman, was also one of her best friends. And after Monica had totally flummoxed Sue by resigning to marry her lovely vicar, they'd made a determined effort to keep in touch and not let their friendship lapse. Of course, Sue kept hinting that Monica's old job was still there if ever she wanted it. So far, though, Monica hadn't been the least bit tempted.

'That Vivienne Goring, the cow!' Carol-Ann, still hissing like a steam kettle, glowered back at her mother ferociously. 'Jenny said she saw her going into the cinema with my Clive.'

Monica felt a twinge of nervousness. 'Your Clive?' she asked, managing not to gulp too much, and Carol-Ann heaved a sigh and shot her mother a fulminating look.

'My boyfriend!' she said scornfully. 'Duh!'

'I thought you were going out with Steve Crawford?' Monica managed faintly.

She'd always rather *liked* Steve Crawford. Mainly because he was football mad and still gauche and awkward around the opposite sex.

'Oh, Steve's old news,' Carol-Ann huffed, then smiled alarmingly. 'Clive's a love-machine on legs.'

Monica blinked again, gave herself a quick lecture on the perils of panicking, and said nonchalantly, 'Why haven't I met him then? He sounds . . .' gulp, 'interesting.'

Carol-Ann snorted. 'Hah! Bring him here to meet the Rev? You must be kidding. I'd never see him for dust!'

Carol-Ann had this fixed idea that any boyfriend, on finding out that his beloved actually had a vicar for a stepfather, was bound to run screaming off into the hills, never to be seen again.

'Mind you, it's not the rev I need to worry about this time,' Carol-Ann continued to mutter darkly. 'It's that man-eater, Vivienne. If she thinks she can snaffle Clive, she can think again!' she warned direly. 'You just wait. Once I've got my summer job, I'll show her.'

Monica, a bit lost now, frowned. 'I'm confused. How is working in a shop going to spike Vivienne's wheels?' But even as she asked the question, she wondered if she really wanted to know the answer.

'Because of the wages, Mother,' Carol-Ann said patiently, wondering if her mother had always been this dim.

'I hope you're not thinking of spending all your money on buying stuff for this Clive,' Monica began hotly. And, it has to be said, rather dimly. 'Because if you are, you'd be a—'

'Oh, Mother, of course I'm not!' Carol-Ann scorned witheringly. 'Trying to buy a man? Ugh, that's really naff.' And to show just how naff she thought this suggestion was, she mimed thrusting her finger down her throat and being very theatrically sick all over the sofa.

Relieved, Monica subsided. 'That's all right then.'

'No, I'm going to use the money I make to go to London and get a professional portfolio taken of me by a fashion photographer,' Carol-Ann explained blithely.

'Carol-Ann!' Monica squeaked. But when her daughter glared at her, Monica quickly read the danger signs and backed off a little. 'Surely there's a photographer in Cheltenham you can use?' she compromised weakly, but on the spur of the moment it was all she could come up with. 'They're bound to be cheaper than in the capital, and they'll be just as good.'

Carol-Ann shook her head sadly.

'Poor old Mum,' she said sympathetically. 'Any wannabe can go to a local hack to get her pics taken. But everyone knows the *real* pros have studios in London.' Then she shot out of the chair as precipitously as she'd landed in it. 'I'll ring Jenny back right now. She's got a mouth like a foghorn, and it'll soon be all over the place that I've been signed on by a modelling agency. See if Clive will want Vivienne then, when he can have a model for a girlfriend!'

'Modelling agency?' Monica yelped. 'What modelling agency?'

'The one I'll get when I start showing my portfolio around!' Carol-Ann tossed back over her shoulder, with a teenager's blithe disregard for the actual facts.

Monica gulped but returned to her email. She was determined that Carol-Ann wasn't going to send her grey before her time. In her own mind, Carol-Ann might already be setting out on the catwalk to fame, but the reality, as every grown-up knew, was far different from the dream. Besides, by the time her daughter had trawled the shops and found herself a summertime job, she'd probably have found herself a new boyfriend who was into computers.

Well, she could but hope.

Turning her attention to her laptop once more, Monica concentrated on the task in hand. Since she had so far resisted the temptation to return to London and the advertising agency, Sue had changed tactics somewhat, and had now written to her about doing some part-time work for the agency from her own home. This, she had pointed out, was an excellent compromise, since Monica could still be the stay-at-home wife and mother, and yet earn a little bit of income and keep her creative and professional juices from drying up altogether. And since they had a big commission for birdseed coming up, was she interested?

And on the whole, Monica rather thought that she was. She knew that Graham would have no objections to her doing whatever made her happy, and with Carol-Ann growing up so fast, she couldn't deny that a little more money in the kitty wouldn't be a welcome bonus. The trouble was, she was having trouble getting her mind back into its old advertising groove.

Pep up Polly's lunchtime with . . . Monica shook her head. No. Too condescending and old hat. Birdseed . . . She tried to do a bit of free association, letting her mind wander vaguely. Birdseed . . . What did that conjure up? Sylvester and Tweety, the cartoon cat and canary. Monica shook her head. No, that was no use — their images were bound to be covered by copyright, and to use them would cost any company a fortune. Birdseed . . . She still thought cartoons, rather than real flesh-and-blood feathery friends, was the way to go, and something with an element of comedy in it, but . . .

Unbidden, an image of Carol-Ann, with her long blonde locks flowing in the breeze created from a wind machine, suddenly flashed across Monica's mind. Her daughter, dressed in a skimpy T-shirt and gracing the latest teen magazine, being salivated over by every hormonal teenage boy in Britain. Then, quick as a flash, that image was superimposed by one of Carol-Ann being led away in cuffs by Jason Dury to face a murder charge.

She shuddered, all thoughts of birdseed utterly forgotten. This was threatening to be one hell of a summer.

* * *

'Think you'd better see this chap, sir,' Jim Greer said.

It was nearly noon on a bright Monday morning and the lab boys were busy sifting the decorators' fingerprints from all those found in flat 2. But Jason wasn't exactly holding his breath to see if they were left with a mystery set when they'd finished. Nowadays even the dopiest of killers knew to wear gloves. Still, you could never be certain.

And so far, no connection was coming to light linking their murder victim with any of the men working for the decorating company. None admitted to even knowing who she was, let alone talking to her, or having any personal or business relationship with her. Which made sense. From what Jason was beginning to learn about Margaret Franklyn, she wouldn't have given a lowly decorator so much as the time of day.

He looked up from the pile of incoming reports he was reading and raised an eyebrow.

'Something interesting, Jim?'

'A farmer, one Mr Clement Jarvis, wants a word. About a missing shotgun,' Jim added heavily.

Jason's pale blue eyes narrowed. 'Does he now? Better show him in then.'

Clem shuffled in, still looking the epitome of misery. His usual demeanour, Jason would have said, was bluff and hearty, but now he looked as downcast as a whipped puppy.

'Mr Jarvis. Please sit down,' Jason said briskly. 'You have something to tell us?'

Clem sat down, took a massive breath, then launched into his story. Jason sat, stiff-backed and disbelieving, as he was told the tale of the pigeon shoot last weekend and the missing gun. When the farmer was finished, the chief inspector looked numbly at Jim, then back to Clem.

Clem was already feeling belittled by the policeman. There was something about a man who actually looked *good* in a suit that had always roused deep misgivings in the down-to-earth farmer. Add to that the look of sheer disbelief in those cold blue eyes of his and. . . . Clem quickly looked down at his work-roughened hands, which were twisting about in his lap.

'And you just left your shotgun in the boot room?' Jason repeated, trying to keep his voice at a normal level. 'In a public room? In a pub? Where anybody could just take it?'

Clem coughed. 'Done it like that for years, mister, me and others too,' he said, just a shade sullenly. 'Nigh on twenty years or more I've been doing that. And it's never been nicked before. Why would anybody want to? It's just an old shotgun.'

Jason opened his mouth, then quickly snapped it shut. It was no good bawling him out now. He'd only turn truculent and uncooperative. Besides, there was something naive and trusting about the man that made him feel jaded by comparison. And no doubt what he'd said about leaving the gun in the pub after a pigeon shoot for the last twenty years was perfectly true. Even now, those born and raised in the country had a different set of expectations of life than those raised in the more nefarious and knowing cities.

'I see,' Jason said heavily. 'This gun of yours. I'll need details. I don't suppose you remember the registration number?'

Clem obligingly described it — an old but able work-horse of a shotgun. He didn't, of course, remember any numbers that might have been on it. He never looked, did he?

Jim wrote down the technical details, then glanced with some sympathy at his superior.

'And you're sure that none of the other members of your shooting party took it?' Jason tried the most obvious answer first.

But Clem shook his head adamantly. 'Rung round, didn't I? First thing I started to do when I heard about the killing, like. None of my pals have it.'

Jason sighed. 'Can you remember who was in the pub at the time you and your friends were there?'

Clem flushed. 'Well. We were all drinking quite a bit. We got over a hundred pigeons that day. You know how it is,' he mumbled, not meeting the chief inspector's eye. 'Well, all the regulars were there. You can ask June. She'll remember more. And a lot of your lot,' he added hastily.

'Our lot?' Jason said, his voice like a whip. 'You mean policemen?'

'Nah, the lot that live here.'

'You mean residents?'

'Yerse. But not the vicar, of course. He doesn't come into the pub very often — or his missus. They weren't there. But I reckon most of the others were. That pretty young girl was there . . .'

Julie Dix, Jason thought. And where Julie was, her mother was sure to follow.

'And that older piece. Mutton dressed up as lamb, with an eye for the men.'

Pauline Weeks, Jim Greer thought, with an inner smile.

'And that chap with muscles who only eats raw carrots, or so he says.'

Paul Waring.

'And the egghead. And the lady who can cook. And that bloke who's always with her. I tell you, they was all there. Ask June if you don't believe me,' he finished self-righteously.

'June?'

'The landlady of the pub,' Clem snorted. Didn't these coppers know anything?

'Ah. And did you remember seeing the Franklyns there?' Jason put in skilfully.

Clem flushed. 'I reckon,' he admitted uncomfortably. 'The skinny woman and her husband, right?'

Jason sighed. Great. They finally get a clue to the murder weapon and it looks as if any one of his prime suspects had the opportunity to steal it.

'I don't suppose you can see the entrance to the boot room from the public bar?' Jason asked, but without much hope.

'Nah,' Clem said. 'It's part of the porch. Right at the entrance.' So it would be child's play to just nip into it on the way out, remove a lethal weapon and walk away with it, Jason mused. Just marvellous.

'Well, thank you, Mr Jarvis. I'd appreciate it if you'd keep this piece of information to yourself. There are reporters wandering about. Don't let them suck you in.'

Clem grumbled something about 'bloody vultures' and got to his feet. He looked relieved that it was all over, as well he might. He was getting away with it lightly. Jason could have made life difficult for him, but he knew his superiors wouldn't have thanked him for it. Nowadays, there was such a backlog in the judicial system that even high-priority cases had trouble being processed. No, he couldn't see the CPS wanting to proceed with charges against the dozy farmer, so he was doing everyone a favour by letting him off with a warning. Besides, he was pretty sure that from now on the farmer would be a damned sight more careful with his firearms.

Jim escorted Clem Jarvis out, then came back shaking his head.

'There's no chance of us keeping it quiet, sir; all his mates will be talking about it by now. It'll be in the papers tomorrow, for sure,' he predicted glumly.

'I know. I suppose we'd better drag the river, Jim,' Jason sighed.

'You think the killer tossed it into the drink, then?'

'It's the most obvious place to dump a weapon, isn't it?'

Jim nodded. 'I'll get on to the divers. Sir, this rather puts the kybosh on our theory that Sean Franklyn might have hired somebody to kill his wife, doesn't it? I mean, a professional would bring his own weapon, not steal one from the local pub.'

Jason grunted. 'I agree. It's looking more and more like a home-grown job.'

'So, we're back to those who were missing at the time of the shot. Pauline Weeks, Maurice Keating, and Julie Dix,' the sergeant sighed.

'Seems so,' Jason concurred. 'But according to our witness statements, all three came on the scene not long after the shot was fired. A few minutes at the most. Would they have had time to kill Margaret, run back to their own flat and change their clothes — don't forget there'd be bloodstains — nip out the back and sprint to the river to toss the gun, and then get back to the party again in just a few minutes? Even supposing that they hid the gun somewhere and then disposed of it later during the night, they would still have to be super-quick.'

'Probably not our professor. He's too old,' Jim said.

'But the other two are fit and healthy enough. And Pauline Weeks did have a bit of a tiff with the victim at the party,' he mused, but even to his own ears it sounded weak. Not many people could commit cold-blooded murder and then show up at a social function just moments later without giving themselves away, surely? 'Well, let's not jump to any conclusions before we know all the facts,' he said flatly. 'Apart from anything else, we still don't have any real motive for any of "our lot" here wanting to kill Margaret in the first place.'

Jim sighed. 'Well, we might get some leads today, sir.'

'Let's hope so,' Jason said grimly. 'Or we'll be having the brass breathing down our necks. Go and check out the pub, will you? Speak to this June woman. See if she can confirm our farmer's memories of that day.'

'Right, sir, and get forensics to give the boot room a once-over?'

Jason grunted. 'For all the good it will do us now, but why not?'

* * *

132

Jason was reading a new report about Margaret's family background when there was a tentative knock on the door. He looked up, showing no surprise to see Paul Waring hovering uncomfortably in the doorway.

'One of the constables outside said I could come in,' Paul explained diffidently, moving further into the room as Jason nodded and indicated a chair.

'Yes, Mr Waring — something I can do for you?'

'Well, I'm not sure. When I was questioned the other afternoon, they asked me if I'd noticed anyone hanging around the vicarage.'

He shuffled himself onto the chair like a big St. Bernard, unsure of his welcome.

Jason's eyes glittered. 'You've thought of something you'd previously forgotten?' he prompted.

The constable who'd interviewed him had made a note in his interview report that he thought this witness might have been holding something back. Looks like the PC had good instincts, and Jason made a mental note to remember his name and keep him in mind when he needed uniform help again.

'Yes. No. I mean, it wasn't anyone I'd seen around the vicarage. That's why I didn't think of it at the time.'

Jason sighed, wishing just for once that a witness could be clear and precise in what they said. Still, not everyone had a neat and tidy mind, he supposed. Then he warned himself not to jump to conclusions about Waring's intelligence. After all, you didn't get to own several gyms and buy a flat here by being dumb.

'Perhaps you could just start at the beginning?' he advised mildly.

Paul brushed the sandy hair off his forehead. 'Well, see, I'm not sure it means anything, and I don't want to, well, make trouble for Maurice. I mean, not when it's probably nothing,' he said, still somewhat incoherently.

Jason sighed again. OK, so witnesses often needed reassuring and cajoling along. That was part of the job.

'Well, Mr Waring, if it's nothing then it won't matter, will it? And if it is relevant, then it's best to tell us.'

Paul flushed. 'Fine,' he said, somewhat testily, sensing the other man's impatience. 'It's just that when I came out of the shop after buying the wine and beer, I noticed a man I'd seen before walking across the square to his car.'

'And you'd seen this man before where? At the vicarage?' Jason asked, feeling himself tense up. This was the first they'd heard of any stranger lurking about the vicinity.

'No. I saw him in town. Cheltenham, I mean. A few weeks ago now, I suppose it would be. He was with Maurice in a pub. They seemed pretty friendly, really talking up a storm, but quiet, like. I didn't recognize him at first — the man in the square, I mean. On the day that Margaret died. It just sort of vaguely registered that I'd seen him somewhere before, you know how it is.'

Jason nodded. 'Yes, I understand. And then?'

Paul looked blank. 'Huh?'

'What happened then?' Jason prodded with infinite patience.

Paul blinked. 'Well, nothing. He just got in his car, I presume, and left. Like I said,' he began angrily, 'it's probably nothing. I just thought I should say something, that's all.'

And what's more, the tone of his voice implied, *I wish I hadn't bothered.* He got to his feet and gave Jason a can-I-go-now look.

Jason nodded, then sat for some time after his visitor had left, twiddling a pen and thinking furiously. Had this stranger been in Heyford Bassett to visit Maurice? And if he had, why had Maurice not mentioned him? The village was not a place that you could just 'pass through' on the way to somewhere else. So if he hadn't been here to see the Oxford don, then just who was he, and what *had* he been doing in the village on the afternoon Margaret Franklyn had been killed?

Unless Paul Waring had been mistaken in his identification, of course. Or lying.

* * *

134

At that moment, Monica was walking along the pavement towards the village shop. She'd run out of milk and needed some stamps. Better to buy a few books' worth now, while they still had a post office at all, she thought gloomily. With all the cuts in post offices going on, she didn't know if their shop would survive the cull for much longer.

'Oh, Mrs Noble, there you are. I was just wondering how you and the vicar are coping. You're all right, I trust?'

Too late, Monica realized that she'd just stumbled into prime Muriel Larner territory — namely, the vicinity of her garden hedge. She'd earned her nickname as the village menace by dint of being able to talk the hind legs off a donkey. And attempting to do so whenever possible.

Monica forced a smile. 'Hello, Muriel, yes, we're fine, thanks.'

'Oh good. I can't imagine it's much fun living in a house where,' her voice dropped dramatically, 'murder's been done.'

Monica bit back a grin. Not for Muriel a sly hint or dig. She'd just come right out with it. It was this trait that almost endeared her to Monica, in a funny kind of way.

'It's the kind of world we seem to live in nowadays, I'm afraid, Muriel,' she said sadly.

Muriel's cat, a disreputable ginger tom with tattered ears, hopped onto her garden gate and began to wash his bent whiskers. Muriel stroked him absently, and he gave a lawn-mower-loud purr.

'I hope you enjoyed the fair, though? Had a nice time?' Monica asked quickly. If she could just sidetrack her, she might be able to get away.

'Oh yes, great fun,' Muriel gushed. 'And we were all so looking forward to going to the fair, and had been for ages, as I told that young chap with all the muscles. If only we'd known! Well, none of us are psychic, are we, so it's no good cutting up now about missing out on things back here, is it?'

Monica found herself fighting off a fit of the giggles. No wonder Muriel was so unpopular with her neighbours! She could well see how her candour could chafe!

'Not that you ever expect something bad to happen on your own back doorstep, obviously,' Muriel continued. 'And none of you people did, either, I 'spect?' she added cunningly. 'Otherwise I'm sure you wouldn't have been having a party in the first place.'

Monica winced at her unintentional callousness. 'No, it came as a dreadful shock,' she managed to say feebly.

'Arr, it would,' Muriel nodded her grey head sagely. 'I saw that divorced woman just the day before it happened and asked her if we'd see her at the fair, you know, all friendly, like, and you should have seen the look she gave me!' Muriel sniffed.

'No. Well, Pauline can be a bit—'

'Still, I hope that nice Mr Franklyn ain't letting himself get too down,' Muriel interrupted, blithely unaware of her rudeness. 'You have to watch new widowers, you know,' she added significantly. And tapped the side of her nose knowingly.

Monica blinked. Now exactly *how* was she supposed to answer *that*?

'Oh, Mr Grantley. Cooo-eeee!' Spotting another victim who'd been unable to take evasive action in time, Muriel waved a hand furiously. Across the road, a man walking his dog blanched.

Monica quickly ducked her head and cowardly walked away, leaving Mr Grantley to his fate, with a muttered farewell. She passed her fellow victim on the way, giving him a rather unchristian sorry-but-rather-you-than-me look in passing. He managed a gallant smile, but his dog looked at her with big, accusing brown eyes.

She made it to the small village shop with a sigh of relief and collected a basket before strolling around the few aisles, immediately popping in her pint of milk. The shop, like most villages lucky enough to still have one, was an all-round convenience store. She selected some notepaper and tried not to wince at the price. It was one of her many 'duties' as a leading light of the community to be seen supporting her local tradesmen and women. The shop did well enough though, since most of the conference-goers from the old manor would

136

wander down for their daily papers and odds and ends, and comment on how 'quaint' it was to be in a 'real' shop again. And most of them, out of sheer nostalgia, bought some of the sweets kept in huge jars that lined the windowsills.

Monica approached the till with a firm smile fixed on her face, for she'd just noticed Madge Tilsbury waiting there, her own shopping basket all but empty. Also watching her approach was Phyllis Cox, the inimitable shopkeeper. Phyllis, at fifty-two, was widowed and spry, and the 'information centre' of the village.

Monica, confronted by two pairs of avid eyes, braced herself. 'Morning, Madge. Phyllis,' she said cheerfully.

'Morning, Mrs Noble,' Phyllis said.

The perpetual use of her married name was one of the few drawbacks of being married to Graham, Monica had discovered. All of Phyllis's other customers were called by their first names, but although Monica had urged her to do the same for herself, she was the vicar's wife, and as such was doomed to be Mrs Noble until judgement day.

'Mrs Noble,' Madge echoed politely, then cast a quick look at Phyllis. Phyllis nodded encouragement. 'I was just saying to Phyllis here,' Madge launched into conversation instantly, 'my old dad was at home Saturday afternoon.'

'Oh?' Monica murmured, wondering where this could be leading.

'Well, he said he'd be all right on his own for a while,' Madge added defensively. 'And he would have it that I was to go off and enjoy myself for a few hours at the fair.'

And Monica suddenly remembered that Madge was Arnold Tilsbury's youngest daughter. Unmarried, she had stayed on at home, first to look after her mother, who was now dead, and just recently to keep an eye on her father, who, unfortunately, had the early stages of Parkinson's.

'I'm sure it made a nice change for you to get out and about on your own for a bit,' Monica said firmly. 'It must have done you the world of good. Did you enjoy the fair?'

Both women unbent a little in obvious approval. Some old biddies didn't like the vicar's wife because she was pretty and younger than her husband. But the jury was still out with the vast majority of villagers, and for Monica to show such understanding and sympathy with a carer's plight went a long way in raising her profile with the shopkeeper and Madge.

'Ah, it was wonderful,' Madge said. 'I won a goldfish.' Then her brow furrowed. 'Anyway, when I got home and found out about, well, all your trouble, Dad said something that sort of stuck in my mind.'

And in a flash, Monica knew why she was being told all this. Madge and her father had been Heyford Bassett residents all their lives, and were honest, hard-working people of an older, simpler order, who'd simply never come into contact with the police before, or ever expected to. And what they needed now was a go-between, someone they could trust to keep their best interests in mind. And Monica made for an ideal conduit.

'I see,' she said softly. 'How very worrying for you. Was it something that might be relevant to the case, do you think?' she asked, very careful to keep any hint of pressure out of her voice.

Again Madge and Phyllis exchanged quick, nervous glances. 'Well, it might be,' Madge said reluctantly. 'You see, when I heard about . . . the trouble, and told Dad, he said he'd actually heard shots that afternoon, about ten minutes apart, he said. Loud as could be, and coming from the vicarage. Or Chandler's Spinney, he wasn't sure.'

Monica nodded encouragingly. 'Yes, somebody said much the same thing to my husband Saturday evening,' she confided craftily. 'I'm sure he's already mentioned it to Chief Inspector Dury. But if he hasn't, I'll be sure to pass on your message to him myself. What time did your father say he thought he heard the shots?'

'Ah, well, there's the thing you see,' Madge said uncomfortably. 'He's not good with his memory, Dad isn't. Not anymore. He thinks the first one was at about three o'clock. But he's sure the shots came ten minutes or so apart.'

Monica nodded, looking grave and concerned. No doubt the Tilsburys were trying to be genuinely helpful. And there was no point in sounding like a know-it-all by saying there was only one shot. That would only negate all the goodwill she was accumulating now.

'I see. Well, thank you for telling me, Madge. I'll be sure it gets passed on to the right quarters.'

Madge heaved a sigh of relief. 'Thanks ever so, Mrs Noble.'

Monica nodded and turned to Phyllis. 'Can I have three books of first-class stamps please, Phyllis?'

She didn't know it then, but that conversation would soon come back to haunt her, and make her wonder how she could ever have been so stupid as to not realize its importance straight away.

But that would come later.

139

CHAPTER 11

Jim Greer had been praying for a break all morning, and those prayers that they get a lead soon were answered at around 2:30 that afternoon, with the ringing of the telephone. The sergeant picked up the receiver, listened for a few moments in silence, then said crisply, 'Right, that's very helpful. Can you give me your exact address?'

Jason, who was going through the background reports on the vicarage residents, concentrating at the moment on Paul Waring's meteoric rise to a bodybuilding fortune, caught the note of excitement in his sergeant's voice and looked up hopefully. Like his sergeant, he too had been hoping, if not for divine intervention exactly, then for a spot of random luck to come his way.

Jim was scribbling away furiously, and after he hung up, he looked across at his superior officer and grinned.

'We've got a nibble, sir. A very nice but discreet lady from a bank just called. She said that she recognized Margaret Franklyn's picture in the paper as being that of a lady who rents a safety deposit box at her bank.'

Jason cursed. 'I thought you got onto their bank on Saturday for their financial records?'

Jim was already getting to his feet. 'I did, sir. But this isn't the Franklyns' usual bank, and the deposit box is in her name only, which leads me to wonder if her husband even knew anything about it.'

Jason reached for his jacket.

'Let's ask him on the way out, shall we?' he murmured. 'He's back in their flat now, isn't he?'

'Yes, sir. He was seen coming back this morning.'

'Been out on the tiles all this time?'

'Spent Sunday night drunk in one of the cells in Cirencester,' Jim said flatly.

Jason nodded without comment. One of the dilemmas in a murder case was that posed by the victim's spouse. On the one hand, they were often a prime suspect. On the other, a police officer had to always be aware that, if innocent, these people were grief-stricken human beings who'd just had their whole world violently turned upside down. And a little compassion and understanding never hurt anything, he'd always thought, as long as you didn't allow it to cloud your judgement.

Sean, when he finally opened the door to their summons, still looked a little the worse for wear.

'Oh,' he said dully, opening the door wider. 'It's you. Come on in.'

'We won't stay long, sir,' Jason said, and didn't miss the relieved look in the other man's eyes.

The picture he was getting of the Franklyns' marriage didn't exactly portray it as being that of a match made in heaven, but you never really knew. Even if they weren't exactly love's young dream, Jason knew that the loss of a person who'd played a major part in your life could still be one hell of a wrench, and leave anyone feeling vulnerable and lost.

'Good. I've got to see the undertaker about things,' Sean said vaguely.

Jason looked at him even more closely, knowing a fudged excuse when he heard it.

'Perhaps it might be a bit premature to be thinking like that, sir,' he said gently. 'I doubt your wife's body will be released any time soon. Besides, it's best to take these things as and when they come.'

'Oh. Right. Er . . . thanks for the advice, Inspector. I'm just—' Sean shrugged helplessly. 'I just don't know what to do with myself, that's all.'

Jason nodded. 'I'm sure it's very difficult, Mr Franklyn. And we'll try not to keep you for long. If you could just answer a simple question for me, we'll be on our way. Did you know that your wife kept a safety deposit box?'

Sean, who'd been looking vaguely around the room, abruptly swung his head towards the policeman. He looked stunned, and then, quite unmistakably, furtive.

'Safety deposit box? Margaret?' he said harshly. 'No. For her jewellery-making materials, you mean? Precious metals and semi-precious stones? That sort of thing? And do you mean at our bank?' Something about his bluster rang a warning bell deep in the back of Jason's mind.

'No, it wasn't at your regular bank,' he said, nothing of his suspicion telling in his voice. 'Thank you, Mr Franklyn, that's all for the moment.'

'Just a minute,' Sean said roughly, reaching out to catch hold of Jason's arm as he turned to leave. 'I have a right to see what's inside it! I am her husband, you know!'

His face was flushed now, but whether with excitement or fear, neither policeman could have said. Jason very carefully disengaged his arm.

'We'll be sure to leave you a receipt for any items taken from it,' he said carefully, and Sean flushed and flung himself away.

'Oh, do what the hell you like,' he muttered ungraciously. Jason nodded to Jim, and both men left the room. But the instant the door was shut behind them, Sean walked to the telephone.

He had to talk to his solicitor. Quickly.

* * *

The bank was one of the main five, with a branch situated in a prime location in the heart of Cheltenham. The lady who'd called quickly identified herself when Jason approached one of the tellers, and hastily showed them through the back and into a small beige room.

'I wasn't expecting you quite this soon,' Mrs Judith Banner said, a shade flustered. Wearing a smart blue suit and neat hairstyle, she was the epitome of a trusted bank employee. 'I do hope, Chief Inspector, that there will be no, er, mention of this bank's connection to Mrs Franklyn in the newspapers?'

Jason assured her there wouldn't be as far as the police public relations office was concerned, and listened to her patiently as she recited the bank's policy on the obligations of privacy towards customers. Eventually, however, she took them into a room down in the vaults.

'Normally, of course, Mrs Franklyn would bring her key and I mine, but in the circumstances . . .' she trailed off hopefully.

'Yes, of course,' Jason said, making a quick mental note. *Find the key.* It had obviously not been kept at the Franklyn flat or amongst Margaret's personal possessions, otherwise the police search would have uncovered it by now.

'We have duplicates made of the customer keys, of course,' Mrs Banner admitted. 'They will lose them. And sometimes they die, and the next of kin can't find them. Perhaps you'd turn this key while I do the same?'

The long, flat box was extracted without any more fuss and Jason carried it to the table provided. It wasn't very heavy. Jim politely thanked the bank employee and walked her to the door and held it open for her. When she was gone, Jason flipped back the lid. Wordlessly he went through the contents.

The box contained papers that related to Margaret's insurance, her passport, some money (£1,600 they were to discover, when they later counted it), some private letters from a lover (the last one dated over two years ago) and a pile of various odds and ends.

The first thing Jason checked was the insurance.

'Hmm, she's insured for £100,000. Not a fortune, but the beneficiary's her husband.'

The passport was current.

Jason next read the love letters with a slightly uneasy feeling that he shouldn't really be doing so (which he quickly quashed) and then passed them on to Jim.

'A job for you, Jim. It looks as if it was all over long ago, and ended amiably, but check him out. Find out where he was on Saturday, and if he thinks the husband knew about the affair.'

'Sean doesn't seem the jealous-husband type to me, sir,' Jim said. 'And why kill her over her infidelity after all this time?'

'Perhaps he only recently found out about it,' Jason said, but without any real conviction. 'I have to say, though, that I'm getting the impression that the Franklyns had a free-range sort of marriage. Now what's this?'

He'd been sorting through the odds and ends — some postcards from abroad, a letter or two from jewellery retailers promising to look her wares over — when he suddenly struck gold.

'Sir?'

'Read over my shoulder, Jim,' Jason said curtly, which the sergeant promptly did.

What he saw was a slightly yellowed piece of ruled paper, written to Margaret in rounded, distinctly feminine handwriting. The author was obviously in terrible pain and anger, and as the missive went on, the language became more and more desperate. But it was the mention of one name in particular that fairly leapt out at the two policemen.

The name was that of Dr Maurice Keating.

* * *

The first thing Jason did after leaving the bank was to drive back to police headquarters, where a computer, given the

144

name of the letter-writer, quickly coughed up several salient details, including the hard, harsh facts of her death.

After reading through the data, the next port of call was to St Francis's College, Oxford, where Maurice Keating had been a tutor of English literature for thirty-two years.

The provost of the college, perhaps not surprisingly, was not pleased to see them, and was even less pleased to discuss Dr Maurice Keating and a certain female student. But he was unfailingly polite. Naturally, nothing had been proved. And Dr Keating had left his post recently solely because he'd reached retirement age, and wanted to devote all his time and effort to the great opus of his life, writing about the work and times of the poet John Donne.

Of course, the college's name mustn't be dragged through the mud.

By the time they left, Jason's skin was crawling. As they walked across the ancient quad, he laughed grimly.

'What a place to live and work. All this quiet, backstabbing, over-intellectualised angst gives me the creeps.'

Jim shrugged. 'Oh I don't know, sir,' he said, looking around at the beautiful quad and baize-like croquet lawn with a mild sense of envy. 'I daresay it suited our professor quite well.'

Just then an ancient woman, ninety if she was a day, and dressed in the full regalia of a don's gown and colourful headwear, walked across the lawn towards the ivy-clad library.

'Reached retirement age, my foot,' Jason growled. 'In these sorts of places they don't retire. They just get retitled as emeritus fellows and put out to pasture until they die of old age.'

'You think he was definitely pushed then, sir?' Jim asked. It had been obvious from the start that the name of Dr Maurice Keating had had the same effect on the provost as that of a whiff of decaying fish.

'Let's say "gently encouraged,"' Jason drawled. 'I don't know that anyone in this place would be so crass as to actively push.'

Back in the car and heading towards the Cotswolds once more, the radio crackled into life. Jim took the call. When he'd finished, he was looking satisfied.

'The search warrant for the Keating flat has been delivered to the vicarage, sir.'

'Good.'

* * *

When Jason tapped on Maurice's door, with Jim and two constables beside him, it was quickly answered. The professor looked as matinee-idol perfect as ever, dressed in a dazzlingly white shirt, dark grey trousers and neat loafers. His white hair looked newly washed, and had been brushed back off his high forehead in true Stewart Granger style. But the sudden panic-stricken look in his eyes shattered the illusion.

'Dr Keating,' Jason greeted him cordially, holding out the paperwork in his hand. 'I have here a warrant to search your premises. We'll be very careful of your things, sir, I assure you,' he added, stepping forwards and thus giving Maurice no other choice but to step back to allow him entry.

'But . . . I think . . . well . . . I shall call my solicitor,' Maurice huffed, watching with alarm as two constables split up and disappeared, one into his bedroom, the other into the spare.

'I think that might be a good idea, sir,' Jason said. 'You can telephone him from the police station.'

Maurice went white. 'Police station?' he echoed faintly.

* * *

Outside, Paul Waring parked his beloved sports car and carefully locked it. At the same moment, Pauline stepped out of the back door with a towel and a bottle of sunscreen.

Monica, who was helping John tame some bushes, glanced up as a police car pulled in to the gravel-lined car park and stopped just beside the back door. And a moment later, Maurice was escorted very carefully to the car and helped into the back seat. As he slipped inside, the Oxford don's eyes slid nervously over those watching him, his gaze lingering over Paul's impressive sports car. Maybe, Monica thought with a pang of sympathy, Maurice was wishing he could jump into it and roar away.

Jason walked around to the front passenger door, and as he did so, his eyes very briefly met those of the startled Monica. Without pausing, he slid into the front of the car, which then reversed and drove away.

Pauline, slack-jawed, walked quickly across to Paul.

'Well! Did you see that?' she gushed. 'Who'd have *thought* it! I mean, *Maurice* of all people!'

Monica noticed John look at Pauline with a strange, almost disdainful expression on his face.

'I mean, I just can't believe it,' Pauline gushed. 'I wonder why he did it?' she asked, carrying on before any of them could reply. 'And to think you helped him get his flat here.' She turned to Paul and laughed. 'So much for attracting the right residents!'

Paul flushed red. 'For Pete's sake, shut up! We don't know he's even been arrested yet, and you have him banged up for life already.' And with that he strode away to the back door.

Pauline quickly trotted after him.

'Paul, I'm sorry,' she wailed. 'I didn't mean to sound so bitchy. It's just the *relief* of it all. Wait!' Her unhappy voice trailed away as she quickly followed him back into the house.

John, without a word, turned back to the bushes and resumed his patient pruning.

'John,' Monica said softly. 'Do you think Maurice really did do it?'

'No,' John said shortly. And his curt tone of voice was so unlike his usual mild live-and-let-live baritone that Monica felt quite unable to ask him anything else.

* * *

At the police station, Maurice did indeed call his solicitor, who arrived promptly. A man in his early sixties, he conferred briefly with his client before sitting beside the professor and watching Jason intently. And it wasn't until the tape recorders were running and all the usual preliminaries were over that Jason was able at last to question his prime suspect.

'Dr Keating, did you know Margaret Franklyn before she moved into her flat at the vicarage where you are also a resident?' he began.

Maurice licked his lips, shot a quick look at his solicitor, who inclined his head indicating permission to answer, and said quickly, 'No.'

Well, that's a lie for a start, thought Jim excitedly. Which made for an excellent start. Being able to point out a lie to the police nearly always took the wind out of most people's sails.

'Did you know a woman called Marilyn Wass?' Jason continued smoothly.

Maurice jerked in his seat. He began, very visibly, to sweat. 'Yes.'

'She was a student at St Francis's College, in fact? Reading English literature?'

'Yes.'

'And you were her tutor?'

'I was one of her tutors,' Maurice corrected quickly. 'She had several others.'

'I see. And can you tell us what happened to her?'

Maurice again shot a quick look at his solicitor. Slowly, the legal expert nodded. When they'd been conferring together they'd obviously been discussing strategy, and what should and should not be admitted. And now the two policemen were about to find out what their suspect and his solicitor had decided was dangerous for Maurice and what was not.

'Yes, it was all very sad.' Maurice cleared his voice and sat a little straighter in his seat. 'Unfortunately, Marilyn was highly strung — that sometimes happens with students who are very bright. I've seen it before. The brightest pupils are often the ones with emotional problems.'

Maurice glanced from Jason to Jim, as if seeking some sign of understanding.

Jason nodded patiently. 'Go on, Dr Keating.'

'Well, there are a lot of pitfalls that young people can fall into, Chief Inspector, as I think you know. There's drugs, and drink, and all kinds of—'

'Are you saying that Miss Wass was a drug addict, sir?' Jason asked coldly.

'Oh no,' Maurice said, instantly sensing the sudden hostility in the room. 'Nothing of the sort. But she was, as I said, highly strung. And she took medication — legally prescribed by a doctor, I have no doubt.'

'So what did happen to her, Dr Keating?' Jason pressed, unwilling to let the man keep on quibbling.

Maurice, finally cornered, said flatly, 'She killed herself, Inspector, one wet and cold November day. The whole college was extremely shocked, as you can imagine. Very shocked. Her family and friends were heartbroken, naturally.'

'Yes. Did you like her, Dr Keating?' Jason asked abruptly.

Maurice went red, then white. 'Well, er . . . what an extraordinary question! She was a good student. She had a fine grasp of understanding when it came to metaphysics, certainly.'

'She was very pretty, wasn't she, Dr Keating?' Jason quickly cut across the waffle.

'Yes. I suppose so.'

'We've heard that she was the kind of girl who preferred older, mature men,' Jason said, although no one had told him any such thing. 'Would you say that was so, Dr Keating?'

Maurice reached for a carafe of water and poured himself a glass. His hands were visibly shaking now.

'I really wouldn't know, Chief Inspector,' he said. 'It was quite a few years ago now, and I've tutored so many students.' He shrugged. 'She didn't make overmuch of an impression on me, I'm afraid. Sad as it is to say it, the thing I tend to remember most about her *was* the fact that she killed herself. It was all such a shocking waste.'

'Yes,' Jason said coldly. 'I agree.'

Time to take off the kid gloves, he thought. He reached for a photocopy of the letter he'd found in Margaret Franklyn's safety deposit box.

'Have you ever seen this letter before, Dr Keating?' he asked silkily. His solicitor leaned forwards as Jason pushed the letter towards him. And he read it far more quickly than his client did. His face, however, remained impassive.

Maurice stared down at the letter with a sick look on his face.

'I want to consult my client privately for a few moments, Chief Inspector,' the solicitor stated firmly. He was a short man, with a balding head and a somewhat straggling moustache, but he had the attitude of a terrier.

Jason sighed heavily, but had to agree. He nodded to Jim, who did the necessary with the tape recorder, then followed his superior outside.

'He looked as sick as a dog when you showed him that letter,' Jim said gleefully. 'All those lies about hardly remembering her! My eye.'

The letter had been from Marilyn Wass to Margaret Franklyn, who'd obviously been an old friend. In it, she poured out her heart about being in love with her tutor. The same tutor who was refusing to marry her. The same tutor who said it would ruin his career and reputation if it should be discovered that he was having a dalliance with one of his own, so very much younger, students.

It was obvious that, by the time of writing the letter, Marilyn Wass had become an increasingly desperate and disturbed young woman. In fact, she'd ended the letter by stating categorically that if Maurice Keating didn't agree to marry her, she'd kill herself.

'I wonder how Margaret reacted when she first got that letter, sir,' Jim asked.

'I don't know,' Jason said. 'More to the point, *why* did she keep the letter? It makes me wonder if she kept other letters as well.'

And there could only be one reason for it, if she had. Namely, because she'd seen some sort of profit in it for herself. If Margaret Franklyn *had* been the blackmailing type, then they finally had what his superiors would call a proper motive for her murder.

Just then a PC called to them that Dr Keating and his solicitor were ready to resume the interview. Once again, they walked into the interview room and restarted the tape recorder.

'Well, Dr Keating. You've had a chance to study the letter. What can you tell me about it?' Jason asked crisply.

'What *can* I say?' Maurice attempted a smile and spread his hands helplessly. 'I did say Miss Wass was a highly strung young woman, but I had no idea her fantasies had gone so far.'

Jason's face hardened. 'Are you trying to tell me, Dr Keating,' he gritted, 'that you *didn't* have an affair with Marilyn Wass? That you never led her to believe that you loved her, and that marriage was a viable option?'

'That's correct, Chief Inspector,' Maurice said earnestly, leaning forwards across the table and crossing his hands anxiously in front of him. 'It was all in her mind. Sometimes young girls do get fixated on their tutors, you know. Doctors and psychiatrists can have the same sort of problems with their patients, so I hear.' Maurice sighed regretfully. 'They get fixated on someone, usually an older man, or a man they may perceive as being in a position of power, which triggers their sexual fantasies. But I was always very careful to give her no encouragement, and I honestly thought that she was over her infatuation.'

Jason shot a quick look at the solicitor, who looked blandly back at him.

'I see,' he said, careful to keep any anger out of his voice. So he was sticking with that story, was he? 'Naturally, we shall be getting in contact with anyone who knew Marilyn during her time at St Francis's. Both her closest friends and other tutors.'

Unspoken lay the threat that if their affair had been made known to anyone else, Jason would soon find out.

Maurice's smile faltered a little, but then beamed right back at him. 'Of course. You must do what you think fit,' he agreed fulsomely.

Quickly, he tried another form of attack. 'Did you know that Margaret had been a friend of Marilyn's?'

Instantly, something hard and ugly flashed across the academic's face, but then just as quickly was gone. 'No.'

'Did you know that she had kept this letter from Marilyn Wass?'

'No. Like I just said, I didn't know they were friends, and I therefore never knew this letter existed.'

Another lie, thought Jason and Jim simultaneously, neither man missing the telltale flicker of panic and rage in the older man's eyes. So she *had* been blackmailing him, Jason thought. And at that moment, he would have bet almost anything that when they started to research Keating's finances in earnest, they'd find that he'd been living very frugally indeed, and for some time. And that large amounts of money would have been regularly withdrawn from his bank account that he couldn't explain away.

'Did Margaret ever tell you she had this letter?' Jason pushed on.

Maurice shifted on his seat. 'No.'

'Did she ever ask you for money in return for keeping the letter a secret?'

'No!' he all but squeaked.

'So, Margaret was blackmailing you,' Jason said softly. At this point the solicitor huffed and puffed, saying something forcefully along the lines that his client had already answered that question, but Jason kept his eyes firmly on Maurice, who winced under the scrutiny.

'Let's return to the day of Mrs Franklyn's murder, shall we?' Jason said, casually changing the subject. 'You have no alibi for the time of the shooting, do you, Dr Keating?'

'I was in my room, I told you,' Maurice said, for the first time beginning to get really heated. 'I was having a wash. It was a hot day. I hate to swe— I mean, perspire.'

They kept on at him for hours, but couldn't break his story. In the end, lacking any concrete evidence against him, they simply had to let him go. To make matters worse, more bad news awaited them back at the vicarage. The search of Maurice Keating's flat had produced no signs of bloodstained clothing, or any other evidence of the crime, and forensic samples had come back negative on his drains, bath and wash basin for evidence of human blood. Needless to say, they hadn't found Clem Jarvis's shotgun hidden in his wardrobe either.

It wasn't until they'd been back in the incident room for a little while that they received news of anything worthwhile at all. A message came through asking them to call a Mrs Judith Banner at the bank. When Jason did so, that discreet lady was full of apologies. She'd meant to mention it at the time but had clean forgot. She didn't know whether or not it was important, but on the Friday afternoon, the day before her murder, Mrs Franklyn had called in to use her safety deposit box.

She'd been quite alone.

But, even when pressed, Mrs Banner simply couldn't tell them whether Mrs Franklyn had made a deposit or a withdrawal, since she'd left the lady alone to complete her business, as per protocol. She could only confirm that Mrs Franklyn had had her handbag with her, and had taken it into the room. So she could have left something, or equally as easily have taken something away with her.

CHAPTER 12

'Sir, I think we've found something,' Jim said early that next Tuesday morning, his voice quivering with excitement.

'Jim, that's the nicest thing you've ever said to me,' Jason grinned, rising stiffly from his chair.

He'd just put in a late night reading through the reports again, but this time with his eyes peeled for any signs of blackmail. But if Margaret had been bleeding dry any of the others living at the vicarage, there'd been no outward signs of it.

The proceeds of Vera's lucrative career had gone straight into her savings account and various canny stocks and bonds. John lived as well as any cartoonist, and Pauline Weeks's alimony seemed to be spent invariably on clothes, make-up and other such necessities. Joan Dix's salary was barely adequate for her needs and left no room for a blackmailer, and her daughter, naturally, wasn't yet earning a penny.

The poorest of the residents by far were the Nobles. Jason had been surprised to learn of Monica's previous high-paid and high-powered job in advertising, and he'd wondered what on earth could have made a woman like that leave London and her career for a fifty-year-old vicar with only a small village parish. Then he'd promptly reminded himself that *that* was none of his business. He'd found no signs that either Monica or Graham were paying out money where it shouldn't go, and that was all that need concern him.

The most interesting of the bunch, as far as he was concerned, was Paul Waring. His gyms weren't doing all that well, and yet he seemed to live very high on the hog.

'I've got some of the financial whizzes looking over Waring's empire,' Jason said, following his eager sergeant out the door. 'His records are such a cleverly complicated mess that it's going to take an accountant to sort them out.'

'Yes, sir,' Jim said, patently not interested. He was forging ahead towards the centre of the big house, reminding Jason of an eager spaniel sighting rabbits. 'When the search party came up empty Saturday, sir, I—'

'This is the search of the public places in the building you're talking about, yes?' Jason asked, getting it clear.

'Yes, sir. The halls, lifts, stairs, corridors, car park, rubbish bin and utilities area and every other stick and stone that wasn't somebody's private residence.'

'And?'

'Well, there seemed to be nothing to my naked eye,' Jim said, mounting the main concrete staircase and taking the steps two at a time. 'But forensics have just gone over everywhere with luminol to show up even the faintest of bloodstains.' They'd just turned the corner on the second staircase and there, gathered in the far, dim corner, was a little knot of excited constables.

'And they've picked up this.'

As Jim spoke, a place opened up for them, and the forensic photographer showed them her viewscreen.

'Are you sure it's blood?' he asked, and she nodded emphatically.

'They've already taken a sample to the lab, sir,' Jim said. 'If it's Mrs Franklyn's blood then it's almost sure that the killer was standing here at some point on Saturday after killing her.'

Jason straightened, congratulated everyone on their diligence, and slowly walked back down the stairs, Jim following.

Back in the incident room, he got the map of the house and studied it. Then, with a little 'x' he marked the spot where the bloodstains had been discovered.

'Well, if it *is* Margaret's blood,' he said, thinking out loud, 'and it's fresh enough to have been there only since Saturday, then that quashes our outside killer theory.'

Jim looked puzzled for a moment, then suddenly twigged. 'Right. Because what would he be doing one flight up?'

'Exactly. Margaret was killed on the ground floor, so his next logical move would be to scarper quickly out the back door and leg it. Not to take a hike upstairs.'

'So it's someone who lives here returning to their flat to clean up after him or herself?' Jim said flatly. 'That means someone who lives on either the second or third floor?'

'It's looking more and more like it.'

'Which lets out the vicar and his family, John Lerwick and Sean Franklyn?' Jim added tentatively.

'Hmm,' Jason said, a little more cautiously now. 'Let's reconstruct it as we think it happened, OK?'

Jim quickly dragged his chair over and they both looked over the map. 'Margaret was the type that blackmailed. No matter how much Maurice might squirm and deny it, he was paying out money to her and, what's more, had been doing so for years. The financial boys have been going over his records and reckon she was squeezing him for at least £3,000 a month, maybe more.'

'Ouch,' Jim said. 'Not even retired Oxford dons can afford to lose that much, not when they don't have a source of income anymore.'

'Quite,' Jason said dryly. 'So let's just suppose that Maurice is our killer. He's fed up of paying blackmail. Then, as luck would have it, fate hands him out a big bonus. His blackmailer comes to live in the same building.'

'Yippee,' Jim said dryly. 'It must have been driving him wild. It also explains why Mrs Franklyn was so mad at her husband for buying a flat here. No wonder she was unhappy.'

'But of the two of them, I imagine it was Maurice who was the most dismayed,' Jason mused. 'It must have been more than flesh and blood could bear, to have to live with the fact that he might accidentally bump into his tormentor at any time. His nerves must have been shot to pieces. So he decides to get rid of her. He knows the house like the back of his hand, and he can observe her movements, and over time he formulates a clever plan.'

'Fine so far,' Jim agreed encouragingly.

'Now. We know, or at least it's reasonable to assume, that the only reason Margaret went willingly to the empty flat on the other side of the house from her own was to meet someone. We've got no evidence that she was forced to go inside, and she certainly left the party of her own volition.'

'Right.'

'Now, let's say she went to the empty flat to meet her blackmail victim. Suppose our professor had promised her one big payoff, once and for all, for the letter. He might have risked a bluff, saying that he'd had enough and that if she wouldn't hand over the letter, she could do her worst. That might have tempted her to go for one last big payment and relinquish the letter.'

'And for that, she'd have to go to the bank and pick up the letter,' Jim said.

'And yet we know that, although she did go to the bank, she left Marilyn Wass's letter in the safety deposit box,' Jason put in quickly.

'So just why *did* she go to the bank?' Jim asked.

Jason sighed. 'Perhaps she went there for a reason totally unconnected to her blackmailing activities. Anyway, that's just hitch number one,' he said gloomily. 'I've got a feeling we'll run across more. Still, let's continue, just for the sake of argument. She goes to the flat, where she finds Maurice waiting for her with a shotgun. What would she do?'

'Run? Scream? Or try and talk him out of it? Those are the only options she's got, as far as I can see,' Jim said grimly.

157

'Right. And running or screaming would almost certainly get her killed. Even someone who doesn't know anything about guns would understand that a blast from a shotgun at a short distance will get you very dead, very quickly.'

'So she tries to talk him around?' Jim agreed.

'But she hasn't got the letter, which is all that Maurice wants.'

'So, in a rage, he kills her?'

'Hmm. And right there is hitch number two,' Jason pointed out. 'How can he be sure that her husband doesn't know about the letter also? What's to stop him from being in on it too, and just carrying on where Margaret left off? In which case, by killing Margaret, he'll be in an even worse spot than before because now Seán would have something even more terrible to hold over him. No, if you're going to murder someone, Jim, you make damned sure you get what you came for first.'

'Unless you're just so mad that you want to kill anyway,' Jim pointed out. 'Out of sheer frustration?'

'Perhaps,' Jason said, patently unconvinced. 'But I've got a feeling, you know, that this killer was as cold as ice. That everything was thoroughly thought out and planned and executed well in advance.'

Jim sighed. 'Well, let's just say for argument's sake that our Maurice killed her in a fit of rage. What next?'

'He stops to cover her body with a tarpaulin,' Jason said softly. 'But why? He must know that the shot has been heard, and that a search will be made.'

'Hitch three,' Jim said drolly.

'Especially when he must have been in one hell of a hurry to get out of there,' Jason added thoughtfully. 'Why waste time on something so futile? Anyway, he goes back to his flat and changes his bloodstained clothes—' Jason paused. 'Except, we know that his flat is clean. And if those bloodstains on the stairs *do* turn out to be Margaret's, maybe our killer doesn't change in his or her room after all, but changes right there on the stairs. Which brings anyone living on the ground floor back into contention. The killer could, at a pinch I suppose, have used wet wipes to clean up any blood on their face and hands. But why? Unless it was just to make sure that no physical evidence would be left in their own flat.'

'Maurice . . . or whoever, could have just dripped a bit of blood there on the way to their flat, sir,' Jim objected.

Jason sighed. 'Jim, think a bit. Were those bloodstains found in the middle of the stairs, where someone running up to their flat would be likely to drip the odd stain? Or were they tucked well back against the angle of the wall, in the darkest corner and out of sight?'

Jim stared at him with renewed respect. 'They were in the corner, sir.'

'So why should anyone stop just there and go and stand in the corner of the stairs for no particular reason?'

'They wouldn't, sir,' Jim said flatly.

'Not unless the killer did so expressly in order to change out of bloodstained clothes and into fresh ones. Right there on the stairs.'

Jim scratched his head. 'Taking a bit of a risk, wasn't he, sir? I mean, he might have been seen.'

'By whom? Those down in the garden at the party couldn't see him. And anyone who just happened to be on the top floor would be more likely to use the lift to return to the party.'

Jim nodded. 'You're right. The chances of him or her changing unseen were pretty good. But, still, he was a cool customer to do it that way.'

'Yes. Tell me, Jim, does Maurice strike you as being a particularly cool customer?'

Jim thought it over. 'No. Not cool. But he's clever. He'd know that if he changed his clothes in his own flat, we'd be able to find even microscopic evidence of blood on the carpet or wherever. What with *CSI* on the telly, and all the latest forensic crime novels, everyone knows about trace evidence. That would tie in with your theory as to why the killer changed on the stairs.'

'Yes, I think we take it as read that that's why the killer changed where he did,' Jason said. 'Our killer isn't giving anything away, is he? Or is it really a she we're after? You know, I can't help but see this as a male crime, somehow.'

Jim nodded. 'Well, I see what you mean about this being carefully thought out, sir.'

'And the killer had probably stashed a set of fresh clothes in the stairwell that he could change into. So what next? The killer's just changed clothes and he's there on the stairs. We'll keep on saying "he," I think, just so long as we always bear in mind that we could be wrong. But what does he do with the bloodstained clothes he's suddenly been lumbered with?'

'Into a plastic bag, sir? Then hide them in his flat?'

'OK. But he'd have to get rid of them at the very first opportunity and before any search could be made.'

'Right. But remember one of the men on duty here Saturday night thought he heard someone sneak out of the building. That could have been the killer, using the opportunity to get rid of the clothes and perhaps even the shotgun as well.'

'Almost certainly, I'd say,' Jason agreed. 'I'll have to order another search of the grounds. See if anyone's had a little bonfire recently. But, to continue. The killer changes his clothes, bags up the bloodstained ones, cleans any trace evidence off himself with wet wipes or a wet towel or whatever he's left there for the purpose. Then he returns to his flat, stashes the shotgun and hides the evidence and returns to the party, all innocence and light.'

'Well, it fits. In a way,' Jim added, a shade dubiously.

'Yes, and in a way it doesn't. Did Maurice have time to do all that, for one thing?'

'Well, sir, none of the witnesses can say *exactly* how long it was before he turned up after the shot was fired,' the sergeant pointed out. 'The shortest time we got was five minutes, the longest nine or ten.'

Jim looked for a long while at his superior's closed face and said tentatively, 'You don't really like him for it, do you, sir?'

Jason sighed and rubbed his tired eyes. 'I don't know, Jim. It's a very clever crime, and our professor *is* a clever man. But it just doesn't sit properly, somehow. Our killer is cold-blooded and must have nerves of steel. And Maurice is a pathetic womaniser clinging on to his image of respectability. The two just don't go together in my mind.'

'But most of the evidence points to him,' Jim said despondently.

Jason's frown, if anything, deepened. 'Yes, it does rather, doesn't it?' he said softly.

* * *

At eleven o'clock, an old Daimler pulled to a halt at the vicarage gates and a man in impressive black and purple clerical robes climbed from the back. David Drabble had been a bishop for only two years, but he enjoyed the job. But not, perhaps, when murder and press coverage was suddenly thrust upon one of his vicars.

He smiled benignly at the constable on the gate, and made his way towards the vicarage.

At that moment, Jim and Jason stepped out of the far wing and headed across the lawn. At the same time, Graham Noble and a young couple stepped out of the other side of the house, discussing an upcoming christening. Suddenly, they all converged.

Graham spotted his bishop first, and smiled.

'David,' he said warmly, knowing the bishop preferred the use of his first name to his full title.

'Graham,' the bishop returned fulsomely, holding out his hand, but aware of the two men walking towards him. 'I've come, of course, to discuss this awful tragedy with you.'

As he was meant to, Jason pricked up his ears, as did the young couple. The girl dug her beloved in the ribs with her elbow.

'We was just leavin', wasn't we? Thanks ever so for the run-through, Vicar. We'll all be there Sunday afternoon then, bright and early for the christenin'. I hope little Venus doesn't cry!' she added with a giggle.

At this, it was the bishop who pricked up his ears. 'Little Venus?' he asked faintly.

The new mother beamed at him proudly. 'My daughter, er . . . Reverend, sir,' she said, not at all sure what you called a man dressed as David Drabble was dressed.

The bishop's eyebrows rose. 'Ah, I see.'

Jason and Jim, who were waiting patiently to talk to the bishop, carefully avoided catching Graham Noble's agonized eye.

'Mr Noble's been trying to talk me around to a different name,' the young mother said, unknowingly making her vicar want to sink to the ground and kiss her feet in gratitude. 'But we like Venus, don't we, sweetpea?' And again the elbow was applied judiciously to her partner's ribs.

'Huh, yeah,' he grunted painfully.

'See you Sunday then,' Graham said firmly, then stood back to indicate the open door. 'David, won't you come in? Oh, this is Chief Inspector Dury and Sergeant Greer.'

'Splendid,' the bishop said heartily. 'Perhaps you'd care to join us for just a short while, Chief Inspector?'

Jason said he'd be delighted.

CHAPTER 13

Paul Waring pulled into the car park and sighed. He'd just spent the last three hours working out at the Stroud gym, giving a demonstration of his prowess to a coterie of dedicated fans, and now, as he climbed out of his car, he felt pleasantly tired.

'You look wilted,' a cheerful voice called to him from the shrubbery. 'I don't suppose I can persuade you to pick up a saw, can I?'

He turned to find a rather weary-looking Monica Noble crouched in front of a particularly woody specimen of rhododendron and walked over to her.

'You look like you're having fun,' he said wryly.

'Oh, huge amounts,' Monica agreed grimly. 'I decided it was time these monsters were tamed. But I think they're getting the better of me.'

'Where do you want it cut?'

Monica handed over the saw with an alacrity that wouldn't have earned her any points with a women's libber, and stood upright. Then she asked, 'Have you heard the latest?'

Paul could see where she'd been sawing, and set to with ease. 'No. Nothing to do with Maurice, is it?' he asked, looking up at her and making Monica fear for his fingers.

163

'No, I'm rather glad to say. It's about bloodstains. Apparently the police have found some.' She passed on the information with studied carelessness, but watched him carefully to see his reaction.

'Here it comes,' Paul grunted, tugging on the woody limb and pulling it free. 'Bloodstains?' he added. 'Where?'

'Oh, on one of the main flights of stairs, or so the rumour goes.'

Paul almost smiled. 'Isn't the grapevine a wonderful thing?' he drawled.

'Oh marvellous,' Monica agreed, then eyed the pale yellow sickly undergrowth that had just been uncovered. 'These bushes are nice when they flower, but nothing else has a chance to grow.' She glanced around as a troop of constables passed by. They were all armed with long sticks. 'I wonder what they're doing?' she asked thoughtfully.

Paul shrugged. 'Searching the grounds inch by inch, according to Sean. He was looking a bit frazzled when I saw him, but then, this thing is getting all of us down, isn't it? Must be far worse for him, of course. Anyway, he reckons they're going to search all of our flats soon. I'm surprised it hasn't happened before now,' he added philosophically.

Monica groaned. 'Me too. They certainly are thorough, aren't they?' she said, her voice just a shade brittle.

'You can say that again,' Paul sighed. He grunted as he tested another bit of dead wood and then reached for the saw again.

'And when they question you, you can't help but get the feeling that they don't believe a word you say,' she added bitterly.

'Well, you've got it easy,' Paul said, sawing on another branch with hard, swift, certain strokes. 'You were in plain sight all afternoon.'

'So were you,' Monica responded.

'Oh no I wasn't,' Paul snorted. 'I had to leave for a while to get the booze, remember?'

'Oh yes. I'd forgotten that,' Monica said.

Paul laughed. 'Well the police haven't, believe me. I had to account for each and every second of being away. I can only thank my lucky stars that good old Phyllis remembered my every move. If she hadn't confirmed my story, I'd probably be sitting in the cells right now instead of Maurice. Or at least, that's the impression I got.'

'But Margaret wasn't killed until later,' Monica objected.

Paul shrugged. 'I know. But I dare say they have to check out every little . . . wait, here it comes.' Another woody branch was removed, and Monica observed the fast-clearing space with satisfaction. She'd have to enlist Paul's robust help more often.

'They even wanted to know who I'd seen and talked to on the way to the shop and back,' Paul continued. 'As if that mattered,' he grunted, setting to with a will on the next piece of demolition Monica pointed out for him. 'Not that there was anybody about — everyone was at the fair. I swear, if it hadn't been for some man going to his car, and a lost driver in an Alfa Romeo, I doubt that I'd have seen anyone. Well, not to talk to, anyway.'

'Alfa Romeo? Someone lost, you say?' Monica prompted sharply.

'Yeah. He wanted to know the best way to get to Warwick, of all places. It took me a while to convince him of the best route.'

'Well, they wanted to know everything I did or said that day too,' Monica commiserated. 'So you're not alone there. I dare say it was the same for all of us.'

Paul grunted. 'I'll be glad when it's over, I can tell you that.'

He wasn't the only one.

* * *

In her bedroom, Julie Dix sat with the debris of her chest of drawers scattered all around her, and the stark truth staring

165

her in the face. Her last love letter from Sean was missing. And there were only three possibilities. The first was that Sean had come up to the flat and taken it back himself, terrified that the police might find them out.

The second, even scarier thought was that the police *had* found it, and did in fact now suspect Sean or herself of Margaret's murder, or both of them acting in collusion.

Or thirdly, and by far the most likely, her mother had discovered the passionate note.

With a sigh, Julie put her clothes back and then walked wearily to the window. Ever since *it* had happened, Sean had been ignoring her. If only things hadn't gone so wrong! They'd be lying on a beach in Spain now, safe and happy and free.

It made her ashamed now to think that she'd once thought that Sean could possibly be the man of her dreams. He was weak. Just like most men, he was spineless when it came to dealing with the reality of things. If she had to do it all over again things would have been different, that's for sure, she thought savagely.

* * *

Pauline heard a door open below her and quickly walked down the stairs, peering over the railings. She was just in time to see the top of John's head appear.

'John,' she called, skipping quickly down the stairs to catch up. 'Have you heard?' she said breathlessly, coming to a halt just above him. 'About the bloodstains?' She gave a sudden start, and lowering her voice to a whisper, looked around. 'What was that?'

'What?' John asked, patently baffled.

'I thought I heard a door . . . never mind. It was right on this second landing where they found them, you know,' she said, and cast a look over her shoulder towards the dark corner. 'Right over there.'

John shifted uncomfortably from foot to foot. 'Oh, well, I'm sure it's all cleaned up now,' he said as heartily as he could, but Pauline wasn't to be denied her drama.

'I dare say, but they were gory enough Saturday afternoon,' she declared firmly. 'You know, I *thought* I noticed something dark in that corner on my way up to get the fruit salad,' she said. 'But I never went to investigate.'

'Oh, right,' he said feebly, thinking how funny it was that after the event, everyone seemed to suddenly remember things. A bit like the way everyone remembered feeling 'something wasn't quite right' only after something had gone wrong. 'Well, I must be off. I've left Monica to the mercy of the rhododendrons, and I can't leave her there all day.' He turned, jogged a few steps down, then reluctantly turned and looked up again. Pauline hadn't moved.

'Are you all right?' he asked her softly.

Pauline nodded. 'Yes, fine,' she said absently. But she was shivering. Again John went down a few more steps, then once more stopped and looked up. He'd been about to tell her that she should be careful, and that going around saying things about what she'd seen on the day of the murder could be dangerous. But Pauline was gone.

He continued down to his own flat, looking worried.

* * *

Maurice was driven back to the vicarage after more questioning, feeling both embarrassed and elated. He got out of the police car and watched it go, then, sensing movement out of his peripheral vision, turned to watch Monica Noble step out from the bushes.

'Hello, Maurice,' she said gently. 'You look whacked. Would you like to come in for a cup of tea?' she offered kindly.

Maurice brushed an imaginary fleck from the sleeve of his jacket and smiled handsomely.

'Thank you, but I think a bath and then a stiff gin and tonic are more in order,' he said. 'These policemen of ours are thorough fellows, but everything's been cleared up now,' he added firmly and loudly, having just spotted Paul over

Monica's shoulder. The younger man was studiously ignoring him by pulling out some particularly stubborn roots.

'That's good news,' Monica said. For all his bluster, she could sense the poor man was a jumble of nerves. 'Paul and I were just saying how gruelling it is to keep answering questions all the time.'

'It certainly is. But at least I've had my turn,' Maurice said, and added a shade spitefully, 'I wonder who'll be next?' And with that rather unnerving statement, he headed for the back door and disappeared inside.

'Poor man,' she said softly. 'He looked shattered.'

Paul sighed. 'I hope he doesn't run into Pauline,' he muttered darkly. 'She'll probably demand to know why they let him out.'

Monica couldn't help but grin.

* * *

John sat at his drawing board, staring at a piece of blank paper. In all the years he'd worked as a cartoonist, he'd never cut a deadline so fine. He sighed and began to draw a swarm of bees looping around a no entry sign, hoping that he could think up a good punchline for them later.

* * *

Walking in the meadow, Carol-Ann followed the bend of the river as it meandered towards Ford Street. The area here was overgrown, prone to flooding in the winter, but alive with wildlife. She'd passed several groups of policemen on her way out, and their concentrated industry had aroused a sense of excitement and adventure in her, which had set her off exploring. Several stinging nettle rashes, two gnat bites and a pair of sweaty armpits later, she was beginning to wish she'd never bothered.

She stopped willingly at the riverbank and looked down at the pretty water crowfoot flowering in the middle of the

168

water, then looked out across the village. Slowly, she followed the river edge, but had only gone a few yards when she noticed how the bank had fallen in at one spot. And just below the overhanging bank there was a wedge of mud that hung out only a few inches above the water. And there, right there in the middle of it, was a small pile of ashes.

Carol-Ann stared at them for quite a while, thinking what a strange place it was to light a bonfire, and then realized that this might be what all those policemen were looking for. She began to grin.

'Yes!' she hissed, giving a clenched-fist salute of victory.

* * *

Pauline watched Monica and Paul from her top-floor flat. If she hadn't thought it would be so obvious, she'd change into a pair of snazzy dungarees and go down and offer to help. But she feared Monica Noble's knowing eyes. And since Paul had flown off the handle at her about that wimp Maurice, she'd have to be cool and aloof at all times from now on. Just until she was sure he'd forgiven her. Men didn't like to be chased too hard, but she'd have him in the end.

Pauline always got what she wanted.

* * *

Still in the incident room, Jason was thinking of calling it a day when they informed him of the find near the river. It was quite a trek out, but the scenery was breathtaking. Beyond the river was a flat meadow, full of peacefully grazing cattle, and rolling hills headed up towards the main road and the dark patch of trees beyond known as Chandler's Spinney. Some rare ragged robins grew near the river, bright pink in the sun, as well as one or two interesting orchids. But his mind very quickly turned back to the job in hand when he suddenly spotted the svelte, blonde-haired form of Carol-Ann Clancy, hovering by a knot of constables.

'What's she doing here?' he said abruptly to Jim, who shook his head.

'I'll find out.' The sergeant beckoned over one of the constables, had a quick, whispered conversation, then relayed the news to his boss before they got to within earshot of the others. 'Apparently it was Miss Clancy who found the ashes and called the uniforms over, sir.'

Jason groaned. 'Great. That's just what I need. A teenager playing Miss Marple.'

Jim grinned.

'Hello, Jason,' Carol-Ann said cheerfully as he walked up beside her.

Jason winced, but wasn't about to ask how she'd discovered his first name. 'Miss Clancy. You've been busy, it seems?' he said mildly.

Carol-Ann grinned. 'Just thought I'd help out,' she said modestly.

'Thank you,' Jason said dryly. 'But I'd be grateful if you would return home now, Miss Clancy, and wait for me. I'll need to ask you some questions later.'

Carol-Ann heaved a massive sigh and sulkily strode off. Jason watched her go, then walked carefully to the bank and looked down.

'A good spot for it,' he noted. 'If we'd had any rain at all, the mud would have disintegrated and the whole lot would have collapsed back into the river before we even knew it was there.'

'It might have done so anyway, sir.' Jim, more of a countryman than his superior, pointed out the very dry conditions that had sent cracks running all around the edge of the bank. 'I reckon the killer must have been lying on his belly and set the fire at arm's length to avoid crumbling this lot in then and there. You have to admire him, in a way.' As Jason had always said, this killer was clever enough to try and think of everything.

'We'll have to be careful then,' Jason mused. 'Cauldicott,' he beckoned over a uniformed PC, 'get your wellies on and get in the water. I don't want anyone setting foot on the bank any-where near those ashes until forensics have bagged them up.'

An hour later, Jim watched as Jason carefully used a pencil to sift through the find. The ashes were now carefully strewn at a safer distance from the river on black plastic bags, and Jason grunted as his pencil hit something solid. He carefully extracted it even though he knew that, after a fire, fingerprints were probably out of the question. With gloved hands he held up a small, round, scorched button.

'Definitely the remains of clothes then, sir,' Jim said flatly.

'Yes.' Jason put the misshapen bit of plastic into an evidence bag. 'Get it back to the lab, Jim. I want to know what kind of button that is.'

'Sir.'

Jason rose and looked towards the vicarage.

'Meanwhile,' he said, without enthusiasm, 'I'd better find out just how Miss Carol-Ann Clancy came to lead us right to it.'

* * *

Joan Dix, confronted by her daughter, admitted to burning the letter.

'Mother, how could you?' Julie asked, but more in hope-lessness than in genuine rage. She was beginning to wonder whether her mother might not have the right attitude towards men after all. 'It was mine! And it was private! What gives you the right—'

And, for the first time ever, Joan raised her hand to her daughter and slapped her — hard. The sound ricocheted around the room like a bullet, and a livid red handprint sprang up on Julie's shocked white face. Her wide-open eyes stared back at a woman she couldn't ever remember seeing before. For Joan's face was as hard as iron. Her eyes glittered, not with love, or pride, or pleading, but with bitter anger.

'You stupid fool,' Joan hissed. 'Don't you know what I've done for you?'

Julie blinked. 'Mum?' she said tentatively.

Joan ran a hand through her hair and began to pace.

'We've got to think what the best thing to do *now* is,' she said, walking agitatedly to and fro. 'Should we go or should we stay?'

Julie shook her head and sank back onto the sofa. As she watched her mother pacing the floor, a sudden look of comprehension flickered across her pretty face.

'Oh, Mum!' she said hopelessly. 'Oh, Mum!' Then, a little while later, 'I'm so sorry.'

And she burst into bitter, ugly tears. For once, Joan simply let her cry and made no move to comfort her. She had some hard thinking to do.

* * *

Monica hovered nervously by the sofa as Carol-Ann, who looked about as much in need of protection as a Rottweiler, swung her legs casually from the end of the sofa and watched Chief Inspector Jason Dury through guileless blue eyes.

'I just wanted to have a look around,' she said, for about the seventh time. 'I saw all the policemen crawling about over the grounds and knew they must be looking for something, so I thought that I'd have a look too.'

Monica bit her lip and glanced at Jason, trying to read from his expression just how convincing he found this explanation. To her mother, who knew her well, it *was* just the sort of thing Carol-Ann would do. But did it make her look even more suspicious in the eyes of the police? Was he wondering, behind those oh-so-enigmatic pale blue eyes of his, if Carol-Ann wasn't being just a shade *too* helpful? If she might be playing games with him? Damn it, she wished she knew.

'I was getting a bit bored, though, to be honest,' Carol-Ann admitted now. 'I was about to give it up and come in for some ice cream, when I just saw it. It looked like a weird place to have a fire, so I yelled to one of your policemen to come and have a look.' She gave a shrug. 'And that was that.'

Jason thought that that was probably just how it had been. Sheer dumb luck.

To Monica, it all sounded pitifully lame and phoney. And her heart sank as she became more and more convinced that her daughter was probably now number one on Jason's suspect list.

Jason sighed, caught Monica's eye, and gave a shrug of his own.

'All right, I think that's all for now,' he said wearily. 'It's getting late — time I headed for home. I'm tired,' Jason admitted suddenly.

And he looked it too, Monica thought sympathetically, with his fair hair flopping limply across his forehead, and deep lines running from his nose to his lips. He smiled and left, and Monica watched him go, gnawing on her bottom lip. For a second there, she'd felt like going over to him and rubbing his aching back. She blinked and shook her head to clear it.

First things first.

How on earth was she going to persuade Jason that Carol-Ann was just an innocent bystander in all this? That she wouldn't steal, especially another woman's diamond earrings, and that she certainly wouldn't murder anyone, and that finding the bonfire site the killer had used had just been sheer bad luck on her part?

She looked down at her daughter and discovered that Carol-Ann was watching Jason's disappearing figure like a thoughtful hawk.

'You know, Mother,' Carol-Ann said dreamily, 'he's really quite dishy.'

Monica groaned. It was less painful than tearing her hair out.

* * *

The next morning, Len Biggs was back, having got permission from both his boss and the police to lead his workforce into battle in flat 12. Monica had no idea they were there until she looked up out of her kitchen window and saw a man walk past carrying two huge tins of paint.

And the sight of him suddenly sparked something in her memory. She'd totally forgotten to tell Jason about what Len had said a couple of days ago!

She quickly finished the quiche she'd been making and popped it in the oven, then made her way up to the top floor. As she stepped off the last stair and looked around, the sound of a radio playing wafted out of an open door. She walked over and asked a vacant-looking youth for Mr Biggs, who blinked and said that the boss was in the toilet.

Monica waited patiently for nearly ten minutes before she realized that he meant Len was *decorating* the premises, not actually using them. Laughing at herself, Monica at last found the foreman, busily grouting tiles.

'Hello, Len,' she said from the open doorway, making him jump.

From his kneeling position, he quickly swivelled around, his face creasing into a smile.

'Oh, hello there, missus. Cup of tea time?' he asked hopefully.

Monica grinned. 'Anytime, Len. You know where my kitchen is.' And that reminded her, her quiche wouldn't do to be left too long. 'Len, I wanted to know if you'd asked around.' And, as he continued to look at her blankly, prompted gently, 'You know, about the tarpaulins still being up in the flat.'

Len shot her a quick, assessing look. 'Yeah, I did. I was right, we *did* take them down, right after lunch on Friday. And nobody admits to putting 'em back up again.' Slowly he laid his platter of grey grouting down and rubbed his hands nervously along the legs of his overalls. 'Is something up, then?' he asked diffidently.

Monica looked at his open, honest face, and sighed. 'Yes, Len, I think there might be. I'll have to tell this to Chief

Inspector Dury. He'll probably be up here to talk to you all again. Sorry about that.'

Len sighed fatalistically. 'Oh well, I suppose you have to expect it,' he replied philosophically. Then he shot another quick look at her. 'And how're you all coping? You and the rev are OK? You look a bit peaky.'

Monica could have kissed him. 'Thanks, Len, I'm fine.'

***

Jason Dury was feeling anything *but* fine. It was day five of the murder inquiry, and although evidence was dribbling in, it didn't seem to be leading them anywhere. Their most promising suspects seemed to be slipping through the net, and new leads were beckoning. His superiors were already beginning to pile on the pressure for a result, and they had nothing concrete on either the husband or the blackmail victim to link them to the crime.

He looked up as a timid tap came on the door, and when Monica looked in, he felt his spirits lift. She was wearing a white wraparound skirt and dark green blouse that clung to her in all the right places. Her dark curls gleamed in the sunlight.

'Come on in, we won't bite,' he said softly. For once the incident room was unusually empty.

'I forgot to tell you something yesterday. No, Monday,' Monica began nervously. 'It was something that Len said, in passing. Len Biggs, the decorator here.'

As she began to explain, Jim Greer left his desk and came up to stand beside her and listen in. Jason's face slowly darkened as she spoke, and when she'd finished, her voice was little more than an apologetic whisper. But Jason wasn't angry with her so much as he was with himself for having missed it.

'I think we'd better go and have a word with Mr Biggs,' he said flatly. Jim, too, felt like kicking himself. He'd been present when they'd interviewed the decorator, and he hadn't picked up on this tarpaulin business either.

After Len Biggs had been visited, and had vociferously assured them that the tarpaulins hadn't been on the walls Friday afternoon when all the decorators had left, the two policemen returned to the incident room.

'It just doesn't make sense, sir,' Jim said peevishly.

Jason retrieved the photographs of the scene of the crime and spread them across his desk, not sure what he was looking for. All they told him was what he knew already: that the tarpaulins *were* in place on the walls, except the one that had been pulled down and used to cover the body. So what did this latest information actually tell them? He was sure it should tell them everything, if only he was smart enough to see it.

* * *

Back in her kitchen, Monica rescued her quiche, thinking that if only she could figure it all out, Carol-Ann would be in the clear. The only trouble was, she felt hopelessly inadequate. And the mystery about the tarpaulins simply had her baffled.

But she wasn't a quitter, either. She'd figure it out if it killed her!

176

CHAPTER 14

John put down his knife and fork and leaned back in his chair, feeling pleasantly replete.

'That's the best breakfast I've had since I came here the last time,' he said, smiling in satisfaction.

Vera smiled back, retrieved his plate, and took it to the sink, running hot water over it and adding a squirt of washing-up liquid. But her mind was clearly on things less domestic.

'I see that Maurice is back,' she said casually.

'Yes, I saw him going to his flat,' he confirmed. 'Not that I was looking out for him or anything.'

Thursday had dawned, as irrepressibly bright and hot as all the previous days. Vera returned to the table with a pot of freshly brewed coffee and a creamer. She pushed the bowl filled with brown sugar a little closer to his place setting.

'The inquest will have to be held soon,' she mused, bringing a newly poured, piping-hot cup of coffee to her lips and blowing on it gently. Slowly, their eyes met and Vera sighed heavily. 'It'll all be over soon, won't it?' she asked softly.

John nodded. 'Yes, I think so,' he said levelly. 'But I'm worried about Pauline.'

'John, do you think we should do something?' she asked worriedly.

John continued to sip his coffee and said nothing.

* * *

Monica, with Carol-Ann chattering non-stop beside her, parked her little runaround in the centre of Cheltenham. And, as usual in these days of budget cuts and swingeing charges, was forced to pay handsomely by the council for the privilege. Sighing, she checked her already denuded purse and nodded.

'Right, we've got seventy pounds between us to blow on an outfit and not a penny more. So choose carefully.'

And after complaining bitterly about her miserly ways, which would have put Mrs Scrooge to shame apparently, choosing carefully was exactly what Carol-Ann did, dragging her mother remorselessly from shop to shop. Eventually, in about the fifth place they tried, Carol-Ann finally decided on a flowered granny frock, (which, for some reason, was back in vogue this season) which left Monica with about half an hour to find her own dress. She knew that Graham liked velvet, and a very pale blue evening gown in just that material which happened to catch her eye on a back rail, and which was on special offer, was undoubtedly the find of the day — no matter how much Carol-Ann made barfing gestures in the changing room about its 'boring' midi-length style and nicely decorous, 'old-maidish' boat-shaped neckline.

On the way home, they chatted about Carol-Ann's unsuccessful search for a job and her upcoming exam propositions. By mutual consent, they made no mention whatsoever of the murder or anything remotely connected with that weekend's events. But as Monica slowed down on the busy main road and indicated to turn off towards Heyford Bassett, she nevertheless felt something suddenly niggle at her. Something important that her subconscious was trying to bring to her attention, if only she could remember, or figure out, what it was.

But then they were home and trying on their purchases again in front of Monica's bedroom mirror, testing certain accessories and different jewellery combinations, once more two giggling, carefree, sated shopaholics. And whatever the vague idea was that had been trying to slip into Monica's consciousness, it slid away again.

* * *

If Monica and Carol-Ann had spent the day in idle pleasure, Jason Dury and his team most certainly hadn't. And at just gone five o'clock, one of the constables, who had been set the task of researching the backgrounds of the residents, came in with something interesting.

'Sir,' the constable approached Jason with eager respect.

'Your hunch that you'd seen Paul Waring somewhere before was right.'

Jason looked up. 'Oh? Let's have it then,' he said eagerly.

'Do you remember about six years ago, when you busted David Friel?'

The name rang a bell. 'Yes. He owned a health club and gym in Shrewsbury. One of his clients died — heart attack I think it was.'

'That's right, sir. But the autopsy was a bit iffy.'

'I remember. Friel had been supplying him with steroids in dangerous amounts. They argued culpable homicide for a while, and his brief cried blue murder and held out for natural causes. In the end, he pulled a ten stretch for manslaughter if I remember rightly.'

'You do, sir. Well, guess who was working at the gym at the time?'

Jason suddenly grinned. 'Is that so? He was one of Friel's boys, was he? I *wondered* where I'd seen him before. He wasn't implicated in the victim's death, though, was he?'

'No, sir. He was just a fitness instructor. I don't think the victim was even one of his clients. They tended to be women, apparently, from what was noted in the file.'

Jason smiled. 'Yes. I can see our Mr Waring being a popular choice with the ladies. Well, Constable . . . er . . . ?'

'Phillips, sir.'

'Well, Constable Phillips, let's go and have a word with our Mr Waring and see what he has to say for himself, shall we?'

And Constable Phillips, who'd never been this close to a murder investigation before, wasn't averse to that suggestion at all.

* * *

In her room on the top floor, Julie, under her mother's watchful eye, sullenly packed her bags.

'I still think this is a mistake,' she said uncertainly. 'Won't the police think it's suspicious, me going away like this all of a sudden?'

'Why should they? You're only taking a summer holiday, nothing suspicious in that,' Joan responded crisply. 'And when you've got a friend living in a Devon village as pretty as Combe Martin, with a mother who does bed and breakfast, it's an obvious place to go.'

Joan had changed out of all recognition these past days, and for once her daughter no longer felt as if she had the upper hand. In fact, Julie was just the littlest bit afraid of Joan now.

'That's everything then,' Julie said feebly, snapping the case shut and hauling it off the bed. 'What time's the train?'

'You've got plenty of time yet. I'll just have a look outside.' The last thing Joan wanted was for the police to spot her daughter sneaking out with a suitcase. Or Sean Franklyn seeing them leave, for that matter. She pulled aside the bedroom curtain and craned her neck to look below and then to the left and the right. There didn't seem to be anybody about.

Behind her, Julie took a big, shaky breath. 'Mum?' she said softly.

Joan turned her head. 'What, love?'

'Oh, nothing I suppose. Just, well . . . thanks,' Julie said humbly.

Joan smiled. 'Don't worry. I won't let anything happen to you, chick. You know that. Come on, let's go, while the coast's clear.' She wouldn't feel happy until her precious baby was safely out of easy reach. Then, whatever happened, Joan would be there to take the flack. And, like a mother tigress, she'd defend her cub to her dying breath.

* * *

Pauline tapped on Paul's door and waited anxiously for a response, hopping a little nervously from one foot to the other. She was wearing an emerald-green silk top with no bra, and a close-fitting pair of denim jeans so stonewashed they were almost white. She smiled brightly as the door opened, and held out the bottle of expensive mineral water that she was carrying.

'Hello.' There was a hint of uncertainty in her voice. 'Truce?'

Paul smiled ruefully and stepped aside to let her pass. 'Of course. Come on in. Look, I'm sorry I snapped your head off the other day. It wasn't right to take it out on you, but I'd just had a rotten day, and everything got on top of me I suppose, and you just happened to be in the wrong place at the wrong time. I'm not usually that grouchy, it's just—'

'I know,' Pauline interrupted his apology quickly — not that she wasn't feeling relieved and gratified by it. 'Things can get on your nerves, can't they? I feel the same. This place just feels really oppressive right now, have you noticed?' She waved the bottle again. 'Have you got some ice and maybe a slice of lime or lemon?'

Ten minutes later they were sat together on the sofa, sipping the water and using fingers of a somewhat dry and tough sourdough loaf to mop up an avocado dip that Paul had got from a health food shop in Cheltenham.

Pauline watched him alertly, wishing the mineral water had a good dash of gin in it. Then she smiled to herself, remembering how she'd sneaked into his apartment on the day of the murder to spice his veggie drink with vodka. Oh, it had seemed like a grand plan at the time. And, once he was nicely drunk, she'd planned to jump his bones.

But then Margaret had gone and got herself murdered, and all that sneaking around had been for nothing. Not even she had been able to think up an excuse to go calling on Paul with all of that going on. And she wondered, with another inner smile, if he'd noticed that that day's batch of veggie juice had gone down rather better than most?

When the doorbell suddenly rang, Pauline groaned.

'Oh, for Pete's sake! Just ignore it. They'll go away, whoever it is,' she snapped.

But the doorbell sounded again, and when Paul reluctantly rose and answered it, it was to find Jason Dury and a blank-faced constable on the other side. He grimaced wryly.

'Come on in, Chief Inspector, and join the party.'

Jason took him at his word and cast Pauline a quick, assessing look. 'I was wondering if I could have a word with you, sir?' Jason said. And looked pointedly at Pauline. 'Alone.'

Pauline's finely plucked brows rose. Sensing fireworks, Paul grimaced again.

He said wearily, 'I'm sure that whatever it is you want to ask me can be talked about in front of Pauline.'

Jason shrugged. 'Very well, Mr Waring.' And on your own head be it, he added silently. 'We've met before, did you know that?'

Paul looked at him, openly surprised. 'Have we? It must have been a long time ago.'

'It was. Eleven years, sir, to be precise. In Shrewsbury.'

Paul's face suddenly shifted. 'Ahh,' he said, on a small sigh. 'That. I was wondering when you'd get around to it,' he added. On the sofa, Pauline moved to the edge of her seat and watched him like a hawk. 'This is about David Friel, isn't it?' Paul asked grimly.

He made no effort to ask them to sit down, or if they wanted refreshments. He himself remained defiantly standing.

Jason nodded. 'Yes.'

'Look,' Paul sighed. 'I don't say I agree with what David did, but as I said in court at the time, and would say again if I had to, Gregory Orland must have *known* what he was doing when he took those steroids. Orland wanted results fast, that much I do remember. He simply wasn't prepared to work at it and get the results he craved by diet and exercise alone. He wanted to look good, and he wanted it fast. If you ask me, he was either trying to impress a woman, or make some bloke jealous. I know his sort. They want abs like Sylvester Stallone in his heyday, but have no real concept of what level of commitment that takes, so they look for a shortcut. It makes you despair sometimes, honest it does. And then when something goes wrong, his family look for a scapegoat to blame.' His voice was heated, but, even to the policeman's ears, he sounded sincere. 'Don't get me wrong, if Dave did supply him with steroids, he was an idiot. But if that was going on at that gym, I had nothing to do with it. Besides, I was way down on the totem pole at the time — me and the aerobics instructor weren't paid as well as the cleaners, let alone given any say in the running or management of the place. That's just one of the reasons why I was so determined to get my own gym.'

To give himself time to think, Jason looked slowly around the room. Waring's flat, number 10, was one of the three big, prestigious flats. Done out in cream with hints of silver and turquoise, with bamboo furnishings, it looked impressive.

'The gym business obviously pays well, Mr Waring?' Jason asked casually.

Paul grinned. 'Yes, I'm glad to say,' he said. 'And you can check up on any of my gyms, Inspector. They're all drug-free, I assure you. Seeing Dave's life ruined and the poor sod go to jail, not to mention having to testify in court, all really made their mark on me. I'll say this for the whole sorry experience, it certainly taught me about some of the pitfalls in this business, and what *not* to do.'

'I see. Well, thank you for the offer to check out your establishments, sir,' Jason said mildly. And he'd probably be taking him up on that. *When* he got the time. 'Well, that's all for now,' he said, and turned away.

But just as he was going out the door, Jason heard Pauline's harping voice demanding to know what all that had been about, and he realized that, wealthy or not, he didn't envy Paul Waring one bit. There was something very hard and tenacious about the predatory divorcée that set his hackles rising.

In the lounge, Pauline watched Paul finish his drink, and began to reach out with her hand to touch him. But Paul suddenly leapt from the sofa.

'Well, I guess I'll put the Nikes on and get in a few miles. Fancy a jog, Pauline?' he asked, with just a hint of malice.

Pauline sighed. That hadn't been the kind of exercise she'd had in mind.

'Thanks, I think I'll pass,' she said drolly.

Paul shrugged and showed her out.

It wasn't until much later, as Pauline was standing at her window and watching Joan park her car and cross the gravel back into the house, that she suddenly remembered something. Just what it had been about the afternoon of the murder, and the clothes, which had been niggling away at the back of her mind ever since.

And remembering it made her thoughtful and curious, when it should have made her scared. Instantly, she reached for the phone.

* * *

Back in the incident room, Jim listened intently as Jason filled him in on the latest news.

'But there was no hint that our friend Waring had anything to do with supplying steroids to this bloke that died?' he asked, when Jason was finished.

'None that came out at the trial, at any rate,' Jason said, rereading the photocopies of the Orland case that had been incorporated in Constable Phillips's report. 'Of course, Friel claimed he'd never even so much as seen a bottle of steroids, let alone passed any on to Gregory Orland.'

'Well, he would, wouldn't he?' Jim said with a grin.

'Hmm. They never found out who Friel's supplier was, though,' he noted quietly.

Jim glanced at Jason thoughtfully. 'Are you thinking that it was Waring who was really behind it all, sir?'

Jason sighed heavily. 'No, not really. And there's not even a hint in the original files that he might have been. But it's *possible*. And if he *has* done it before, perhaps he's doing it now. In which case, Margaret *might* have found out about it. She was the sort that did find out things, remember? Blackmailers have long noses, and they make a point of sticking them in where they don't belong. That way they find out all sorts of useful things. Or maybe she was a member at one of his gyms, and was offered a little something to help her get her weight down? She was very slim, and maybe could have been a bit obsessive about that. Not steroids, of course, but something. Check it out anyway, will you?'

'Right away, sir. And if it turns out that she *did* have a membership at one of his gyms? Does it really follow that she was blackmailing him as well?' Jim sounded doubtful.

It all sounded very tenuous to him. He hated to think it, but perhaps his boss was starting to clutch at straws? After all, they were now well past that magic milestone, the first forty-eight hours, and as every copper well knew, if a case wasn't solved by then, the chances of it getting solved at all slowly diminished.

'I really don't know,' Jason sighed. 'It's worth consideration, I suppose. And while you're at it, find Phillips and ask him if he can find any connection between the man who died, this Orland character, and Margaret Franklyn.'

'Sir.'

Jason went through the report again. Apart from Waring's one very tenuous brush with the law, the man's life had been perfectly straightforward. After a pretty standard education, he'd got into weightlifting, and from that sport went on to win a few minor bodybuilding trophies in his early twenties. He'd then travelled about the world a bit before finally settling down to set up his first gym here in the Cotswolds. That had been founded on the strength of his trophies and his ability to convince a bank manager that the market would continue to grow. And so it had. And from there he'd never looked back. The financial boys had had time to go through his complicated books now, and had discovered nothing more incriminating than the fact that he was a little on the optimistic side when it came to predicting profit margins. That, and the fact that he was about to sell off one of his less-profitable gyms.

The only other piece of information the painstaking constable had been able to uncover was that Paul had a certain reputation as a 'star-maker' in the bodybuilding world. No doubt putting his own knowledge of competitions to use, he'd produced several 'champions' over the years. His gym in Stroud in particular had sponsored one or two competitors in last year's 'Mr England' competition. Moreover, one of his customers *had* won a male body-modelling contract with one of the big London agencies not so long ago.

'Well, yip-de-doo,' Jason said disgustedly, throwing down the file and rubbing a tired hand across his forehead. He was getting nowhere, and he knew it. Despite all the leads, and the promise of Maurice Keating, who was still their prime suspect, he still felt as if he was just spinning his wheels. House-to-house interviews were finished now, and as expected had been a bit of a bust. Whereas usually they could rely on somebody, somewhere, having seen something, nearly all the residents of Heyford Bassett had been at that bloody fair.

His eyes narrowed as he thought about that. The timing was just too good to be a coincidence, wasn't it? It made sense that the killer had chosen his time well. He'd know that the village would be practically deserted. So did that suggest an outsider had done this, after all? Someone had come in from outside, killed Margaret and left, confident in the knowledge that nobody would be around in the deserted village to notice his passing through?

Perhaps in Jason concentrating his efforts so close to home, so to speak, he was making a mistake? But then, constantly second-guessing himself was pointless. He was covering every angle that he could think of. What more could he do? Besides, there was the issue of the clothes in the stairwell again.

Wearily, he leaned back in his chair, and as he did so, found his eye resting on a photograph of Margaret. It was a picture of her on her wedding day, and she looked young and fresh, and not so distressingly thin as she'd become in later years. As he met her smiling celluloid eyes, he shook his head.

'Margaret, Margaret,' he said softly. 'Just who did you go to see that afternoon? And why? And how come someone as smart as you didn't see that shotgun coming?'

* * *

In one of the flats in the attractive vicarage, a killer paced the floor, thinking furiously. It had all been going so well. The execution had been flawless, the timing perfect. There should have been no mistakes, but a mistake *must* have been made somewhere, for now there was danger.

And so the mistake must be rectified, and the danger nullified.

Quickly.

CHAPTER 15

Jason stood on the bank of the river, watching the progress of a silvery stream of bubbles that were rising steadily from a police diver's breathing apparatus.

He'd been ready to call it a day, when the news came through that the diver had signalled that at last he'd found something in the river.

'Here he comes,' Jim said unnecessarily, as a dark figure began to emerge from underneath the carpet of water crow-foot and held aloft his trophy.

A double-barrelled shotgun.

'Right, bag and tag it,' Jason said crisply. 'And then get Clem Jarvis in to identify it. Then send it straight back to HQ for testing, although just how much use it'll be to us is debatable. Being in the water will have severely compromised the fingerprints, even if the killer had been dumb enough not to wear gloves. And you can't get a ballistics match on a shotgun shell.' He turned to Jim. 'Still no luck in tracing that "mystery friend" of Maurice that Paul Waring saw?' he asked, but the sergeant shook his head.

'Not so far, guv. Everybody and their granny was at that bloody fair. Not even the lady running the shop saw him.'

The Oxford don had flatly denied knowing anything about him when asked his identity, saying that Paul Waring must have been mistaken. But the old man had gone very pale, and had started to sweat profusely when Jason and his sergeant had questioned him, and both policemen had been sure he was lying. So although they only had Paul Waring's word for it that the unknown man had been hanging around at all, Jason was very much inclined to believe him. Which opened the field to an awful lot of speculation. Had the Oxford don, and not Sean Franklyn, been the one to hire a hitman to kill Margaret Franklyn? It certainly made a lot of sense. He was the one being blackmailed, after all. And it enabled him to stay at the party and keep his hands clean of the actual dirty work, which was something that would undoubtedly appeal to a fastidious man like Maurice. But without knowing the identity of the man the police were helpless — and there was the question of those damned clothes in the stairwell again. So Maurice Keating was sitting pretty, and he knew it. All he had to do was keep his mouth shut and hope for the best. Unless something else had been going on that they didn't know about.

'You know, Jim, I can't help but get the feeling that some-one in this house is leading us down the garden path somehow,' he said softly.

Jim nodded. 'Maybe you're right, sir,' he agreed uneasily. 'You can't help but get the feeling that someone's been dead clever, can you?'

Jason grunted and together, in morose silence, they headed back to the small, equipment-filled room that was beginning to feel like home. And there they found a very eager constable waiting for them.

'PC Bennington, sir,' he said smartly.

'Detailed to check into the erring husband,' Jim added in a helpful aside to Jason.

'Sir, I finally managed to speak to one of Mr Sean Franklyn's closest friends. He admitted that just recently Mr

189

Franklyn had been boasting about how he'd got himself a real young looker. But he was in a bit of a lather about it, on account of it being so dangerous.'

'Dangerous? How?' Jason asked quickly.

'That's what I asked him, sir. He was a bit reluctant at first, but then he said that this latest bird of Sean's was literally right on his doorstep. And that Maggie — that's Mrs Franklyn, sir — knew all about it, and didn't like it one little bit, and was cutting up something awful about it, threatening divorce and all sorts.' The young PC paused to take a much-needed breath. 'Sean Franklyn also told his friend that it wasn't worth the hassle anymore, what with what's happened and everything, and that he'd have to give this bird the old heave-ho.' The constable flushed a little over his notes, and cleared his throat. 'That's verbatim, sir,' he added nervously. He wouldn't like his superior officer to think that was all his own language.

Jason gave a long, slow whistle.

'Thank you, Constable,' he said at last, and nodded a dismissal. And Bennington, his moment of fame over for the day, shuffled off dejectedly.

'It has to be Julie Dix, doesn't it, sir?' Jim asked quietly after a short, thoughtful pause.

'She's the only one that fits the description,' Jason agreed. 'Pauline Weeks is too old, and Monica Noble may be younger than him, but only by a few years, I'd say. Carol-Ann is far too young, and if it was her we'd have a different kind of issue on our hands. No, unless it was someone from his workplace then it has to be Julie Dix. It explains why her mother is so anxious and protective too.'

'Do you think Franklyn had already told her she had to go?' Jim asked ominously. 'Maybe it was clear that he was getting tired of her, and had been for some time?'

'He might have done. And yes, she might have sensed that he was getting tired of her,' Jason agreed, meeting his eye.

'And she might not have liked it,' Jim went on.

'She's young and the young can be very passionate about things,' Jason agreed. 'They get things out of proportion, and do silly things they later regret.'

'And she might have seen Margaret as the one standing in her way of happiness and the path of true love,' Jim followed the argument on to its inexorable conclusion.

'And aside from Carol-Ann, of all of those who weren't present when the shot was heard, she's the youngest and quickest,' Jason mused. 'So she might have had time to do it. Just. But did she have the brains for it? And remember, that shotgun was stolen a week ago. So this murder has been planned for some time. You think she's that cold-blooded?'

'Well, perhaps she's been working herself up to it, sir,' Jim said, playing devil's advocate. 'Perhaps it wasn't cold-blooded at all, but a crime of passion.'

But he didn't sound all that convinced either.

'Perhaps,' Jason said. 'Anyway, I think it's time we had a longer, closer word with Miss Julie Dix.'

* * *

In her flat, Vera slowly put down the phone and bit her lip. Although Pauline had been very roundabout during their little talk just now, Vera knew when she was being pumped for information. And Vera was too wily not to know what Pauline had been getting at. Oh, she'd talked a little bit about anything and everything, but it was obvious, to Vera at least, what it was that she'd really wanted to pick her brains about.

Clothes. And what everyone had been wearing on the afternoon that Margaret had been killed.

Vera sighed heavily. 'Damn,' she said softly. Then, more forcefully, '*Damn!*'

Picking up the receiver again, she dialled a familiar number.

* * *

Joan glanced up from her book as the doorbell rang, rose without hurrying, and walked through to the front door. She did not look particularly surprised to see Jason Dury and his sergeant on the other side, but her backbone stiffened instinctively. She'd known this moment could come at any time, and she was determined to rise to the challenge.

'Chief Inspector,' she said with a small, tight smile. 'Please, do come in.'

'Thank you. We'd like to have a word with your daughter, please, Mrs Dix,' Jason said, following her into a pleasant room, decorated predominantly in cream and lilac.

'What on earth for? She's already given you a statement, hasn't she?' Joan played for time.

'Is she in her room?' Jason asked abruptly, in no mood to be messed about.

'No,' Joan said shortly. If this very capable young man thought he could bully her, he was in for a nasty surprise!

'Can you tell me when she'll be in?'

'No.'

Jim glanced uneasily at his superior, sensing trouble. Jason's eyes narrowed.

'Mrs Dix, just where is your daughter?' he demanded softly.

Joan smiled. 'She's on holiday, Chief Inspector. Why shouldn't she be?' Joan stuck her chin out defiantly.

'People don't usually take holidays in the middle of a murder investigation, Mrs Dix,' Jason pointed out softly. 'And I consider it a very suspicious circumstance that your daughter has absented herself without telling me first.'

'The last time I looked, this wasn't a police state,' Joan flared.

'Mrs Dix,' Jason said quietly, 'are you going to tell me where your daughter is, or do I have to find her myself?'

Joan shrugged. 'I don't see why I should tell you anything, Chief Inspector. The murder of that awful woman has nothing to do with us. Why should I let it spoil our life?' She returned to the sofa and held her book in readiness on her lap. Obviously she was trying to indicate that this interview was now over.

Jason nodded. 'You're very protective of your daughter, aren't you, Mrs Dix?' he asked softly.

Joan's face hardened. 'I'm all she has,' she said flatly, but Jason understood at once that she'd got that backwards. Julie was all that *she* had. 'Her father was no damned use to her, or to me,' Joan snapped, feeling suddenly afraid.

There was something determined and quietly *hard* about this handsome blonde policeman that scared her.

'And you saw to it that she had everything she ever wanted,' he mused out loud, his voice gentle now.

'Well, naturally.'

'And her education,' Jason continued softly. 'You made sure she had the best. Am I right?'

'Of course,' Joan said. 'My Julie's got a bright future ahead of her. She's a clever girl.'

'Yes. But not clever enough to avoid falling for a married man,' he landed the bombshell softly. 'We know that Sean Franklyn was having an affair with your daughter, Mrs Dix.'

Still Joan said nothing, but her hands clenched into fists on her lap, and her knuckles showed white.

'We have it on good authority that Mrs Franklyn didn't like it, and had demanded that her husband break the affair off.'

Joan could finally stand no more, and sprang to her feet. '*She* demanded it?' she shrieked. 'Who was she to demand anything? She was a viper! She was a parasite who deserved exactly what she got!'

Suddenly, Joan fell silent, her lips held in a thin, grim line.

'Parasite, Mrs Dix?' Jason pounced. 'In what way?'

Joan gave a shocking half-laugh, half-snarl. 'Oh go to hell,' she said bitterly, and Jason wondered if this twisted, hate-filled visage was the last thing that Margaret Franklyn had ever seen in this world.

Then he remembered that Joan had an alibi. She'd been in full sight of the rest of the garden party when the shotgun had been fired.

'Where is she, Mrs Dix?' Jason demanded. 'Where's your daughter?'

Joan smiled grimly. 'You're the detective,' she jeered softly. 'You find her.'

Jason shook his head. 'Do you really want us to go on the telly and flash a great big picture of your daughter, Mrs Dix? Asking the public if they've seen her? Because then everyone will know—'

'Sir!' Jim yelled in warning, but Jason, who'd been watching Joan closely, was ready for her.

As Joan sprang at him, snarling and half-sobbing, he caught her raised fist easily. Nevertheless she fought him like someone demented, managing to land one or two painful kicks to his shin, her fingers curled into talons as they sought out his eyes.

As a display of rage it was chilling.

But when the storm was over, and Joan was once more sat on the sofa, weeping uncontrollably, Jason offered her a big white square handkerchief.

'Now, where is she, Mrs Dix?' he asked insistently. He could, of course, charge her with assaulting a police officer, but he knew it would be pointless. She was far beyond caring about any personal threat to her liberty. 'You know we have to speak to her. We won't bully her, I promise.'

Joan heaved a shuddering sigh. 'She's in Combe Martin,' she admitted at last, realizing that it was hopeless to hold out on this. She'd have to start thinking in terms of solicitors and barristers and things like that instead. The fight hadn't totally left her yet. 'She's staying with a friend.' Reluctantly, she cited the address. 'But she had nothing to do with the death of that woman. Nothing,' Joan insisted, turning her tear-ravaged, desperate face towards the policemen.

Jason nodded, realizing that this woman was absolutely terrified that her daughter *had* had something to do with it. No wonder she was so fraught.

'Then she has nothing to worry about,' he said quietly. But Julie Dix did have something to worry about, of course.

As did Sean Franklyn, who was roused from his flat and taken in to Gloucester police station for further questioning.

* * *

In their kitchen, with Graham washing up and Monica wiping, it was a scene of domestic bliss in the Noble household. They'd heard the latest from Pauline Weeks of course, and wondered how long the police would keep Sean and Julie in for questioning. It seemed as if Maurice's prediction that someone else would soon be put through the wringer was proving all too true. And now most of those living at the vicarage were wondering if they'd be next.

Except for Graham, whose conscience was blissfully clear. In his mind, he was running over the christening of baby Venus.

Monica, however, was distinctly agitated. As someone who'd been right there on the scene, she should have some ideas of who'd killed Margaret by now, surely, she told herself grimly. She'd heard things from the others, and her subconscious mind had been processing all the information for days now. And there was no denying that *something* was niggling at her more and more. She felt as if she should *know* who had killed Margaret. She felt, in fact, as if she was being awfully dim.

It was a horrible feeling, and one she would have given anything not to have. She retired to the bedroom where she could find some peace and quiet and think without interruption. And for the next few hours she replayed everything in her mind.

The day of the party. The sound of the shot. The things people had said to her since. Len Biggs. The sound of the shot again. She kept coming back to that. The sound of the shot. Why?

She sighed and headed for the shower. It was no use. But the feeling that she was on the verge of understanding everything was growing stronger and stronger. And it scared her.

That night, she held Graham very close.

* * *

Police stations never slept, and neither, it seemed, did chief inspectors investigating murders. It was nearing midnight when Jason closed the door on Interview Room 3 and its occupant, Sean Franklyn. He looked grimly at his sergeant.

'Do you believe him, sir?' Jim asked.

Jason nodded gloomily. 'Yes. I think I do. But we'd better see what Julie Dix has to say for herself before we write them off, though.'

A squad car had been sent to collect Julie from Devon, and she now sat ensconced in a separate interview room, having rejected the solicitor her mother had called in. Joan was beside herself, and clearly wanted the solicitor to be present to ensure that Julie said nothing incriminating, but the teenager was showing remarkable fortitude. Jason could only hope that she talked before she changed her mind. It wasn't often the police got to interview such co-operative suspects.

Inside, they set up the recorder, ran through the usual procedure, and Jason slowly leaned back in his chair and smiled at Julie. She was looking pale and nervous, but calm.

'So, Julie, what can you tell us about the day of the murder of Margaret Franklyn?' he started off gently.

Julie sighed heavily. 'Sean and I are . . . were . . . in love,' she began, and beside him, he could feel Jim relax. It was a good start, and far better than they could have hoped for. It looked as if they were in for a straightforward time, after all.

'It had been going on for some time,' Julie continued, her voice as exhausted as she looked. 'And it got to the point where we wanted to spend some quality time together. It was hard, what with Margaret right there at the vicarage, and Mum watching me like a hawk.' Julie pushed a wing of hair behind one ear, and stared down at her pale hands. 'Then Sean came up with this plan. He told Margaret that there was this week-long conference in Scotland that he had to go to, but he'd really booked us a villa in Spain for the week.'

'So what was the plan?' Jason asked.

'On the day of the party, I was to go inside and pack my bags, leaving a note for Mum saying that I'd gone to stay with friends for a week and would call her later. I was to catch the 4:30 train to London, and book into a hotel in Paddington for the night. It was all arranged, and Sean tapped his watch at the party to remind me. Then he was going to join me there on Sunday, and we'd fly out to Spain that afternoon. But, well, as you know, things happened, and we never got to go,' she finished lamely.

'I see. And did Margaret know about all this?'

Julie flushed. 'Not about the Spanish thing. I don't think so anyway. But I think she might have guessed about me and Sean. She was always so nasty to me. It drove Mum wild.'

Jim bet it did. But Joan's alibi was airtight. Everybody at the party said she was in plain sight when the shot was fired. Pity. Because if ever a woman had murder in her, it was Joan Dix, Jim mused.

'I see. And tell me again where you were when the shot was fired?' Jason prompted.

Julie looked at him bleakly.

'You think I did it, don't you?' she queried flatly. 'Because of Sean, and because I don't have an alibi. But I *was* in my flat, changing, like I told you, and I was also packing my bags.' She shrugged, obviously too exhausted to care, for the moment at least, whether or not they believed her.

'And Sean never talked about killing his wife?' Jason pressed her, watching her head snap up, a look almost of contempt crossing her face. 'Or of hiring someone else to do it for him?'

'Don't be daft,' she said bitterly. 'Why would he? Never heard of divorce, Inspector? It's far more simple and much less risky,' she said scornfully, and with a sudden show of spirit. 'Besides, the greatest stroke of cunning Sean ever pulled off was renting a safety deposit box and skimming off enough money every week to stash away in order to afford the villa without Margaret knowing about it. I think he was dead scared that you'd find out about it and discover the money and his passport and other stuff, and arrest him for the murder.'

Which explained why Sean had reacted so badly to the mention of Margaret's safety deposit box, Jason suddenly realized. He must have assumed we'd got our wires crossed somehow, and had discovered *his* little secret stash instead.

Eventually the interview was over, and outside, Jim sighed heavily.

'Well, they both tell the same tale, sir,' he pointed out. Of course, Franklyn had neglected to mention the safety deposit box, but they could soon discover the truth about that.

'Yes, but if they were in it together, they *would* be careful to get the details right, wouldn't they?' Jason said flatly. 'Anyway, check and see if they really did have flights booked, and that this villa they were on about was all paid for.'

Jim rubbed the back of his head. It was getting on for the wee small hours now, and he wanted his bed. 'It wouldn't be the first time a husband and his mistress got together to get rid of an unwanted wife, would it?' he said. 'And if there were two of them in it, it might have made the logistics of the thing easier.'

'Yeah,' Jason said. 'But I've got a feeling, when you check out their story, that it'll all gel.'

'They might have still gone through with that, sir — the Spain thing I mean — as a getaway, like,' Jim said, but his heart wasn't really in it.

'Rather obvious, though, don't you think? Margaret gets killed, and her husband and a young female resident of the house disappear at the same time. It'd be like sticking a big notice on their foreheads saying, "We did it!" Besides, it's not as if you can't get extradited from Spain, is it?'

'Oh, I'm going to bed,' Jim said crossly. Like his boss, he didn't really see Julie and Sean as the killers, but he was too damned tired to worry about it now.

Jason grunted, not unsympathetic with his sergeant's sudden bad mood.

'Good idea, Jim. We'll pick it up again in the morning,' he agreed. And yawned widely.

CHAPTER 16

Jason arrived at the vicarage at a little after nine the next morning, and as he locked the car door, his sergeant pulled in behind him. When they walked into the incident room, John and Vera rose quickly from a pair of chairs where they'd been waiting, the nervous but resolute looks on their faces instantly putting Jason on the alert.

'Good morning. Is there something I can do for you?' he asked pleasantly, taking a seat behind his desk. Jim sat where he was able to see both their faces, and got out his notebook.

John cleared his throat, then abruptly sat down as Jason gestured him back into his chair. Vera did likewise.

'We,' John shot the plump blonde woman beside him an anxious look, and plunged right in. 'We're rather worried about Pauline,' he said bluntly.

Whatever Jason had been expecting, it wasn't that. 'Oh? Why?'

Again John shot Vera a look, and she obligingly took over. 'It's not anything definite,' she began. 'By that I mean it's not any one thing we can put our finger on. It's sort of complicated.'

'To begin with,' John chipped in, 'she's been going around saying that she noticed the bloodstains on the stairs when she went back to her flat to get some fruit, on the day of the murder. Now we know that can't be right, because, according to her, she was in her flat when she heard the shot. So what would bloodstains be doing on the stairs then?'

Jason shot a startled glance at Jim. This was the first he'd heard about this. Why hadn't Pauline been talking to *them* about it?

'So of course, we didn't really take much notice of her,' Vera picked up the baton. 'Pauline has a way of bragging, just to make you take notice of her. Personally, I think she's just lacking in self-esteem.'

Jason didn't give a fig for Pauline Weeks's self-esteem. He was, instead, going over what he knew about the couple in front of him. According to what research on their background had picked up, they'd only met when buying their respective flats at the vicarage. Both had been single, never having married, both were self-employed in a creative field, and they had evidently hit it off and were now more or less an established couple. There wasn't so much as a hint of any criminal activity in either of their backgrounds, and so far neither of them had any connection to Margaret Franklyn that the police had been able to discern. They seemed to be a pair of responsible, intelligent people, and since they were well down on his suspect list, he was inclined to listen to their evidence with an open mind. Quite why they should have been watching Pauline Weeks so closely, he wasn't yet sure.

'Of course, even though we quickly learned what she was like,' Vera carried on, 'it still worried us that she was going around saying things about the murder, and what happened that day. I mean, not only could it skew the facts, but it could be dangerous, couldn't it? If the murderer happened to hear her?'

Jason's slightly puzzled frown cleared. Ah, so that was it. And they were quite right — it was a very dangerous thing to go around claiming knowledge when a murder had been committed. They'd have to speak to the divorcée as a matter of urgency.

'So when she called me up last night and tried to pump me about clothes, well, then I became really worried,' Vera swept on.

'What's this about clothes?' Jason interrupted sharply. As far as he was aware, it wasn't yet common knowledge within the vicarage that the ashes from the bonfire site had contained articles of clothing.

'Pauline rang me up last night, and it was weird, but I'm sure she was trying to pump me for information without letting on exactly what it was that she wanted to know about,' Vera said. Aware she was being somewhat less than clear, she made an effort to marshal her thoughts, pushing a hand nervously through her hair before trying again. 'Let me try to make it clearer,' she said. 'The first time she mentioned something about clothes to me was when we were both putting some rubbish out. But it was very vague — she just said something was niggling at her, but she didn't know what. Then, last night, I was sure she was trying to find out if I'd noticed if somebody at the party had been wearing a different shirt or blouse later on in the day. She was full of things like, "Do you remember the colour of Joan's blouse? Wasn't it a ghastly pink?" And then I'd say something about being sure it was pale yellow, or whatever, and then she'd skip to something else, but then come back to a question about somebody else's clothes. She almost went through the entire group of us who were there, trying to get my take on what they were wearing.' Vera shrugged helplessly. 'As I said, I thought it was strange, and after she hung up, I called John.'

'And I told her we should see you first thing,' John put in bluntly. 'You see, we've both come to think of this place as our safe haven,' he explained, blushing a little as he admitted to such sentimentality. 'You know, Vera and me meeting here and all. And at our time of life. It was like we were blessed. It seems so ideal that we think of it as our bit of paradise.' He looked across at the cook, who smiled back at him. 'So when poor Margaret was killed, everything seemed to be in danger of falling apart somehow. And then this thing with Pauline sounded so . . . well . . . risky. Odd. So we thought we'd better bring it to you, to see what you make of it.'

Jason nodded. 'I'm glad that you did. I think Jim and I will go and speak to Mrs Weeks now and get this thing cleared up once and for all.'

Vera beamed in relief. As they all left, Vera and John to go back to his place, Jason and Jim to the stairs, a rare cloud passed across the sun, briefly darkening the interior of the big house. But when the two policemen got to Pauline's flat, there was no answer. As he knocked on the door for the third time, Jim restlessly stirring beside him, Jason began to get a bad feeling about the whole thing.

He tried the door, surprised to find it open. He shot Jim a quick look. His sergeant had gone a slightly greener shade of pale.

'Mrs Weeks,' Jason called, pushing open the door and looking in. 'It's Chief Inspector Dury. Are you decent?'

They stepped into the hall, and Jim pushed open the door nearest to him. It was the master bedroom, but the bed hadn't been slept in. Jason walked the length of the short vestibule, and pushed open the door to the lounge. In the doorway he stopped, heaved a heavy sigh, then moved quickly but carefully forwards.

Pauline lay almost exactly in the centre of the room. She was sprawled, face down on the carpet, her blonde hair making a stark contrast against the grey and blue colour scheme. Jason put two fingers to the side of her neck and pressed, feeling for a pulse as Jim looked at him pale-faced and questioning. Briefly, Jason shook his head.

'Get the team in,' he said flatly.

When Jim had left, Jason stood staring down at the dead body at his feet, feeling both guilty and angry. Damn it, why hadn't she come to him sooner? There was no need for her to be dead. If only she'd told them what she'd known.

The question was, what *had* she known? And was it all just a sad coincidence that Vera and John had come to him just that little bit too late?

* * *

203

Graham accepted a cup and saucer from Mrs Sheila Marsh, and carefully took a sip of the tea it contained.

'Hmm, lovely,' he said, smiling brightly at the comfortably padded, middle-aged woman beside him.

He'd called on baby Venus's parents one last time in order to make a final attempt at changing their minds about her name, but his presence at the Marsh family home was obviously causing a bit of puzzlement. Best to get on with it, he thought ruefully.

'So, you're hoping to get a place of your own soon?' he asked Linsey conversationally, but it was Mrs Marsh, the proud new grandmother, who replied.

'Well, that's easier said than done, isn't it?' she asked grimly. 'It's tragic, it is, the way youngsters have trouble getting places to live nowadays.'

Graham's face clouded. 'Yes, I know,' he said, in genuine sympathy.

'Biscuit, Vicar?' Mrs Marsh asked, thrusting a packet of ginger nuts under his nose.

'Lovely.' He took one — although he wasn't fond of them — then turned once more to Linsey. 'So, we're all set for Sunday then?'

'Oh yeah,' Linsey said, obviously wondering why the vicar had called around.

And Graham, sensing her puzzlement, cleared his throat. Last night he'd made up a list of all the unusual girls' names he could think of, since it was obviously the strange and unusual that attracted Linsey, and wondered now how best to dangle the bait under her nose. They were due to get the birth registered the following day, so this was his last chance to convince her. Taking a deep breath, he launched his gambit.

'I was talking to a friend of mine the other day who has a parish in Oxford, and he was telling me how he'd recently christened a child called Pandora Gwendolyn. I thought that was really pretty.'

'Yeah, it's OK,' Linsey agreed grudgingly.

'Of course, nowadays unusual names are very popular,' Graham tried a bit of reverse psychology, 'and everyone's looking for individualistic names for their children.'

Mrs Marsh, who was nobody's fool, caught on quickly and shot the clergyman a grateful glance, confirming his guess that she was probably none too happy to have a granddaughter called Venus either.

'Mind you, there's only one name I came across in an old parish registry that I'd never heard of before . . .' He took a sip, saw Linsey's head turn interestedly his way, and summoning up a mental list of names, picked one at random. 'And that's Halcyone.'

'Halcyone,' Mrs Marsh said cautiously. 'Oh, I don't know that I like that much.' Her eyes, however, were twinkling, giving Graham quite a start. The old girl was already one step ahead of him! Of course, Mrs Marsh's disapproval was all the encouragement that Linsey needed.

'Mr Noble, that's really great! It sounds like a heroine from a comic strip. Halcyone the Hellcat or somethin'. Yeah, I really like that! It's great. Steve, whaddya think?'

Steve, well trained, quickly nodded. He never argued with either his mother or Linsey if he could help it.

'Yeah, I think I've changed my mind. We'll call her Halcyone. Halcyone Venus Pandora,' Linsey said, with real enthusiasm.

Graham inwardly winced, but decided a partial victory was better than none at all, and began to make getting-ready-to-leave gestures. In the hallway they heard the baby crying in an upstairs room, and Mrs Marsh quickly excused herself, leaving Linsey to show him to the door.

'Any news about the murder then, Mr Noble?' Linsey asked blatantly, and Graham sighed and shook his head.

'I'm afraid not.'

'It gave me the creeps, it did,' Linsey said, walking with him to the garden gate. 'To think I'd been there that morning, and might have passed the killer, waiting in the bushes or something.'

'Of course. Your appointment was at lunchtime, wasn't it?' He opened the gate and stepped out onto the pavement.

'Yeah. Then we came back here. We took Venus, I mean Halcyone, out in her pram, she was grizzling so. Couldn't take her to the fair like that, could we? Besides, we didn't have the dosh to spend to make a real proper day of it anyway. Far better to stay home, I thought. I said so to Steve. Save our pennies.'

'A good idea,' Graham sighed. And one that a lot of people seemed to be adopting nowadays. Then, when Linsey looked at him with disconcertingly shrewd eyes, he smiled in apology. 'Sorry. I was thinking of the appeal for the church bells.'

'Not going well, huh? You oughta ask that bloke who drives the big fancy Jag for a touch-up then. He must have a quid or two,' she advised.

'Jag?' Graham mused thoughtfully. He knew several people who drove Jaguars.

'Yeah, a big blue one. One minute we was walking down the path, moaning about not being at the fair, and the next minute, this mouth-watering car comes cruising past us and disappears up the road.' And she pointed vaguely towards the road behind her. 'All right for some, ain't it?' she added with a sigh.

Graham, however, was still looking up the road she'd indicated, a puzzled look on his face. The Marshes had a little house in the square, and the road Linsey indicated petered out onto a dirt track that led to nowhere except to Chandler's Spinney. But why on earth would a car go up there?

* * *

Once he left the Marsh household, and still in blissful ignorance of the grim discovery that had just been made back at his vicarage, he drove instead to a town not too far away.

Trisha Lancer answered the door quickly, unaware of how worn-down she looked.

'Hello, Vicar. Thanks for coming,' she said listlessly. She'd called him first thing that morning, asking him if he might call round, but such was her state of gloom she'd been half-expecting him to either put her off or simply not show up at all.

'That's all right,' Graham said, successfully hiding how shocked he felt at her haggard appearance. 'You know I'm always only a telephone call away.'

He stepped inside, and followed her through to a neat and cosy lounge, done out in pale oranges and blues. He noticed, with a pang, that there was a large square dent in the carpet, probably where a cabinet had once stood. Were things so financially dire for the Lancers that they were reduced to selling off bits of furniture? Graham rather thought that they might be.

Once he was settled comfortably in an armchair, he tentatively broached the subject they both knew he'd come to discuss.

'I've had a chat with that therapist friend of mine I told you about,' Graham began, and pulled out several leaflets issued by self-help groups from his pockets. 'I was surprised how common this problem is,' he continued gently. 'Your husband isn't alone in his addiction, I promise you.' Trisha took a deep breath and reached for the leaflets.

'He's an insurance agent if I remember rightly?' he asked conversationally.

'Yes, Wilkins & White.'

The name of the big insurance company rang a bell, but Graham couldn't quite place it.

'You have a nice place here,' he said softly, looking around, and realized at once that it had been the wrong thing to say. Trisha shot him an agonized look and her lower lip began to wobble alarmingly.

'Yes, if we can keep it,' she said, her voice cracking.

'Trisha,' Graham said gently, leaning forwards and looking her levelly in the eye. 'If you can persuade your husband to come to the six-a-side football and fête at Middleton Barrow tomorrow, I can arrange to be there too. I can start a conversation with him, apparently purely by chance, and—'

But Trisha was already shaking her head.

'It's too late for all that now, Vicar,' she said, and let the leaflets fall back onto the table. 'And for these,' she nodded down at them. 'He wouldn't listen to you, no matter who you are. Or what you said. He's too far gone.'

'I know sometimes it's hard to—' Graham began patiently, but Trisha once again shook her head.

'No, Vicar,' she said flatly. 'I've found something else out. Something that makes it all so hopeless and so much worse.' She closed her eyes for a moment and then opened them again. 'Would you come with me?' she asked, her voice strangely calm now. 'I need to show you something.'

Getting up, she walked into the hall then up the stairs, her slow movements reminding Graham of someone who was sleepwalking. She had an air about her of hopeless fatalism that sent chills through him.

Graham, without hesitation, followed her. She led him to what was obviously the main bedroom, where she ignored the unmade bed and took him straight to a big wardrobe. There she bent down, retrieved a shoebox, and put it on the bed. Then she lifted the lid.

'Look,' she said flatly. And Graham looked.

* * *

Monica glanced at her watch, wondered when her husband would be home, then decided she had time for a few hours' sunbathing. She got a towel, some sun block and a raunchy paperback blockbuster that she'd have to hide double-quick if any of Graham's fan club came a-calling, and headed for the garden on the far side from her flat.

There seemed to be a lot of activity at the back of the house all of a sudden, but this bit of the garden was the least used, and it didn't take her long to set herself up. With her skin gleaming from the oil, and her elbows dug contentedly into the grass as she read from her book, the rest of the morning looked set to idle along nicely. Until she became slowly aware of the sound of voices. They weren't loud, or particularly intrusive, but once her ears had picked them up, she simply couldn't tune them out again. Especially when one of the voices belonged to Jason Dury.

She didn't know it, but they'd just left Pauline's flat to the SOCO team, and were waiting for reinforcements to come in order to start a whole new round of interviews. The residents of the vicarage were about to be put through the wringer once more. In the meantime, however, Jim had been too restless to sit and wait and had pounced with alacrity on a new report just in.

'The lab report about the ashes has come back, sir.' Jim, standing by the open window of the incident room, had no idea that he was being overheard.

'Oh? Any help?'

'Not on the button, sir. Could have come from anything — from a man's pair of shorts or a woman's blouse. But there was something else they picked up that's interesting. It seems that our killer didn't just burn his clothes. Look.'

In the garden, Monica turned over on her towel and sighed.

'Cassette tape,' Jason said. 'A bit low-tech, isn't it?'

'It certainly is,' Jim confirmed. 'What do you make of it?'

'It's got to be what the killer came for, Jim.'

'Sir?'

'We know that Margaret went into that room to meet someone. We know that she was blackmailing Maurice, and probably several others. We know that she'd paid a visit to her safety deposit box the previous day.'

'So you think she took a cassette tape out?'

'Why not? You can blackmail people with cassette tapes just as easily as with the written word or photographs. Perhaps she recorded someone's private conversation?'

'But what could have been on it that was so important that she was killed for it?' Jim asked rhetorically.

'I don't know. Two people discussing a crooked financial deal perhaps? Something damning anyway. And, if a tape *was* used, it was probably done some years ago now. So she may have been blackmailing this particular victim for a long, long time.'

Jim whistled.

'That's pretty cold-blooded stuff, sir,' Jim said. 'I wonder how many people she had her claws into? And how long she'd been making a living from it?'

Monica gathered her things together, her peace shattered, and stepped into the central garden. So Margaret had been a blackmailer? Somehow, she wasn't surprised. She looked up and saw a man in white overalls go into the house, and felt gooseflesh ripple up her arms. The last time she'd seen a man dressed like that had been on the day of the murder. A forensics officer. But she thought the SOCO team had finally finished with the building. What was another one doing coming back now? What were they hoping to find?

Monica was so stunned she found herself staring into the darker interior of the house. The door to flat 2 opened, and she saw Jason come out. 'Phelps. What have you got?'

He glanced over the SOCO's shoulder as he spoke and noticed Monica Noble, barefoot, lightly tanned and looking stunning in a modest one-piece peach swimming suit. In the sunlight, her hair gleamed, and her startled eyes met his in a clash of blue-on-blue that he could feel reaching right down to his toenails.

Suddenly Monica blushed and quickly walked on. Jason listened as the SOCO officer told him that the police surgeon had arrived, and had given preliminary cause of death as being due to strangulation.

He and Jim headed straight back to Pauline's flat.

* * *

Back in her own flat, Monica headed for the shower, her mind churning over the latest bits of the puzzle. She knew that Julie and Sean had been taken in for questioning, but had no idea why. And what did a burnt bit of cassette tape actually mean? Was it really more of Margaret's blackmail evidence, or could it be down to something else entirely?

She didn't know it, but as she stood under the spray, on the brink of a revelation, her husband was returning home with two very big pieces of the jigsaw puzzle in his possession.

And once they put all the pieces together, they'd know exactly who had killed Margaret Franklyn. And how and why.

CHAPTER 17

Jason Dury knocked impatiently on the Nobles' front door and was instantly confronted by a vision in high-heeled spikes and tight-fitting leather. Carol-Ann, on her way out, stepped obligingly to one side and gestured vaguely towards her stepfather's study.

'They're in there, and I have to warn you, looking unbearably smug,' she drawled disgustedly.

Jason raised an eyebrow. 'Does your mother know you're dressed like that?' he asked quizzically.

'Not yet, but she will,' Carol-Ann said ominously, and left, slamming the door behind her.

Jason grinned and made his way to the study, where Graham and Monica were waiting for him.

'You wanted to see me?' Jason asked mildly, shutting the door behind him and sitting down in the large armchair that Graham ushered him to. 'I have to tell you, I don't have much time.'

Since they obviously didn't know yet about the second murder, Jason was not about to tell them. He looked at them curiously, wondering what could be so urgent. The married couple were sitting side by side on the sofa opposite him, holding hands tightly.

'You two look very serious,' he added. Monica glanced at Graham, then cleared her throat.

'We think we know who killed Margaret,' she said boldly.

When Graham had returned just over an hour ago, and told her what he'd learned from Trisha Lancer, it had sparked off a brainstorming session between them that had left them both bewildered and totally out of their depth. But their conclusions seemed solid, no matter how hard they tried to pick their newly constructed theories apart. Consequently, they'd decided that the only thing they could do was to lay all their suppositions at Jason's feet and hope he could tell them how daft they were. Or arrest a killer. Neither Graham nor Monica was quite sure which they hoped it would turn out to be.

Jason blinked at her words. He looked neither amused nor angry, but merely watchful. At least he wasn't laughing them off out of hand, Monica thought with relief. But she wondered what he, a professional, must think of amateurs trying to tell him his business.

'Oh?' He turned to Monica first. 'Perhaps you can start by telling me who you think did it?' he asked, his voice flat.

'Paul Waring,' she said. Then she took a deep breath at having said it out loud.

'And why him, in particular?' Jason asked, with genuine curiosity. Deep down, he didn't think the Nobles could have solved the case. The vicar seemed almost too innocent to be able to understand such evil, let alone track down and solve the root cause of it. And as for Monica Noble — to Jason at least — she was the last woman in the world who should ever have to worry about such things.

'Please, can I just tell it my way?' Monica asked. 'I'll get confused if I don't.'

Jason smiled briefly and nodded. 'Oh, by all means. But I should just like to point out that you yourself told me that Waring was standing right in front of you when the gun went off,' he felt obliged to remind her.

Monica nodded. 'I know, I know.' She waved a hand helplessly in her lap. 'On the face of it, it sounds so absurd doesn't it?' Then she gave her husband a quick look, and turned her attention back once more to the policeman. 'All right. Here's how I think it happened,' she said, beyond caring now how ridiculous she might sound.

'I think Paul has been planning this murder for quite some time,' she ventured. 'And it all began with Paul helping Maurice Keating to get a flat here. And then, later, with him persuading Sean Franklyn that he should also buy a flat here.'

Jason began to lean forwards in his chair, for the first time feeling truly hopeful that the Nobles might, at the very least, provide him with some useful information. Because this was something new. Although how it could possibly relate to Pauline's killing was another matter. But first things first.

'Go on,' he encouraged.

'You see, a man called Jim Lancer runs the estate agents' office that was in charge of selling these flats,' Monica explained. 'And we've just learned that he's also an avid, even obsessive member of Paul Waring's gyms.'

'Wait a minute, how do you know all this?' Jason cut across ruthlessly.

Graham cleared his throat, attracting Jason's attention back to himself.

'Several days ago, Mrs Lancer came to me to ask for my help. She told me that her husband was obsessed with body-building, to the point where she was afraid they were going to lose the house, her husband was spending so much money on feeding his obsession. On exercise equipment, gym fees, and other . . . er . . . things,' he trailed off, still not happy about telling this policeman confidences that should have remained between himself and his parishioner alone.

'And I overheard Pauline talking to Paul,' Monica quickly came to her husband's rescue, 'just after you'd taken Maurice away for questioning. John was with me, and he heard her too. Pauline said that she bet Paul was sorry now for helping Maurice get a flat here. And Paul was so angry with her! Until then, I had no idea that Paul was such a great friend of Maurice's.'

'No, neither did I,' Jason said softly, his eyes glittering.

So Pauline had been making waves even then, had she? But surely that wouldn't have been enough for someone to feel threatened enough to kill her. Would it?

'If you talk to Pauline,' Monica carried on, still blissfully unaware of just how impossible that would be, 'she'll tell you all about it. And I bet if you ask Sean how he came to buy the flat here, he'll tell you that it was Paul who put him on to it as well. And don't forget, it was Sean's insurance company that handled all the business on the flats. You know, covered the insurance for the building work, and so on. I think Paul was probably the one who tipped Sean Franklyn the wink that his company could be on to a good thing here. You see how it all ties in?'

'Also, Chief Inspector,' Graham said, 'if you look into the sale of these flats, I suspect you'll find that Jim Lancer gave both Maurice Keating and the Franklyns a far better deal than any of us others received.'

'Either that,' Monica chipped in, 'or Paul put in some money of his own, to make up any deficit.'

'And just why would he do that?' Jason asked, thinking of Paul's unnecessarily fiddly books. Was it possible that these two unlikely sleuths had actually stumbled onto something with real potential?

'Because he needed both the Franklyns and Maurice Keating right here, where he could both keep an eye on them and set them up,' Monica explained. 'Maurice to take the fall for the murder, or at the very least to become a chief suspect, and Margaret to, well, be killed.'

The room was strangely silent for a few seconds after that stark pronouncement. Then Jason slowly scratched his cheek, and looked from Graham to his wife, then back again to Graham.

'And why did he want to kill Margaret?' he asked softly.

Graham looked down at his hands. 'Because, as I'm sure you've already guessed, Chief Inspector, she was blackmailing him.'

'About what?' Jason demanded.

Monica shifted uneasily in her seat. This was the worst part. She knew Graham hated divulging Trisha Lancer's confidences. But there was nothing else they could do. Besides, the shock of what he'd done — albeit unknowingly — might just be enough to shake Jim Lancer free from his obsession.

'I went to see Mrs Lancer a few hours ago, Chief Inspector,' Graham admitted softly. 'And she showed me a stash of drugs she'd found in her husband's wardrobe. Steroids, to be exact.'

'Ah.' Jason's eyes narrowed. So, Waring *was* into supplying his clients with chemical help. And had probably been responsible for the death of a man several years ago — a crime for which another man had then been convicted. If so, that old case would have to be reopened and re-examined. Which would not go down well with the brass, Jason mused with an inner wince. Still, it had to be done. With grim satisfaction, he added, 'Well, we'll be able to get him for supplying steroids, provided Mr Lancer can be persuaded to testify. But we're still a long way from proving a murder conviction.'

Actually, *two* murder convictions, he reminded himself. He wasn't, by any means, forgetting about Pauline Weeks.

Monica nodded. 'We don't know very much about Maurice, I'll admit,' she said. 'We're guessing, though, that you found some kind of evidence that Margaret was blackmailing him too?' Her voice rose at the end, making it a question, and Jason smiled grimly.

'Let's just suppose that for a moment,' he said agreeably.

Monica took a deep breath. 'So, it goes like this. Margaret has something on both Maurice and Paul. Both are paying up, but Paul decides he's had enough. He sees these flats for sale, and hits upon an idea. First he buys his own flat — and remember, he was the first one to do so. Then he helps Maurice get his. He knows Margaret is blackmailing him too.' She quickly held up a hand as Jason was about to interrupt. 'I know, that's only guesswork. But it's not beyond the realms of possibility that Margaret let it slip that she had another

216

victim on her hook, or maybe Paul even found evidence that she was getting money from somewhere else and tracked it back to Maurice. Whatever, he wants an obvious suspect right on hand. And Maurice, with his vanity and his liking for the good life, isn't about to turn down one of the best flats going, and at such a reasonable price, is he?'

Jason nodded. 'And this he does with the help of Jim Lancer, right?'

'Right. Remember, Jim Lancer is desperate to please the owner of the gym, the successful bodybuilder and the man who's going to help him become the next Mr Universe, or whatever,' Monica confirmed grimly.

'OK. Then his next move is to bring in the Franklyns?' Jason was willing enough to play along with the scenario, just to see where it led.

'Yes, but he has to do it through Sean Franklyn alone,' Monica pointed out. 'Do you remember I told you how angry and dissatisfied Margaret was about living here? How I overheard them arguing about it one day? Well, that all now makes perfect sense.'

'Of course. She moved in, only to find two of her blackmail victims right on her doorstep,' Jason said, beginning to feel himself swept along by the argument, and warning himself to keep an open mind. Though he couldn't help adding, 'I'll bet that gave her a nasty turn.'

'No wonder she was threatening to divorce Sean,' Graham agreed. 'The poor woman must have been enraged. Or frightened.'

'No, darling, I don't think she was ever frightened,' Monica corrected gently. 'Annoyed maybe. Or discomfited. But Margaret didn't strike me as the type to scare easily. She might still be alive if only she had been,' she added sadly.

'All right, so he's got them all where he wants them,' Jason cut across all these suppositions. 'Now what? How did he kill Margaret when he was standing right in front of you, and in full view of all the other partygoers that afternoon?'

'Well, of course he didn't,' Monica said. Then added hastily, 'Kill her then, I mean. When we all heard the shot.'

'I'm confused,' Jason said flatly.

Monica nodded. 'I know — I was too for a long time. But this is how I think it went. He told Margaret that he'd just sold one of his gyms and that he wanted to buy back whatever she had on him in one final, last-shot deal. That way she could afford to divorce her husband and move away from the vicarage. Obviously, she agreed. He asked her to meet him on the afternoon of the party, not in flat 2, but up at Chandler's Spinney, where there was no possibility of them being disturbed.'

Jason was staring at Monica in fascination now. 'Go on.'

'He knew the village would be deserted because of the fair, which was a real bonus as far as he was concerned. So, sometime, and I'm guessing it was very early in the morning on the day of the party, he went into the empty flat and removed the tarpaulins. He then took them to Chandler's Spinney and hung them from the branches of the trees, in the shape of a square, to make an enclosure. He then returned to the vicarage and parked his car right out in the sun. That bit's important, and I'll tell you why later,' she said quickly, as once again Jason opened his mouth to ask a question. 'Anyway, I know for a fact that's what he did, because that morning I saw his Jaguar standing out in the direct sunlight. I remember thinking at the time how sweltering it would have been inside, but didn't think anything of it. *Then.*'

Graham felt himself listening in appalled fascination as his wife described the mind and workings of a killer.

'All he had to do then was set up a few things,' Monica continued determinedly. 'You know there are always shotguns being heard going off in Chandler's Spinney, right?' Monica asked, apparently off the cuff.

Jason nodded. 'Pigeon shooters. Kids mucking about. Right.'

'Right. So how easy would it have been for Paul to take Clem Jarvis's stolen shotgun up to the Spinney with a tape

218

recorder, and record the sound of a shotgun blast, without attracting attention?'

Jason blinked. 'Not hard at all,' he said slowly, thinking of the burnt cassette tape found at the bonfire site.

'Incidentally,' Graham put in, 'I think, if you question the people at the pub on the day that Clem's gun went missing, you'll find that Paul must have been wearing a long coat. It's the only way I can think of that he could have hidden the gun. He could hardly walk out of the pub carrying it in full sight under his arm, after all,' he added.

'I never thought of that,' Monica said admiringly.

Graham smiled modestly back at her.

'Back to Chandler's Spinney,' Jason said abruptly. 'He tapes the sound of a shotgun blast?'

'Yes. All he has to do is wind on the blank tape for about five minutes, then fire the gun and record it. And there he is, with the perfect alibi all set up. On the day of the murder, Margaret leaves for Chandler's Spinney where she thinks she's going to be handed a briefcase full of money. Meanwhile, back at the party, Paul makes a great show of forgetting to get in the booze. He leaves to go to the shop, not on foot, as we all thought, but in the car, which is swelteringly hot. He drives up to the Spinney, with the gun in the back.'

'And he was seen,' Graham put in quietly. 'If you'd like to have a word with young Linsey Drew, she saw the car drive past her house in the square, and go up the road that only leads to Chandler's Spinney. It was a blue Jag.'

'Did she see who was driving?' Jason asked sharply, and Graham shrugged and spread his hands. He hadn't thought to ask. Not at the time.

Monica sighed. 'So. He meets Margaret, but he's got a gun, not the money. He forces her to walk into the middle of the tarpaulins that are hung up to imitate the four sides of the room in the empty flat, and then kills her.'

'Which is why the blood spatter on the tarpaulins is consistent,' Jason muttered.

'Yes. That's important, you see. To fool everyone into thinking that she was killed inside the house. In that very room where she was found, in fact. Then he folds the tarpaulins up,' Monica said.

Which is where the mirror images of the bloodstains come in, Jason thought. And why he had to use one of them to cover her body. Not to hide her, as we all thought, but to explain any smudges of the bloodstains.

'He carries the body and puts it into the boot,' Monica swept on. 'Remember, he's very fit and very fast. Then he drives to the shop, buys the booze and returns to the vicarage.'

Jason nodded. 'There he takes the body out of the boot, the only truly risky part of the whole procedure as he might be seen, and lays her out in the flat. Then he hangs the tarpaulins back up on the walls, runs upstairs, changes his clothes on the stairs, where he unwittingly leaves a slight bloodstain, goes into his flat and puts the tape in the tape deck and switches it on.'

'Then he walks back to the party with the booze, knowing that the body won't have lost any body heat at all, having been transported in a hot car,' Monica said. 'Which is important. The body must still be very warm when it's found.'

'And five minutes later, while he's in plain view of everyone, you hear the sound of a shot,' Jason finished.

'But not the real shot. The shot that actually killed Margaret has already been heard by several villagers,' Monica said. 'Except that it was up in Chandler's Spinney, so no one thought anything of it. But you might like to speak to a certain old gentleman with good ears, despite a touch of Parkinson's disease,' Monica recommended softly.

'So, you make a search of the house, find Margaret and there you go.' Jason sighed. It all fit. 'Very clever,' he said softly. Dead clever, in fact.

'But there were mistakes made,' Monica pointed out. 'Because of all that he had to do whilst he was gone, supposedly getting the drinks, Paul had to account for his time, in case someone remembered exactly how long he'd been gone. So he told me that he spent a long time helping a lost motorist find the way to Warwick.'

Both Graham, who hadn't heard that bit, and Jason looked at her in puzzlement.

'For a while now, something's been niggling at me, but I couldn't think what it was,' Monica said. 'Then I finally realized. Why would a motorist, on his way to Warwick, get lost here? I mean, why turn off the main road at all? And especially down a road that's signposted as being a village only and a no through road?'

'That's a bit tenuous,' Jason said cautiously.

'But it all makes sense,' Monica added. Then she looked up at him out of wide, miserable blue eyes. 'Doesn't it?'

And Jason was forced to agree. Because it did add up, and fit all the known facts. In spite of his doubt, the Nobles had come up trumps. 'I'm afraid it does. Yes. And,' he took a deep breath, 'he made another mistake as well. One that got Pauline Weeks killed.'

Monica gave a gasp of dismay. 'Pauline's dead?' she whispered, appalled.

Graham leaned forward, his face pale. 'How?' he croaked.

'Strangled,' Jason said flatly. 'We found her body in her flat this morning.'

'But why?' Monica cried.

Jason shrugged. 'I think because she'd been going around telling everyone that she'd seen the bloodstain on the stairs when she went back to her flat that afternoon.'

Monica shot Graham a quick look.

'Yes, we'd heard that too,' Graham admitted. 'But I'm afraid we didn't really believe her,' he added quietly. 'Or pay it that much attention.' Quickly, Monica reached out and grabbed his hand.

'Don't feel so bad about it, Mr Noble,' Jason said gruffly, sensing his distress. 'Nobody else did either.'

'Except Paul,' Monica put in darkly.

'Yes,' Jason agreed heavily. 'Paul believed her, because he knew that she really *could* have seen the stains; he was the only one who knew that Margaret was already dead and that he'd changed on the stairs, *before* the sound of the shot was heard. And there was something else she knew. Something we haven't been quite able to track down yet, but something to do with clothes.'

At his words, Monica abruptly frowned. Something nipped, then leapt into her mind. 'The panther!' she cried suddenly, and both men looked at her as if she'd suddenly grown another head. 'I know what it was,' Monica stared at Jason triumphantly. 'It was the panther on his T-shirt.'

'Come again?' Jason said softly.

'When Paul went to get the booze, he was wearing a pair of shorts and a plain white T-shirt. When he came back, he was still wearing the same coloured shorts and a plain white T-shirt except for a little navy-blue panther logo on one shoulder. I must have registered it without ever really knowing that I had. If you know what I mean.'

'But Pauline would notice everything about Paul.' It was Graham who spoke up now, his voice sad. 'The way she felt about him, she'd have noticed every little thing about him. Including the fact that his shirt wasn't quite the same.'

'And those two things got her killed,' Jason said flatly.

* * *

It didn't take long, once they knew where to look, to find all the evidence that they needed to arrest and charge Paul Waring with double murder. The forensics team found traces which proved that Margaret Franklyn and the tarpaulins had been in the boot of Waring's car, despite the vacuuming and cleaning he'd since done on it. And once the spot was found in Chandler's Spinney where Margaret had actually been killed, they came up with a footprint in the dust fitting the markings on one of Paul Waring's trainers. The 'moss, lichens and other green matter' found on the tarpaulins were matched to those

222

of the lichens and other growths found on the trees in the wood. And traces of Margaret's blood were found in the turf in sufficient quantities to convince Jason's superior that his detective had got it right. A raid on Paul's gyms also produced evidence of widespread steroid abuse, and under questioning, several dedicated clients confessed that they were taking steroids, supplied by Paul Waring.

The estate agency's records were confiscated, and it was discovered that Monica was right about the deal on the flats. Both Sean Franklyn, when questioned, and Maurice, reluctantly admitted how much they'd paid for their flats. Both prices were well below that which showed up on the estate agents' books.

Paul Waring, when arrested, refused to speak, and demanded a solicitor.

* * *

Neither Monica nor Graham wanted to witness Paul's arrest, and kept to the flat that day. They didn't want to venture far for the next few days in fact, since the press was back and practically camped on their doorstep, but they had no choice — Graham had to give his Sunday service as usual, and it was also the weekend of baby Halcyone's christening. He also paid a visit to Trisha Lancer and her husband, and returned with a certain sense of optimism.

As expected, Jim Lancer had been appalled at what his mentor had done. Sure, Jim had desperately wanted the house sales, but his admiration for Paul had led to severely misplaced trust, and now being sacked by his firm was the least of his worries — he was facing prosecution for fraud, as well as the illegal use of steroids. His wife was vowing to stand by him, but his dreams of being the next Sylvester Stallone were well and truly down the pan.

Pauline Weeks's body was eventually released for burial. Joan Dix moved out of the vicarage, taking a contrite Julie with her.

Jason, feeling he owed it to them, explained to Monica and Graham how, on the day of the murder, Maurice Keating had met a man in his flat, a known criminal, and had paid him a lot of money for a false set of documents.

For once, Paul Waring had been telling the truth about seeing a stranger — and an old acquaintance of Maurice's — in the vicinity. Of course, he'd only told the police about him in order to hammer another nail into the Oxford don's coffin.

But with the arrest of the true killer, Maurice had decided it was safe to come clean, and had confessed to Jason how, just like Paul, he'd had enough of Margaret's blackmailing. He had decided to try and start a new life elsewhere under a false name, in the hopes that she'd never find him again.

As it turned out, he need not have gone to all the trouble.

Maurice also revealed that he'd seen a car identical to Paul's when he'd been leaving Margaret's place around a year ago, fuming after yet another outrageous extortion. Concerned as to who may have seen him, the vehicle had stuck in his mind, but it wasn't until Maurice was being ushered into the police car for questioning that his eyes had alighted on Paul's Jag and got him wondering whether the young man had been keeping dark secrets of his own.

'I was really angry that day and no doubt had a face like thunder,' he recounted to Jason. 'Paul must have seen me and got curious, wondering if he was the only blackmail victim.'

And sure enough, that's exactly when Paul Waring's master plan must have come together, Jason thought grimly. After seizing the gym buff's phone and laptop they had found evidence of him hiring a private investigator, who had no doubt been given a car registration number for the unsuspecting Maurice.

And it was this lack of suspicion that Paul had counted on. He knew the old man wouldn't have the backbone or the knowhow to cover up his blackmail under close scrutiny; he was the perfect scapegoat. But Paul Waring had thought himself just a touch too clever.

* * *

It was Saturday morning again, two weeks to the day after the murder of Margaret Franklyn, when Jason and the last of his team finally cleared out of the incident room for good, and left Heyford Bassett to return to its normal, sleepy existence.

John Lerwick and Vera Ainsley were back in the gardens and weeding steadily when Jason took a final look around and headed for the gravel path to the main gates.

Jason had politely and somewhat awkwardly thanked the Nobles for all their help, taking Monica's hand reluctantly and quickly letting it go again. Even so, it felt as if he could still feel her fingers resting sweetly in his palm.

Jim was already in the car, waiting to leave. The weather had finally broken, and although it wasn't raining, the sun was banked behind thick clouds, and there was a pleasant coolness in the air.

Monica was in the kitchen, looking out of the window, when she saw Jason cross the lawn in front of her. She reached out to fling wide the catch, and was about to call out to him, when something stopped her.

Jason, sensing the movement, swung his head, and found himself looking into a pair of wide, smoky blue eyes. He smiled. He took a single step towards her, then something stopped him. Perhaps not. Better not. He smiled sadly at the vicar's wife, just the once, then turned and walked away.

Monica watched him leave, then went back to the plum and raspberry tart that she was making. She reached for the sugar canister and lightly sprinkled some on top the way that Graham liked it.

From her daughter's bedroom came the sudden blare of the latest pop sensation.

Life, as it always did, had to return to normal.

Stiff-backed, Jason Dury got into the car, and nodded at Jim. 'Right. Let's get out of here,' he said firmly.

THE END

THE END

THE JOFFE BOOKS STORY

We began in 2014 when Jasper agreed to publish his mum's much-rejected romance novel and it became a bestseller.

Since then we've grown into the largest independent publisher in the UK. We're extremely proud to publish some of the very best writers in the world, including Joy Ellis, Faith Martin, Caro Ramsay, Helen Forrester, Simon Brett and Robert Goddard. Everyone at Joffe Books loves reading and we never forget that it all begins with the magic of an author telling a story.

We are proud to publish talented first-time authors, as well as established writers whose books we love introducing to a new generation of readers.

We won Trade Publisher of the Year at the Independent Publishing Awards in 2023. We have been shortlisted for Independent Publisher of the Year at the British Book Awards for the last four years, and were shortlisted for the Diversity and Inclusivity Award at the 2022 Independent Publishing Awards. In 2023 we were shortlisted for Publisher of the Year at the RNA Industry Awards.

We built this company with your help, and we love to hear from you, so please email us about absolutely anything bookish at feedback@joffebooks.com

If you want to receive free books every Friday and hear about all our new releases, join our mailing list: www.joffebooks.com/contact

And when you tell your friends about us, just remember: it's pronounced Joffe as in coffee or toffee!

Milton Keynes UK
Ingram Content Group UK Ltd.
UKHW041406250924
448735UK00009B/80